AN AVALON WESTERN

PAHGOSA
The O'Malley Saga: Book Three

Tom Austin

The O'Malley clan has always bonded together when trouble is on the horizon. So when the Burdett gang threatens young Tom O'Malley and his sweetheart Lee Conall, his cousins, uncles and brothers come from all over to help.

The first run in with the Burdett gang started over a puppy that Tom rescued. In an act of revenge the Burdett gang attacked some of the O'Malleys' friends and war was declared between the two rivals.

Burdett begins to gather his ne'er-do-wells as the O'Malleys catch wind of the forthcoming trouble. From all over the Midwest and as far as California and Boston, the O'Malley clan bands together to defend their name and bring justice to the Burdett crew.

PAHGOSA

•

Tom Austin

AVALON BOOKS
NEW YORK

PRINTED IN THE UNITED STATES OF AMERICA
ON ACID-FREE PAPER
BY HADDON CRAFTSMEN, BLOOMSBURG, PENNSYLVANIA

This book is dedicated to my Aunt, Eula York, who
is the greatest teacher ever born, and to
Brenda Robinson and the Fillmore Junior High
School Sixth Grade of 2002/2003

ACKNOWLEDGMENTS

As with my other novels I had plenty of help getting to the finish line with *Pahgosa*. Thanks to my long-suffering editor, Erin Cartwright-Niumata, my longer suffering wife, Karalee, and my sister and personal editor, Merry Palmer. Between these three women they know all my shortcomings and weaknesses, and love to exploit them. A special thanks to my biggest fan, my mother, Norma Austin (even though she harshly criticizes my writing when one of the good guys bites the dirt!).

Tirley's Father

Fergus O'Malley

FERGUS' KIDS BELOW

Tobias
Peter
Tirley*
Trian
Chagrin
John
Emma
Josian
Ellen
Rebecca

Edith O'Malley

Tirley's Mother

Tirley O'Malley

Eva O'Malley

Matt's Father

Matt's Mother

Matthew's Brothers

Dan
Owen
Mike

Matthew O'Malley

Our hero

The Beginning

Pa leaned his hay fork against the barn and took off his hat. He looked toward the west and wiped his brow with a red rag. "Well, let's get hold of Stone-Cold Phillips and Chris Silva. I got a yen to see some new country."

"Mike saw Stoney camped in La Garrida Canyon yesterday," I told Pa. "He says he's just waitin' on us. Chris was over at Garland a week ago when I delivered those steers. I told him to meet us here tomorrow. I figured we'd be 'bout ready."

"It'll take me ten minutes to pack," Pa said, tuckin' the rag back in his pocket, "then we'll discuss my plan."

"I didn't know you had a plan," I said. "I just figured we'd head out and end up someplace."

"Anywhere is better than a hundred-acre hay meadow," Pa said. He was quiet a minute, looked at me and then toward the mountains. "I don't have any plan particular, but me and Stoney talked about goin' down to Taos and seein' if any of the old folks remember us. Then eventually I want to come back up to the country the Utes call Pahgosa. I remember an old story I heard durin' the war that I want to check out, and it gives us a couple of places to point at and something to look for."

1

"Lookin' for what?" I asked.

Pa reached under his shirt and took out his medicine bag. He pulled open the little leather bag and dug deep with his finger and thumb. He fished something out and held it up for me to see. It was a gold nugget as big as a walnut.

"I think I have a fair idea of where there's more just like this," Pa said with a smile. "Maybe a lot more. I mean to go after it. I got to put somethin' by for when I cain't do nothin' but sit in a rockin' chair."

The thought of Pa sitting in a rockin' chair made me want to laugh, but he had a point. Huntin' gold would give us a reason for the ride, but I remembered somethin' Pa had told me a while back when we'd found some Spanish gold.

"Boy," he'd said, "gold is a thing hard found, but it's even harder to keep." I wondered if he remembered what he'd said. I reckoned he did, but he was surely gonna ignore it. I had an inklin' of trouble comin', but I'd ignored the feelin' before and likely would again.

"There's somethin' else, Matthew," Pa said. "I've got a thing to do besides hunt gold. I got a place to go." He fell silent, not turnin' toward me. He was still starin' at the high lonesome country, and he had a funny look on his face. "I got some folks to see one more time 'fore I go under, and I need to take you with me 'cause there's somethin' you got to hear." He walked away from me, heading for the house.

I was almighty curious about what he had to tell me, but knew better than to push. He'd come to it when the time was right.

I looked toward the Storm King Mountain and thought of my Lee girl for the hundredth time that day. I remembered the way she looked the first time I saw her crawlin' out from under a dead drummer in the shot-up coach of the Butterfield Stage, all covered in blood and tryin' not to cry. I remembered her chestnut hair, her wide green eyes, her trim shape, her good cookin', and her easy laugh. I remembered her savin' my life when Falcon Beck was about to do for me. I remembered the last time I saw her. She ran from me on a Denver street. She'd figured I'd betrayed her when she'd seen me kissin' Ara Turbech, one of my old friends. It had been a good-bye kiss, but all Lee saw was the two of us together. Lee had taken out east and not just to Kansas City. She'd told some folks she was goin' east to have her aunt teach her how to be a lady like Ara. She was gone, and I figured I might not see her again.

My heart still felt like a lump of lead in my chest, and I knew Pa was sick of hearin' me sigh, but I just couldn't help it. I reckoned a trek in the hills might shake me out of it.

"You gonna stand there lookin' at the sky or are you gonna pack?" Pa hollered from the main cabin.

I waved at him and turned toward the barn. I surely missed Lee. I surely did.

I walked over to the main cabin and went to my room. I was proud of what we'd accomplished since comin' West. We had three cabins up, a barn, and several outbuildings. It seemed like most of our cows was havin' twins to make up for the cows we lost durin' the winter, and we had nearly two hundred head of horses on our twenty thousand acres of grass, forest, and mountain. The Storm King Ranch had been deeded to us by the Ute tribe and recognized by the government with a patent. We'd fought for it and we'd lost some friends while buildin' it. We'd come together as a family here on the ranch for the first time since the beginning of the war, and this was our home.

I packed my duds, which didn't take long 'cause I didn't have much, and walked out into the main room. This cabin, the one we called the main cabin, had been the first we'd raised when we'd got to the Valley of the Utes, and it was the biggest by far of the three. It was usually where we came together if we were havin' a meetin' of the partnership. The word had went out that Pa and I were leavin' so folks started driftin' in to see us off.

"I got some bread fresh baked I'll send with you," Patty

O'Malley said, comin' in from the kitchen. She'd married my
brother Owen when we'd still been in Kansas, and she was
the best thing ever happened to him. The door swung open
and Patty's brother, Wedge, and his wife, Jessie May, came
in. They were a strange-lookin' couple. Wedge was way over
six foot, weighed nigh on to three hundred muscled pounds,
and was uglier than a moss-backed snappin' turtle. There'd
been a time when he'd made a practice of tearin' the ears off
folks he didn't like, but Jess had cured him of that. Jessie was
something under five foot, weighed maybe a hundred pounds,
and was purtier than a spring mornin'. They'd hit it off from
the first time they'd seen each other not long after we'd rescued her from some renegades and wasn't long 'fore they
married up.

My brothers Mike, Dan, and Owen came in the front door
just as Pa came in the back door. We all gathered in the big
front room.

"Looks like we're all here," Pa said in a quiet voice. He
walked over to the flagstone fireplace and leaned against the
wall. "Matt and I are leavin' out on a trek. Looks like you got
enough help to get ready for the winter and that Spanish gold
we brought off the mountain ought to help lay in supplies."

"We figured you'd be going soon," Dan said. He'd been a
captain in the army for some years, and was the oldest of us
boys. He usually took the lead. "You goin' anyplace in particular?"

"South and west," Pa said. "Maybe Taos to begin with, then
back up to Pahgosa."

"When you comin' back?" Mike asked. He'd lost an arm
in the war, but was still one of the best cowboys on the place.

"I hope we can start back this direction come spring," Pa
said. "Maybe we'll be here to help with the summer work."

"Gonna miss you boys," Wedge said in his surprisingly
sweet voice. Him and Owen had sung many a close harmony
song together, and they was known far and wide.

"We won't be gone forever," Pa said. "I just want to show

Matthew some country 'fore you boys get him all settled down."

"Matthew, you take care of this old man," Owen said. "Ma would be put out with you if you let somethin' happen to him."

I nodded, not darin' to speak. These were my friends and family, and we had been through a powerful lot together. Ma had been killed by guerilla raiders toward the end of the war, and I'd sworn a blood oath to get them that done it. I'd made my oath good, but it had cost us.

Patty walked over to me and kissed me on the cheek, then Jessie did the same. The men all shook hands with us as we went out the front door. I threw my pack up behind my saddle on my black horse. We mounted, waved, and rode out. I stopped by the gate and looked back. They was all still standin' there. I missed my Lee, and I was surely gonna miss these folks. Who knew if we'd ever come ridin' back this way again?

Chapter One

He was the biggest man on the street, standing head and shoulders over Pa. He was at least a head taller than me, and he had a half-dozen buddies standin' behind him on the boardwalk in front of the general store. He weren't only almighty big, he was downright ugly. He had an overhangin' forehead that gave shade enough to his little pig eyes that he didn't need a hat. His jaw was square and bristled with a week's worth of greasy whiskers, and I reckoned he'd wore the clothes on his back since the day they was new, which had been on his birthday a year past.

I'd told Pa as we were ridin' into Del Norte that I thought we ought to pass it by, but Stoney had run out of pipe tobacco, and we was in need of some coffee, so I was outvoted. I'd argued a little, but when we was about a mile out of town a fall squall hit us with a whistlin' north wind. The arguin' went out of me when the ice started to drip off my hat and down the neck of my shirt.

Now I was wishin' I'd a pushed the point a little. We was facin' up to Mister Trouble and his pack of no-good friends, and they was all belted and booted men carryin' short guns with a couple of rifles thrown in for good measure. One of 'em, the one standin' closest to the Big Ugly, had the darnest growth of hair under his nose. Lots of us wore lip hair, but it looked like this fella had been growin' this special for about twenty years without any trimmin'.

"Mister, where I come from we don't take kindly to them folks that hurt dumb animals," Pa said in that quiet, icy voice he had when he was comin' to trouble.

The big ugly man raised his eyes up from the dog he was chokin' and looked at Pa like he was a bloated tick on a cow's hind end.

"I don't much care what they do where you come from," the man said, "and if you don't stay out of my business, I'm gonna slip this rope off'n this worthless dog and put it on you." The man's voice sounded like sand in a grindin' wheel, and he didn't appear the least bit friendly.

I had an idea what was comin' next, and it weren't gonna be a purty thing. Pa had a short fuse, and when he blew, it was usually root hog or die.

I stepped up 'tween Mister Big Ugly and Pa, and put my hand on Pa's arm, which was wanderin' down toward his tomahawk.

"How 'bout I buy that dog from ya, Mister," I said. We were in a strange town full of folks we didn't know. If we started a shootin' fracas, we might just get in trouble with the law, not to mention that the odds was six to four in their favor. We might get 'em all, but some of us was surely gonna get hurt.

Big Ugly laughed deep from his belly and looked at me.

"Kid, I wouldn't sell this dog for all the gold in California. This here is a pure-blood Airedale terrier, and he's gonna grow up to be the meanest thing, next to me, in this town."

He loosened his hold on the rope and the dog sucked in a huge gulp of mountain air. He blowed out, took in another chest full of air, and then cut loose with a roar that fair took me by surprise. The black-and-rust-colored dog started fightin' the rope and did his durndest to take a bite out of Big Ugly.

"See what I mean, kid? He already has the makin's, and

he's only a pup." He squeezed the loop down on the rope again and the dog began to thrash and kick as his air was shut off.

Both me and Pa had hunted and killed many an animal, but we was never mean about it. Pa'd raised me to take what I needed, but never to cause sufferin' to an animal. I'd passed up many a shot 'cause I didn't think I could make a clean kill.

I knew Pa was about to pop the granny knot in his rope belt, and I had to admit I was feelin' a little hostile myself. My partner, Chris Silva, and Pa's trappin' buddy, Stone-Cold Phillips, was standin' behind us and off to one side. They had their rifles in their hands. It looked like things were about to get real interestin'.

I took a step back so I could clear my gun, and Pa's hand took hold of his tomahawk. Then suddenly he stopped.

"I'll tell you what, Mister," Pa said in a half friendly voice. "You fight this here kid of mine and if you whup him I give you twenty-five dollars. If'n he whips you, we take the dog."

I kinda jerked at the suggestion and got hold of Pa's arm again. I could see Big Ugly was rollin' the idea around in his head, and that give me cause for worry. I squeezed Pa's arm and then half drug him back toward Chris and Stoney.

"Pa, what are ya doin'?" I hissed at him. "Look at that feller."

Pa grinned at me and then looked over at Big Ugly, who was still studyin' Pa's suggestion. "He is a big'un, ain't he?" He looked hard at me and grinned even bigger. "Come on, Matthew. You whupped worse than him in Denver, then tore down a saloon, and done it all in the same day."

"They give me cause, Pa. They'd been comin' at me." I glanced over Pa's shoulder at Big Ugly and saw him kinda nod his head.

"Pa, I've only seen one man bigger than this one, and I always been thankful that I never had to fight him." I was thinkin' of my friend Wedge that was back on our ranch under the shadow of the Storm King Mountain. I stopped a minute and took in some air and looked Pa fair in the eye. "Besides, it's mighty convenient of you to volunteer me to do the fightin'. It was you that started it."

"I'm sorry, Matt, but I couldn't stand him disabusin' that dog."

"You fight him then."

"You know I can't, Matthew. My rheumatiz has been actin' up terrible with this wet weather, and I'm gettin' too old fer that kinda thing." Pa looked at Big Ugly, then back at me. "When I was your age I could a took him with one arm busted and the other one tied to my belt." He give me a half smile.

I could hear voices comin' from the boardwalk and realized that Big Ugly's friends was urgin' him on to take the fight.

"All right," Big Ugly finally said. "You got yourself a deal, old man." He handed the rope and dog to one of the other men and popped his knuckles one by one as he started toward me. He had a plum nasty grin on his face.

Sometimes it seemed to me that a man ought to just get rid of all his relations. He'd surely live a longer and happier life.

Chapter Two

"**S**he's doing very well, Mrs. Wilkes. She seems to have a natural bent for refinement."

Edna Wilkes disliked this little man intensely. His hair was slicked down with grease and he had an oily smile on his face. Edna detested him, but his academy for young women was considered to be the best in New England.

"You promised me that she would be finished in eighteen months if she applied herself," Edna reminded him. She'd learned over the years that all contracts should have a limitation of time.

"And so she shall, madam." His tone was slightly condescending. "As I said, she seems to have a natural affinity for embracing things of culture, and considering her condition when you brought her to me . . ." A momentary look of disgust came over his face at the memory.

Edna almost laughed at the foppish little man. Lewara had been rough around the edges when she'd appeared on Edna's doorstep, but no more so than she herself had been in the gold camps of northern California in the old days. If the schoolmaster had known her then . . .

"You have six more months, Mr. Degan," she reminded him.

"Yes, madam," he said, rising with her as she headed for the door.

"And I want her sent to my home on the weekends from now on," Edna added. "Bring her to my home every Friday evening by carriage."

"But, madam . . ." Degan began to protest.

"I am not a madam, Mr. Degan. My name is Mrs. Wilkes, and I want her on the weekends. I need to judge her progress." Edna knew that Degan's school policy was that the girls would be residents at the school for the entire eighteen months of their training. She didn't disagree with the philosophy, but in this case she'd made up her mind. She needed her niece on the weekends. Edna viewed herself as a strong and independent woman, but since her husband's death she'd been painfully alone.

Edna Wilkes possessed more money, and therefore more power, than most of the men in Boston. She and her husband had amassed a considerable fortune during their years in California, and she'd not been carried along on her husband's coattails. She and Charles had formed a business partnership before they'd fallen in love. Now Edna found that the men of influence in Boston not only resented her self-reliance, but they also closed doors to her that had been open to her husband. She was determined to extend her power base and wealth despite the petty desires of the men who thought they were in control. Edna also realized that her niece had awakened something in her. She felt the old drive to accomplish something constructive with her life, and she felt there was something to live for once again.

She stopped a moment and turned back to Mr. Degan. "Friday evenings, Mr. Degan, or I shall remove her from the academy." She closed the door behind her, cutting off Degan's protests, and walked briskly to her carriage.

Despite the time she and Lee had spent together over the past year, they still barely knew each other. Edna had always been honest with herself, and she knew she needed her young niece in her life. She was also sensitive enough to realize that she couldn't smother Lee. Edna had seen the strength and independence in the girl. Lewara was her sister's daughter, but she also recognized some of her own traits in her young niece.

The carriage jerked as it started forward and the steel rims of the wheels rattled as they rolled over the paving stones on the street.

Edna thought she and Lee might become very good friends, given a little time. She had never been blessed with children, which only heightened the special kinship she felt with her niece.

"You want to go to the market, Edna?" Clayton called down to her from the elevated carriage seat.

"No, just home, Clayton, please," Edna said, raising her voice to be heard above the wheels.

Clayton had been with her since the early days in California. His nationality was a mystery, which had never been an issue to Edna or anyone else once they'd looked in his eyes. He projected the aura of being a dangerous man despite the fact he was of medium size. Maybe it was the saber scar that split his left ear and cheek, or the gold ring in his right ear, or perhaps even the five pounds of knife that was visible at his waist. Whatever the reason, other men stepped wide of him. His skin was the color of caramel, his hair was midnight black, straight, and blocked midway down his back. His chin was square, his cheekbones high, and he had a massive black mustache that she thought he might have been born with because she had never seen him without it. Edna assumed that he was older than she, but he'd always looked the same so his age was indeterminate. Clayt drove her carriage now, but he was more than her employee. He was her friend. She gave him a wage and occasionally a bonus for special services he rendered to her in the course of business. He was attached to her, but he'd always been free to leave at any time. He just never had. There had been a persistent rumor that Clayt had been a pirate of the worst stripe at one time, but again that mattered little to Edna. Clayton had saved her life more than once, and he had killed men in the process. She had also killed a man a long time ago, and in a place separated by most of a continent from Boston.

Edna shook her head to clear the memories, looked from the carriage window at the houses and stores they drove past, and thought of Lee. She wanted the very best for Lewara, but she knew she must go slowly. She didn't want to create the impression that she was trying to buy Lee's affection. They'd reached an agreement early on that the tuition at the academy was a loan, and Edna had executed a contract that both she and Lee had signed. Edna planned on giving the contract to Lee as a graduation gift, but again she had to be careful. Lee was fiercely independent, just as her father had been, and she would never consider accepting something for free. But the work at the school was hard, and by the time Lee was finished she would have earned being free of the contract.

Edna felt the covered carriage turn left and stop. She heard the familiar creak of the gate as the footman opened it, and again a jerk as the carriage started down the lane to the estate. She lifted the scarlet curtain that covered the window once again and looked at her home. "We've come many a mile since that first day, Edna MacLoy Wilkes," she said softly.

"That was her?" the man asked. His voice gave the impression that he wasn't impressed. The woman he'd watched coming and going from the school had been smallish and something above forty years old.

"Yes. That was Edna Wilkes, and don't underestimate her. We know very little about her, but the rumors persist that she can be very hard to deal with."

Degan had come to the front door of the school to answer a knock shortly after Edna Wilkes left. The man that had knocked was dirty, with a weasel face and skinny arms. The individual that stood behind the weasel was a filthy, hulking brute with hunched shoulders. Degan hated dealing with the pair, but their association had proved to be profitable on several occasions. The weasel was named Morgan. Degan didn't know the name of the musclehead, and he didn't care. They were his employees and he didn't need to know much about them.

"So what you want done?" Morgan asked.

"My client wants her incapacitated for a number of days," Degan responded.

"What the hell does that mean? You want her dead?"

"From what he said I don't think he'd mind, but . . . no," he replied after a moment of reflection. "I think a beating that puts her in the hospital for a period of time would be sufficient."

"How soon you want it done?"

"The sooner the better."

"Half now, and the rest when we finish," Morgan said, holding out his hand.

"The same arrangement as always," Degan agreed, reaching into his jacket pocket for the envelope. "Another thing, don't come back here to the academy, Morgan. When it's done, I'll pay you the other half at the tavern."

Morgan nodded, took the envelope from Degan, turned, and walked down the street without a backward glance. Degan rubbed his hand on his pants leg as he watched the two criminals walk away. He always felt dirtied after he'd been in their presence. He closed the door quietly and turned back to his desk. He stopped a moment and allowed himself a wolfish smile. Edna Wilkes was going to regret having acted so superior to him. He was going to accomplish two tasks with one blow. He'd gain a measure of revenge, and he'd fulfill the wishes of his client.

There was also the small matter of a woman, an older woman, who had contacted him with regard to Edna Wilkes' niece. The woman's name was Marilyn Beck, and she harbored a virulent hatred for Lee. Something about her son, a

man named Falcon, and some violence out West. He hadn't
followed the story very well after he'd seen the gold money
she'd slapped on the table. Five thousand dollars in double
eagles was a lot of money, and all he had to do was arrange
an accident for Lewara Conall.

To certain people in positions of power, Degan was a fa-
cilitator. They would tell him of a problem, and he would
arrange for a solution. Sometimes the solution involved violence, or theft, or perhaps forgery. Unfortunately, being a fa-
cilitator put him in contact with the scum of the earth. It was
a necessity, but the criminals he dealt with sometimes gave
him the creeps.

He studied the ledger and allowed himself another self-
satisfied smile. Soon he would have enough money to make
the move he'd planned for some time. When he did, he'd
become a man of substance that people like Edna Wilkes
would bow to. He looked up from the ledger and glanced out
the window. On second thought he doubted if Edna Wilkes
had ever bowed to anyone, or ever would.

Lee watched as her aunt had entered the academy and then,
a short time later, left. The building which housed the school
sat on a corner of two intersecting streets and had a porch that
projected at an angle to both streets. As a result of the peculiar
construction, the front entry of the school could be seen from
the second-story window, next to which Lee now sat. Her aunt
visited her every Saturday, and Lee had learned to both love
the older woman and respect her. Lee was curious as to what
had brought her to see Mr. Degan on a Wednesday. She was
about to return her attention to the sampler she was struggling
with when she saw two men walking from an alley across the
street toward the school. They walked purposely up the four
steps to the porch and knocked. Mr. Degan answered, and she
could see him speaking to them.

Lee had seen Mr. Degan talking to these two once before.
She supposed the reason she'd noticed was that they abso-

lutely didn't fit the mold of people that she assumed Mr. Degan would socialize with. They instead reminded her of men who were better suited to the inside of a jail.

"Miss Conall, are you finished with your assignment?" a stern-faced older woman asked Lee.

"Nearly . . ."

"I'm quite sure you would finish much faster if you would pay attention to your needlework and quit staring from the window," the woman interrupted.

"Yes, ma'am," Lee replied in a contrite tone. She found the needlework class boring, and much preferred the speech and etiquette classes. The choice, of course, was not hers to make. Every weekday the girls at the school spent nine fruitful and inspiring hours learning how to be ladies, at least by the academy standard.

Lee was determined to finish the course. She'd been at the school for a year and had learned much about the niceties of the gentry, but she realized she still had much to learn. She could see no earthly purpose for ninety percent of what they were taught, but she also recognized that learning the specifics gave her an overall polish. Besides, it went against her grain to quit something before it was finished, regardless of how stupid most of the instruction seemed.

"All right, ladies, move down to the music room, and Master Barton will give today's instruction on piano," the stern-faced woman said. The girls in the room rose almost as one, careful that their dresses were arranged in proper fashion, and one-by-one placed their samplers neatly in the wall cupboard.

Lee happened to glance from the window again, and noticed that the two men were walking away. Something about the meeting made her curious, but she cleared it from her mind and walked with the rest of the young women down the hall to the music room. As she entered, she wondered if she could honestly stand six more months of the routine. She desperately missed the open country.

"Miss Conall, may I speak with you, please." Mr. Degan was standing in the hall motioning for her.

"Of course," she replied as she approached him.

"From now on you will be going to Mrs. Wilkes' home on Friday evenings instead of staying at the school," Degan said. His voice was vexed, and Lee thought him angry.

"Yes, sir," was all she could think to say in reply.

"At six o'clock, before the evening meal on Friday, you will meet one of the school's carriages out front and the driver will escort you to your aunt's home. As you know, this is against school policy, but your aunt was quite insistent . . ." his voice trailed off. "While you are away from the academy, I expect your conduct to be above reproach and your activities to reflect what you have learned while here."

"Yes, sir," she replied again, more than a little confused.

"Also, I forbid you to speak of this breach of the rules with any of the other students. Do you understand?"

"Yes, sir."

"Back to class, then," he said. He turned quickly away from her and strode down the hall. His shoes squeaked horribly as he walked, and Lee stifled the urge to laugh. His squalling shoes completely destroyed the image he was trying to project.

Lee again walked toward the music room. She was thrilled that she was being allowed to go to her aunt's on the weekends. It gave her something to look forward to and might make the remaining six months tolerable. She could scarcely wait for Friday.

Chapter Three

Del Norte, Colorado, was a one-street, four-store town with a few houses thrown up here and yon. When we rode in, I didn't figure the whole town would boast a population of more than fifty poor and starvin' souls.

I was wrong. Soon as one of Big Ugly's friends started hollerin' 'bout a fight, people seemed to come right up out of the ground.

"That big kid surely ain't plannin' on fightin' Burdett, is he?" I heard one of 'em ask.

"They fightin' fer twenty-five dollars or the dog," I heard another one answer.

"Kid," a man with a bushy black beard said to me, "there's nobody ever fought Bloody Bull Burdett and won. He's killed at least three men with his hands, and I seen one of those fights myself."

"Thanks, Pa," I said under my breath as I took off my gun belt and handed it to Chris.

I knew I was in shape. We'd been trekkin' for the past three months, and I'd done some of it on foot. I'd always liked hikin', and I'd done a passel of it down in the mountains around Taos where we'd spent the summer. I reckoned that would help my stayin' power.

I'd also learned the basics of fightin' from two men that had reputations for rough fightin'. Wedge had been prone to rippin' ears off folks before we'd settled him down, and a friend of mine who'd been killed out in the high plains of Kansas had taught me the Kiowa's ways of fightin', with some English boxin' thrown in for good measure. Bloody Bull Ugly, or whatever his name was, had been standin' next to a bar drinkin' rattlesnake whiskey and homemade beer durin' the same three months I'd been gettin' in shape. I reckoned I had a chance to at least stay alive against him.

I looked around. There must a been near a hundred people gathered up about us, and there was a good bit of money bein' passed back and forth. Fall in high-country towns meant that they was almost snowed in 'til spring, and they was already starved for entertainment. It looked like I was gonna provide them with at least five minutes of excitement. I 'sposed there wasn't much money bein' put on me.

"Come on, kid," Big Ugly said in his raspy voice. "I got better things to do then stand 'round here and wait on you to start bawlin'."

I turned to face him, and he come on me with a rush. He hit me in the chest with his shoulder so hard it flung me into the crowd. It fair knocked the air out of me, and he had me half whipped before I'd ever raised a hand. He come at me fast and hard again. I managed to jump away, but I was clumsy on my feet. I was suckin' hard tryin' to get my wind back, and my chest burned like fire. I'd somehow turned away from him as I jumped back. As I turned, he hit me so fast I had no chance to dodge the blows. I was on my back lookin' at the sky, and I saw his boots comin' at me as he jumped stiff-legged. He surely planned on stompin' the life out of me. I rolled, then rolled again. It put me out of his range and my head started to clear. I could hear people yellin' and screamin' as I pushed up from the ground and got my feet under me. Big Ugly was standin' in the middle of the muddy street with his hands on his hips smilin' at me.

One of my best friends had been a major in the Confederate Army. He'd told me, "Never underestimate your enemy, Matt. It will cost you the battle." I surely hoped that Big Ugly was doin' just that. I'd been clumsy, and he'd taken me by surprise, but now I was warmed up, and the blood was pumpin' through my veins.

He bellered like a bee-stung opera singer and come at me again, slower this time. I hit him with a punch that would have dropped a bull elk, then followed it with a fast roundhouse that nailed him just over the ear. I knew both punches stung him, but he just smiled and shook his head. I was gettin' worried.

He swung at me, and I slipped inside. I hit him hard three times with left-right combinations in the gut, then danced away before he could react. I was faster than he was, and I thought he might still be underestimatin' me. That happens with a man who's never been beat. I had to make it work to my advantage.

Big Ugly turned as I worked my way around him, then he came with a rush again. I managed to avoid him, but barely. He missed with a swing that would have surely taken my head off had it connected. He swung again, a wicked fast punch I just managed to miss, then I stepped inside his reach again. I nailed him good in the gut with my left, then caught him with a right upper cut under the chin. It hurt him, but not enough. He grabbed me in his arms before I could get away, and he started squeezin' me like a griz would squeeze a milk cow. I kicked, strained, bent my back, and tried to suck some wind in. He started bearin' down more, and I began to panic. My air had left me, and I could feel my backbone poppin'. I started seeing green and blue lights, and my ears were full of a sound like a strong wind in a tall cottonwood. I stomped down on his instep as hard as I could and his arms dropped. I took in a double helpin' of air, and we stood toe-to-toe swappin' punches as fast as we could swing. Burdett stepped back to get some space, and I followed him. He hit me hard in the stomach, and I fell over on my back again.

Burdett figured me done in, and he took a step back tryin' to catch his air. I started feelin' my legs again, did a half roll, then climbed to my feet. I was hurt. My nose was drippin' blood, and I had a nasty cut over my eye that I had no recollection of gettin'. My head was hangin' down, and I was as close to bein' beat as I'd ever been.

Burdett took another step back from me. I could tell he was gatherin' himself up to finish me off, and there just didn't seem to be much I could do about it. I looked around me and saw Pa standin' at the inner edge of the crowd fingering his 'hawk. I knew he'd not let Burdett kill me without a fight, but that would mean that Pa, Chris, and Stoney was likely to get killed or bad hurt along with me. I turned back toward Big Ugly, and he had that nasty grin on his face again. Then I heard the dog whine.

That ol' black rage that I hated but had little control over started fillin' my gut. The poor excuse for a man in front of me had walked hard-heeled around his little piece of territory terrorizing one and all. He was nothing but an overgrown schoolyard bully that everybody was scared of. On top of that he was mean to dogs and probably kids and little old ladies.

I let loose a roar, ducked my head, and took off running right at him. If he wouldn't have been so surprised, he could've stepped aside, and I'd have run my head right through the store behind him. As it was, I took him right below the breastbone with my hard head. It knocked him off his feet and pushed his air out. He jumped to get up, but I kicked him right under the chin and laid him back down. I jumped onto his chest pinnin' him to the ground. I started seein' red and just took to punchin', kickin', screamin', slappin', spittin', and blowin' snot. I hit Bloody Bull Burdett until I couldn't lift my arms to hit no more. Then I stood and kicked him half-a-dozen times more. I'd never given him a chance to get his feet back under him 'cause I knew if he did, he'd have me.

I backed away from him and swayed on my feet. I was hurt, maybe bad, the rage that had drained out of me leavin' me weak, shaky, and sick. The crowd standin' around me was deadly still.

"By gosh, I never seen the likes of that," I heard a man say in near a whisper. They started leavin' in ones and twos, quietly talkin' 'mongst themselves. I looked down at the man I'd whipped. He was breathin', but it was labored and sounded painful. He was out cold as a frozen grasshopper, and his face was unrecognizable.

"I reckon this pup belongs to us," I heard Pa say as he took the dog from the man holdin' the rope. The pup came along willingly as if he knew that things was gonna get better for him. "Let's head on fer the hills," Pa said, "before some of Burdett's friends get the notion to try and start somethin'."

Chris had brought the horses over and they mounted up. For the life of me I couldn't muster the strength to climb into my saddle. Pa and Chris finally got down from their horses and half pushed, half lifted me 'til I felt the saddle under my tail. I was in a daze, and I was seein' two or three of everything.

"I know where there's an old trappin' cabin in a side canyon along the river west of here," Stone-Cold said. "We'd best get him there. He's not gonna be in any shape to ride for a few days, and if I ain't wrong we're in for a spot of nasty weather. We'd better hole up somewhere warm."

"You thinkin' 'bout ol' Three-Finger's place up at the head of that box canyon?" I heard Pa ask.

"That's the one," Stoney replied.

"That's a likely place," Pa agreed. "It's hid and yet not too far out."

Pa led us west out of town up the canyon of the Rio Grande. I was in and out for most of the ride, but I knew when it started snowin' and when the wind started blowin' the snow sideways in front of us. We rode for what seemed like hours. I was disoriented, and my eyes had swollen so bad I could barely see. My horse, Sin, was followin' Pa along, and it's a good thing he was. I had no hope of givin' direction of any kind. Then somethin' happened that hadn't happened to me since I'd been knee high to a short duck. I fell off my horse. I just lay there in the snow kinda hopin' I'd die and get it over with.

"It's just ahead of us, Tirley," I heard Stoney say to Pa. "We can drag him that far if we need to."

"Get on your feet, amigo," I heard Chris say quietly in my ear. "We are at the cabin." I felt his arm around my shoulder liftin', urgin' me to stand. I struggled and finally half stood. I had a stitch in my side, and each breath I took made me shudder with pain. Chris led me to a rough-cut pine door and then guided me in. I was done up, and I fell face down on the plank floor. I just lay there with misery shootin' through every part of my body. I heard a whine and felt a warm tongue on my face.

"You can tell that dog ain't gonna amount to much. He's already taken with Matthew," Pa said. I heard Stoney and Chris laugh, but I surely wasn't gonna join in. Laughin' was the last thing I wanted to do.

"He's in tough shape, Tirley," I heard Stone-Cold Phillips remark as he leaned over me.

"He is that," Pa agreed. "Soon as the weather breaks I 'spect we'd better take him over to Pahgosa and soak him in the springs."

"The Navajos won't take kindly to that," Stoney said.

"It ain't Navajo territory no more," Pa said. He bent over me and started to lift me by the shoulders. I tried to help, but I was just no good. "Give me a hand and let's get him into the bunk."

I felt Chris and Stoney get hold of me and kinda half lift and half drag me, and then dump me onto a bunk built into the cabin wall. I heard one of 'em start to build a fire in the stacked rock fireplace. I was nearly gone when I felt a weight jump on the bunk, then a warm body snuggled up to me. My eyes was stuck shut so I couldn't see, but from the smell I figured it for the dog. He let out a big sigh, snuggled in a little tighter. Just before I drifted out, I thought of an auburn-haired gal named Lewara Conall. I surely wished she was here with me. I surely did.

"How are you, my friend?" Chris asked as we rode down the box canyon toward the Rio Grande River.

"I been better," I replied carefully. Talkin' was downright painful, so I'd been avoidin' it as much as I could.

"You have looked better," Chris said with a smile. I figured that was probably fact. It was six days removed from the fight in Del Norte. My eyes had opened up some, but I still had trouble seein', and sittin' on my horse was pure torture.

Chris and I was ridin' side by side behind Pa and Stone-Cold Phillips. I had the dog layin' on a blanket on the saddle in front of me. We'd had 'bout a foot of snow while I'd been down, and I figured he'd have a hard time in snow that deep. Pa reckoned I was just spoilin' him. Maybe I was, but it was clear that the dog had picked me for his partner. He'd laid beside me for most of the days I'd been stove up and moved only when I did. He followed close behind me no matter what I was doin' or how slow I was doin' it. Soon as I lay back down he was there beside me.

I think Pa was a little put out that the Airedale had picked me over him. He supposed that since he'd stopped Big Ugly from disabusin' him that the dog just natural ought to've picked him to partner with. Pa seemed to forget that it was me that got my guts stomped, and the dog seemed to know it.

Pa and Stoney pulled up, waitin' on us. It was early mornin', and my head hurt so bad I was certain sure I could hear the sun comin' up over the mountains.

"How ya makin' it, boy?" Pa asked. I didn't bother to answer. I just nodded my head. Pa looked a trifle concerned, then turned his face toward the big canyon ahead of us where the river flowed.

"We'll make South Fork by night, and it's probably a good thing," Stoney said to no one in particular. "Gets mighty cold up here this time of the year."

"It snows any more and we ain't gonna make the pass at Wolf Creek," Pa said. His voice had a little worry in it.

"Looks like we're out of snow," Stoney said, lookin' at the sky. "I'd bet it gets warm enough today fer the horses to break a sweat on the climb and melt the snow."

We went slow comin' down out of the box canyon, but when we hit the main trail going up the hill west we picked up the pace.

My horse, Sin, had always been an easy ridin' horse, and I was plumb thankful that he had an even gait. My ribs was creakin' and crackin', and my knees felt loose as quicksand. Even with a good horse it was gonna be a mighty long day.

We made South Fork just as night closed in. It wasn't all that far from Del Norte to South Fork, but some of it had been a purty good climb into the high country. The trail had been passable but muddy, and we'd only made fair time.

As we rode into South Fork, I figured it to be smaller than Del Norte. The Fork, as most folks called it, boasted a stage station, a corral, maybe three stores, and five houses.

I handed the dog down to Chris before I tried to get out of the saddle. I'd done purty well when we stopped at midday, but it had turned mighty cold as the sun went down. I seemed to be stuck to the saddle, and my legs just didn't want to work. I finally half fell and slid, then stood on the ground with my knees shakin'.

"I'll take care of your horse, amigo," Chris said. I usually wouldn't have stood for that. I figure a man ought to do his own chores, but I nodded my head to him, thankful that I had an understandin' partner.

"You go on in the station, Matthew," Pa said. "See if they'll let us bed down on the floor out of the cold."

Chris handed me the dog, and I set him on his feet. I turned and took my Henry from the boot on my saddle. They took the horses and walked around the back of the station to the livery. I got my legs to workin' and walked onto the split-log porch, then pushed my way into the station. The warmth of the room hit me like an open hand, and I had to blink my swollen eyes a couple times to adjust 'em to the light. The big central room was overshadowed by heavy log beams that held up the low roof. A giant stacked rock fireplace completely filled one end of the room, and both light and heat poured from the roaring fire. A dark-haired, bearded man was standing behind a counter that probably doubled as a bar. He had a curious look on his face.

"Looks like you tangled with a San Juan griz and lost," he said in a deep-toned, friendly voice.

"I think I won, but I couldn't feel much worse if I'd lost," I replied.

"If you won, I'd surely hate to see the guy that lost."

"It weren't a purty thing," I said. "There's four of us, and we was wonderin' if we could bag out here on the floor?" I asked.

"Glad to have ya," he replied. "Gets kinda lonely around here when the weather starts to close down. It'll be nice to have somebody to talk to."

"Well, you're gonna appreciate this old hoss then," Pa said as the three of them came stompin' through the door, " 'cause all he does is talk, and most of that's lies." Pa was pointin' at Stone-Cold Phillips.

"Why, I'll be . . ." the stage master said. "I never knew you ol' boys to ever trek together before." The bearded man obviously knew both Pa and Stoney.

"That's 'cause we can't stand each other's company fer more than a few hours at a time," Stoney said, laughing.

"Trouble is we outlived all our friends, so now we got to hang out with each other."

"Lite and sit," the man said, pointing at a long, heavy, wooden slab table with benches pulled up close to it. "The coffee's on, and I'll throw some meat on the fire." He disappeared into a room hid behind a hangin', brightly colored Hudson Bay blanket, and we sat down.

"Man's name is Rosebud Charlie," Pa explained to Chris and me. "His pa was up in the Three Forks Country with us a long time back. His pap married a Crow gal and stayed on with the tribe. He went under fightin' the Blackfeet back in the early forties."

"Rosie here also married himself a Crow gal and brung her down here to what he calls civilization." Stoney picked up the story. "They got 'em a good little business here, but Rosie's learned to leave his woman behind the blanket when he's got company. Lots of folks don't take to a man havin' an Injun wife, even if he is a breed, and he figures it saves him havin' to kill someone for treatin' her bad."

Just as Stoney finished, Rosebud Charlie threw the curtain back and walked over to the table.

"Sky will bring out some feed in a minute, and I think I can find a small jug around here somewheres."

"The feed sounds right good," Pa agreed, "but I need to hold back on the jug. This miserable lookin' fella here is my boy, Matthew," he said, pointin' to me, "and I got to set a good example fer him." Rosie looked at me for a minute, and I could tell he'd heard my name somewhere before.

"You never was much of a drinker anyhow," Rosie said, movin' his attention back to Pa. He looked over at Stoney and Chris. "This old coot speakin' fer you boys as well?"

"I could use a taste of good sippin' cider," Stoney said. Chris just raised his hand and shook his head no.

A pleasantly round, dark-haired, coppery-skinned woman with a lovely face came in with platters of elk steaks and thick cuts of homemade bread. I near fainted, the smell of good food was so strong, and the dog pulled himself off my feet and took a long whiff of what was on the table.

"This is my wife, Sky," Rosie said as she started throwin' down plates and fillin' 'em with grub. "Her name is Morning Star in the Sky, but that's a little long if I need to fetch her in a hurry," he explained. "I just call her Sky."

I pulled my Spanish steel from my belt and tested it on a two-inch-thick steak. It cut through it like soft butter, and I popped a small slice into my slaverin' mouth. My jaws was almighty sore so I chewed slow and easy. The dog sat beside me on the floor, not beggin', but surely expectin' me to share. I cut off a little bigger piece and handed it down to him. He took it from me like a real gentleman, even though I knew he was hungry.

"Dog's got better manners than your pa," Stoney said, bringin' a laugh from everyone includin' Sky.

"What's your dog's name?" Rosie asked me.

"I don't know if he really belongs to me," I said. "I think he's one of them animals that ain't really owned by nobody. He's more of a partner, and he tolerates me long as I keep him fed. Far as a name . . . I'd not given it much study."

"Ain't proper to just call him somethin' like 'dog'," Stoney said, working around a mouthful of bread.

"Naw, that ain't fittin'," Pa agreed. We fell quiet, eatin' and thinkin'.

"Killer's a little much," Stoney said, "and Rowdy don't sound right neither."

"Hombre," Chris said from behind an enormous slice of meat.

"Naw, he don't look like he's got that much Mexican in him," Pa said, and everyone laughed again.

"I think Bucklin's 'bout right," Pa said. "Means somethin' like 'great fighter in the Celtic'."

"Bucklin's a mighty fine name," I agreed.

There was nods all around the table, and the dog was officially named. I threw him the two-pound-bone out of my steak, and he crawled under the table by my feet chewin' and mutterin' to hisself.

We was just finishin' up the feed when we heard the sound of horses in the yard, followed by loud voices. Bucklin come out from under the table and growled low in his chest.

"Easy boy," I said to him, and he crowded up against my leg with his kinky back hair standin' right up. I twisted around a little so my back leaned against the log wall, and I was half facin' the front door. Chris got up and moved around the table and sat down with Stoney and Pa so he was facin' the door. Sky went back into the room behind the blanket, and Rosie walked over behind the bar.

They come stompin' in, bringin' the frigid air with 'em. There was five of them, and they was surely polecats from the looks and smell of them. Bucklin's growlin' got louder, and I dropped my hand to his back to quiet him. The men crowded in and then walked toward the bar. I recognized 'em as soon as the lantern light fell on their faces. One of 'em had a giant growth of hair under his nose, and he'd been standin' with Bloody Bull Burdett in Del Norte. It surely looked like trouble had found us, and this time it could be gun trouble.

Chapter Four

"We have a problem, Mrs. Wilkes."

"You always seem to have a problem, Mr. Jensen. What is it this time?" Edna knew she should pay attention to the banker, but she was distracted. It was Friday, and Lee would be arriving any moment. This was the fourth consecutive weekend Lee had come home from the boarding school.

"Mrs. Wilkes, did you hear me?"

"No, I'm sorry. I'm waiting for my niece to arrive. What were you saying?"

"Your property on the west side will essentially become useless for either homes or businesses should the stockyards be allowed to locate adjacent to your holdings. Useless translates to worthless in this case." Mr. Jensen now had her attention. He cleared his throat, but remained quiet.

Edna stood and walked to the window of the parlor. She'd always thought better on her feet. She had more than half of her cash assets invested in the six hundred and forty acres on the west side of the city. If she lost on this endeavor, the wolves would be at the door, and she wouldn't last long.

"Wingate surely has the support of the city since he sits on the city council, and the man that owns the property told me this morning that he is considering selling to Wingate."

"So what are the particulars?" Edna asked, as she turned to face the banker. "Why does Wingate want to locate the stock-yards and slaughterhouse in that particular spot?"

"The railroad," he answered quickly. "John O'Malley is running a rail line across the property that Wingate is trying to buy."

Edna was silent a moment, then turned to the banker. "It seems we must either buy the land before Wingate does, or we must convince Mr. O'Malley that he shouldn't run his railroad line on that particular alignment," she said. Edna had always possessed the ability to clean a business problem to the naked bones.

"That seems simplified, but yes . . . I would say those are the alternatives," Jensen agreed.

"Buy the land," Edna said. "I will pay a premium for it."

Mr. Jensen hesitated a moment, then looked away from her.

"What is it, Mr. Jensen?"

"The man will not sell to you, Mrs. Wilkes. I've already spoken to him, and he says he would rather give the land away as to sell to a woman."

Edna was not particularly surprised. She'd met with the same attitude on a number of occasions since she'd lived in the East.

"Mr. O'Malley . . ."

"A very hard man, and one not given to changing his mind. I've watched him over the past few years. He's honest but will not change his mind once he's decided on a course." Jensen hesitated a moment, then continued. "There is also the persistent rumor that he's related to a clan of Colorado gun-men."

Edna raised an eyebrow at the mention of Colorado. She knew that Lee had been in Colorado just before she'd come to Boston. Edna and Lee had not talked much about their personal histories during their short time together. She knew that Lee had either owned or managed an eating establishment and had also been involved with a ranch, both located in Colorado.

"How soon do we need to move, Mr. Jensen?" Edna asked.

"The city council meeting is Tuesday. They'll undoubtedly vote to allow the development to proceed, which clears the last obstacle for Wingate. His option on the purchase of the ground is conditional based on approval of the city council and O'Malley bringing the rail line through the property. The O'Malley condition is assured, since I know the engineering for the roadbed is complete, and if the council votes to approve, which they will, he clears title on Wednesday."

"So we have the weekend . . ."

"Only that and Monday," he agreed.

"I will be in contact with you no later than Tuesday at noon," Edna said.

"Very well," Jensen said as he rose to leave. "Oh, I might add that Wingate indicated to me that he would be happy to purchase your property," he said as an aside. He looked toward the front door rather than meet her eyes.

So this was the punchline. The serpent had raised his ugly head, and it came in the form of collusion between her banker and a crooked city councilman.

"And what did Mr. Wingate offer?" Edna asked carefully.

"He said he'd give you a hundred dollars an acre."

Edna almost laughed in his face, but kept her composure. "You realize that I paid a great deal more than that on the original purchase?"

"Of course, but in light of the options it seems a fair offer."

"And one I will consider over the weekend," Edna said sweetly.

She ushered the banker to the front door and showed him out. "Thank you, Mr. Jensen. I'll be in touch with you early next week." Jensen touched the brim of his hat and walked to his buggy.

Edna's mind was working furiously as she watched him drive off. Her problem clearly was that she had not paid close enough attention to business. She'd left her affairs in the hands of a person she barely knew, and now she was paying the price. It was the first time in her entire life that she had not handled a business deal either in company with Charles or on her own. Obviously she was about to be defrauded by two men who had set her up for a fleecing. Jensen had talked her originally into the purchase of the land, and he and Wingate had been in it together from the beginning. She had simply asked Jensen in passing if he knew of any property that might be for sale. He replied that he thought he knew of some prime land that was just coming out of an estate settlement. That had been the beginning.

What would happen next, unless she could find a way to prevent it, was that Wingate and Jensen would purchase her land for a song, then turn about and develop not only the land Wingate was about to buy from the man who wouldn't sell to a woman, but also the land they would acquire from her. Absolutely no one wanted to build in the proximity of a large stockyard and slaughterhouse. If they could force her to sell her six hundred and forty acres cheaply, they would be able to develop both parcels. Her land was probably destined to become a shantytown which would hold the immigrant families of the men that would work at the stockyards and slaughterhouse. Regardless of how Wingate used the land, the railroad played a prominent role, and Wingate, the city councilman, and Jensen stood to gain greatly from the development.

Edna looked up as a carriage pulled to a stop in the spot the banker had just vacated. She grappled for her poise, struggling to overcome her anger. Lee was helped down from the carriage by the driver, and Edna realized that she had become a classically beautiful woman. She was wearing a stylish white gown, her chestnut hair was up, and the small amount of makeup she wore was carefully applied. Her cheekbones were more prominent now than when she had first arrived, an indication that she had lost some weight. The driver grabbed her bag, and they walked up the brick walkway toward Edna. Lee had a tremendous smile on her face as she looked at her aunt. Edna again realized that Lee was absolutely beautiful, and certainly now every inch a lady. She had changed so much during the past year . . . Edna thought again of Wingate and the banker Jensen. She felt a cloud move in front of her sun.

"Are you feeling well, Aunt Edna?" The smile had melted from Lee's face.

"I'm fine, Lee. I just have a small business problem."

"Can I help?"

"No it's something very complicated . . ." Suddenly Edna stopped in mid-sentence. Lee was standing three feet away, and Edna could see the deep intelligence in her niece's eyes. Edna needed a sounding board she trusted, and, in truth, she had been younger than Lee when she'd begun making her own business decisions.

"On second thought," she said, "maybe together we can come up with a solution. I'm in a bit of a bind."

Lee took her bag from the driver, thanked him, then walked into the house with her aunt.

"Ruth, would you please bring us some tea, then close the parlor doors," Edna said to the maid. After the tea was served and the doors closed, Edna told Lee the situation in detail.

Lee watched her aunt intently during the recital and stopped her twice for clarification. The two women sat at a small table covered by a lace tablecloth nestled in the bay window of the parlor. Lee sipped tea, ate a muffin, and by the end of Edna's dissertation she had a tiny smile in the corner of her mouth. Edna thought Lee understood the details of the predicament, but not the seriousness of the consequences.

"What it means, Lee, is that I will have lost most of my liquid assets. It also means that other people I have business dealings with will be less likely to trust my judgement, and by extension their friends will not trust me, and soon I will be frozen out. By this one stupid oversight I could possibly lose everything."

Edna's words seemed to ring in the air, as she had delivered them with more force then she intended, but the smile stayed on Lee's face.

Lee stood, walked over to her aunt, and took the older woman's hand.

"I may now be nearly a lady, but there's still nothin' better than kickin' the stuffin' out of a couple of city boys," she said reverting back to the careless speech of her first days in Boston, and then she laughed.

Edna was confused. She had no idea what Lee was talking about.

"What happens if John O'Malley decides to run the rail line in a place that doesn't involve the Wingate property?" Lee asked.

Edna thought for a moment and then replied, "If he changes the route, it would make the property Wingate is trying to buy much less attractive, and it certainly wouldn't work for the purpose he has planned. The railroad is the means by which the animals are moved from the point where they are bought to the place of processing. No railroad, no animals. Also, Jensen said that the purchase of the land was conditional on the railroad being put across the property."

"Well, I happen to know that Uncle John O'Malley would never let something happen that would lead to innocent people being hurt, particularly if there is something dishonest about the transaction."

"Uncle John O'Malley?" Edna asked, surprised.

"I happen to know John O'Malley well," Lee said. "His nephew is the reason I'm here."

Edna's hand went to her mouth in surprise. "Your young man?"

"Well, he's not mine, but yes . . . Matthew O'Malley," Lee replied. She was silent a moment and then added, "Without the O'Malley family helping me, I might not have survived those first months after Daddy died." Lee walked to the window and pulled the lace curtain back, looking into the street.

"Do you think . . ." Edna began.

"I'm sure he'll help us, Aunt Edna," Lee said as she turned back to her aunt. "Do you know where he is?"

"No, but I know someone who can find him." Edna pulled on the bell cord, and Ruth almost immediately opened the parlor door. "Ruth, would you tell Clayton that I need his assistance, please?"

"Of course, Mrs. Wilkes," Ruth replied.

As the maid left, Edna turned once again to her niece. "Clayt has been critical to my life since I was only slightly older than you are now. He taught me many years ago that information is the grease which allows business to move smoothly forward. If you have the correct information at the right time . . ."

The parlor door opened again, and Clayton stood framed in the doorway. "Edna?" Clayton said.

"We have a spot of trouble, Clayt," Edna said. "I need to find a man by the name of John O'Malley. I need to find him quickly."

"He's at the Copley Inn over by Back Bay," Clayton replied. "I spoke with him yesterday."

Nothing about Clayton astonished Edna anymore, but Lee was obviously surprised.

"You spoke with Uncle John?" Lee asked. "He's here?"

"He's been in the city for several days," Clayton replied. "He plans on building a railroad on the west side."

"Do you suppose you might arrange a meeting between us and Mr. O'Malley?" Edna asked.

"Of course," Clayton replied. "I have an appointment with him and one of his sons for dinner tomorrow evening. I know they'd welcome your company."

"Thank you, Clayton. Please advise him that the meeting is not social. It is a matter of business," Edna said.

"I'll speak with him in the morning, Edna," Clayton replied.

"Thank you, Clayt. As usual you have come to my rescue." Edna smiled at him.

Clayton nodded to her and moved to leave.

"Sir," Lee said, stopping him, "can you tell me how you happen to know John O'Malley?"

Edna looked at Lee, startled. Edna herself would never have asked such as personal question of her friend.

"Let's just say that John O'Malley and I sailed on a ship together many years ago. We've stayed in touch since."

"Thank you," Lee replied, smiling at him. He closed the door to the parlor as he left.

"The rumor is that Clayton is not his real name, and he was at one time a pirate," Edna said quietly. "I have never asked, and he has never volunteered his history."

"I shouldn't have," Lee said. "It was impulsive and rude."

"You're learning," Edna said with a smile, "and no harm done." She stood and walked to the door. "Lets go to dinner, and I have tickets to the theater this evening," she said, holding out her hand to her niece.

Lee took her aunt's hand. Edna turned the ornate knob on the parlor door, and then stopped.

"Uncle John O'Malley," she said, chuckling and looking over her shoulder at Lee. "You're certainly full of surprises, young lady. If this goes the way you think it will, there are a couple of crooks about to get an expensive surprise."

Chapter Five

"Well, look what we got here," the guy with the lip hair said.

I didn't much care for the tone in his voice. "This ain't my place," I said to him, "but if it was, the likes of you wouldn't be welcome." I'd said it quiet, so he acted like he hadn't heard me plain. He'd heard me right enough, but he wanted his buddies to hear.

"I don't think I heard you right, boy," he said.

I must of looked a sight. I knew my face was all black and blue, my nose was still swollen, and I had a barely closed cut over my eye. I don't 'spose I looked like anything that would be a threat to a man that could grow lip hair like he could.

"Why don't you lean over here a little," I said. "I'm havin' trouble talkin'."

His eyes was bright and his hand was hanging over his gun in his belt. He glanced over his shoulder at his buddies and grinned. He was meanin' to kill me, then go back to Del Norte and tell his friend Big Ugly that he'd evened the score. Trouble was ol' Lip Hair just wasn't ready for what happened next.

He leaned over me waiting for me to talk. Instead my right hand streaked for my knife that was still on the table, and my left hand grabbed the collar of his coat. I jerked him down to my level. Before he could twitch, I had my Toledo steel blade rubbin' his Adam's apple. If he'd a swallowed hard, he'd a cut himself. I heard guns cock around me and then silence. Then I heard Bucklin startin' that rumble down in his chest from under the table.

"Mister, me and my friends here just finished a mighty fine meal, and we was just kickin' back to smoke a pipe and jaw about the old days. You spoiled all that for us." I went quiet, and my dog kept gettin' louder. I didn't know what the rest of the boys was doin', but I knew if the piper started playin' Mister Lip Hair wasn't gonna be able to grow no more hair or hear the music, 'cause his throat was gonna be cut from front to back. I think he knew I was serious, 'cause his eyes was as big as a full moon in August.

"Now it'd be my choice," I continued, "that you fellas just say you're sorry, back right on out the door, and head for Del Norte. If you don't like that idea, then I reckon we gonna have to get crossways with each other, and I'm gonna kill you first." I hadn't raised my voice, but I did have his attention.

Bucklin was growlin' so loud that he was vibratin' the dishes on the table. "Buck," I said, and he went quiet. He'd either figured out what his name was or he understood the tone of my voice.

Lip Hair was breakin' a sweat. He dearly wanted to pull his short gun, but there was no way he was gonna make it, and he knew it. I decided I'd had all his polecat smell I could stand, and I made the decision for him. In a single quick motion I moved my knife from his throat to his lip, and cut off the left half of his mustache. In the process I took about a quarter of an inch of nostril, and most of his lip. Then I reversed the knife and nailed him with the heavy butt right 'tween the eyes. He fell like he'd been shot.

Buck walked over to him stiff-legged and took a sniff of him. The other four men stood facing Pa, Stoney, and Chris, with their hands out away from their bodies. They was looking down the barrels of two Colts, one Hawken fifty, and a double-barrel ten-gauge sawed down to long-pistol length which was bein' held by Rosebud Charlie. They might try and take Pa, Chris, and Stoney, but they surely wasn't gonna try Rosie and his shotgun.

"I'd like to invite you men to pick your smelly buddy up and head back down the trail, just like Matt suggested," Rosie said. "You ain't welcome here."

"He cut his lip off," one of the men protested.

"Likely, but you got to admit he come askin' for it," Rosie said. There wasn't much sympathy in his voice.

They didn't say another word. They just picked up Half-Lip Hair and went out the door.

"That boy of yours always that sudden, Tirley?" Rosebud Charlie asked after they'd closed the door.

"I thought he was a mite slow this time," Pa replied. "Must still be stiff from that fight."

Stoney laughed and that broke the tension. We heard their horses head back down the trail toward Del Norte.

"Gonna be a long, cold ride," Rosie said.

"They brung it on themselves," Pa said. "They lucky to be leavin' here at all."

"So where you boys headin'?" Rosie asked, changin' the subject.

"Gonna take Matthew down to Pahgosa and soak him in the springs. Try and heal him up," Pa replied.

"We'd heard the springs weren't claimed by the Navajos no more," Stoney said.

"You heard right," Rosie replied. "The Utes ended up with 'em."

"I figured there'd be a scad of killin' 'fore the Navajos would ever give up claim to them hot springs, or the Utes either for that matter," Pa said.

"Well, there was, from time to time over the years. I'd venture there was maybe ten little skirmishes, and at least two major battles fought over that water between the two tribes, and neither one of 'em ever won a clear victory."

"So how'd the Utes end up with 'em?" Stoney asked Rosie.

Chris stood up and come around on my side of the table, and Bucklin pushed out a big sigh from under the table like he was plum bored. I leaned back on the wall behind me and got all relaxed for a story.

"You boys know how it's been. Probably goes back a hundred years with both tribes makin' a claim to the springs at Pahgosa." Rosie stopped a minute, took a gentle pull from the cider jug, and set it back down on the table.

"I always reckoned the Utes had the better claim to the place than the Navajos. They was the ones that named it Pahgosa, which means boilin', healin' water, or somethin' like that in Ute. They was also the ones that had the medicine story about the spring healin' the tribe when they was struck by a sickness. The Utes seemed to be the folks that spent the most time there, but the Navajos said it was in their territory." Rosie rubbed his whiskers with his hand and thought quietly for a minute as he got the story straight in his mind.

"Anyhow, they fought back and forth, killing each other off with neither ever really winnin' a victory. Finally, the two medicine chiefs got together and decided to settle the issue once and for all by single combat."

"You mean like David and Goliath in the Bible?" Stoney asked.

"Same thing exactly," Rosie replied.

Pa was lookin' hard at Stoney. "When'd you ever spend time readin' the Bible?" he asked.

"Got snowed in up in the Sierras with Jed Smith one time. He was a Bible reader, and read it out loud fer the rest of us. Learned us all a thing or two." Pa gave out a chuckle, as did the rest of us. "Didn't say it changed any of us," Stoney said, a little testy. "I just said we learned a thing or two. That story about David kinda stuck with me."

"Well, it was more like that then you'd believe," Rosie said. "The Navajos picked the biggest brave in the tribe. Some say he was seven foot tall and weighed more than a medium-sized horse. The Utes picked Al Pfeiffer for their champion."

"You got to be kiddin'," Pa exploded.

"You mean that little colonel that was with Phil Sheridan?" Stoney asked.

"That's him," Rosie said. "He's been hangin' with the Utes almost since the war's been over."

"Well, dip me in hog slobber," Pa exclaimed. "He can't stand over maybe five foot three."

"Lucky if he stretches that far," Rosie said. "Probably don't weigh more that a hundred and fifty pounds either."

"What made them pick a white man?" I asked curiously.

"Some folks say he told the Utes the story of David right from the Bible, and Injuns, being superstitious like they are, reckoned that Colonel Al might have some kind of heavy spirit help. Other folks say they didn't want to get a Ute brave killed fightin' that giant Navajo."

"Sounds like Al must've won," Stoney remarked.

"He was so much faster than the Navajo that he danced circles around him. Cut him to shreds with his Bowie, and he finally tipped over dead." Rosie said. "The Colonel never got a scratch on him."

"Well, I'll be . . ." Pa said. "And the Navajos just left out and ain't been back?"

"They know it'd be an all-out war with the Utes if they went back on their word, and they also know that there ain't much worse than a mad Ute, 'less maybe it's a whole tribe of 'em," Rosie said with a smile. He looked at me and then back to Pa. "The Utes gonna stand for you soakin' Matthew in their healin' water?"

"Matthew gets on with the Utes, and so does Silva. I even got a bit friendly with 'em," Pa replied.

"I thought you had a blood feud goin' with 'em," Rosie said.

"I decided it was time to bury the tomahawk," Pa replied. " 'Sides, I've outlived all them I swore to kill. It weren't the whole tribe, just half of 'em."

Stoney laughed and stood up from the bench. "I'm gonna go check the animals and then hit the blankets."

"I will go with you, señor," Chris said, standing up from the table and slipping into his heavy, fur-lined canvas coat. Bucklin walked out from under the table as they opened the door. He looked up at me.

"Go on ahead, Buck," I said. He joined the two men as they went outside.

"I swear, Matt. I think that dog's smarter than most people," Pa said.

"Looks like he's gonna be a good one," I agreed.

I spread out my bedroll not far from the fire, leavin' room for the other men to get close as well. I sat down on the floor slow and struggled to get my boots off. Pa grunted as he did the same.

"Where you boys headed after you soak Matthew?" Rosie asked.

"After the springs, I thought we might go up toward La Ventana and see if we can find Stewart's gold," Pa said. He looked plum serious when he said it.

"I don't put much credit in Captain Stewart's story, but there's plenty of mines around in this country that's been found and then lost again," Rosie remarked.

"Where's this Stewart's mine supposed to be, Pa?" I asked.

"Well, it ain't rightly a mine," Pa replied. "It's a placer find in the bottom of a creek. Fact, is, the captain told me that the bottom of the creek was covered with fine black sand and gold nuggets.

"What creek?" I asked.

"I don't rightly know that either," he replied. "I been told some of the landmarks, so I think I can get us in close."

Chris and Stoney had come in from the livery just in time to hear what Pa said.

"You finally get around to tellin' Matthew what your hare-brained idea is?" Stoney asked Pa as he hung his coat on wooden pegs driven in to the log walls. Bucklin come over to me and lay down on the foot of my blankets nearest the fire.

"It must not be completely harebrained," Pa replied. "I got you to come along."

"I had nothin better to do this winter, and I figured I'd better come along to wet-nurse you. You're gettin' up there in years," Stoney said.

"Why, you old buzzard . . ." Pa started to say.

"Pa, where is the creek?" I asked, interrupin' him.

Pa spluttered a little bit, still put out with Stoney, and then looked at me.

"It's up above the hot springs at Pahgosa. Up north and west of Chimney Rock," he said.

"High up?" I asked.

"I'd say she's middlin' high. How 'bout you, Stoney?"

"Maybe a tad higher than middlin'," Stoney replied. "Where's he's talkin' about is just under the main spine of the San Juans. You get any higher and you fall off the other side."

"Gonna be closed down purty quick, if it ain't already. They get a powerful lot of snow up there," Rosie said.

"It ain't closed down yet, but the next storm will surely do it," Pa agreed. "I'd hate to get caught up there when one of the big ones hit. Me and Bridger got caught in a big storm up on a saddle pass not far out of Cherry Creek. Took us two weeks to get out, and we had to eat our mules 'fore it was over."

Chris laid his blankets out next to mine, pulled off his boots, and crawled in. "Your Sin horse is well, and I gave him oats and a handful of corn," he said.

"Thanks, Chris. I owe ya."

"One day maybe I am down, and you will help me with the chores," he replied with a smile.

"You can count on it." He knew I meant it.

My blankets were warm and the quiet tones of the conversation started makin' my eyes sag. I pulled the blankets up to my chin and dreamed of gold nuggets bigger than my fist.

* * *

"There's steam comin' out of it," I said, mostly to myself. We were on a bluff overlooking the San Juan river. It was cold, and there was a plume of steam comin' out of a small, bowl-shaped hole in the slick rock. Through the curtain of steam I thought I could see a bluish green sheet of water in the bowl.

"She's hot," Stoney said. "I crawled in it one night a few years back and it near boiled my hide off."

"The best place to soak is down by the river in a catch basin. It's probably a hundred feet from the main pot, and the water has a chance to cool down a little," Pa said. "Then, if you get too hot, you can slide down the rock into the river."

I looked at ice that rimmed the river on both sides and figured the river water would surely catch your breath if you was to flop into it.

"Looks like the Utes have set up housekeepin'," Stoney said, pointing down the river. I could see some smoke risin' against the mountain, and if I squinted my eyes down I could make out some shelters scattered in the cottonwoods.

"Let's go down and see if they gonna welcome us," Pa said.

We nosed our horses down off the bluff and headed for the Ute camp. When we rode in, the kids and dogs started gatherin' around us. I had Bucklin up on the saddle with me again, and he was shakin' like a cat poopin' a peach pit. He surely wanted to get down and fight. We wanted just the opposite. We was plumb peaceful.

I saw the flap on one of the hogans fly open and a barrel-chested, dark-faced Ute warrior come stridin' out. He stopped dead still when he seen my horse, then looked up at me. A huge smile split his face.

"O'Malley Man," he said loudly and came walking toward me with big steps.

I climbed down off Sin painfully, leavin' one hand on my dog to hold him on the saddle, and reached my free arm out. He gave me a fierce hug that made my sore ribs hurt worse and made me grunt.

"O'Malley Man, I have not seen you for many moons."

"It's good to see you, Ignacio," I replied.

"You have been fighting again, O'Malley Man," he said lookin' at my face.

"He put near as much punishment on me as you did back in Kansas," I said.

"Ah, yes, that was a fight. We do that again maybe?" he asked, with a smile on his face.

"No, my friend. Fightin' you once is plenty."

"We figured to soak him in the springs, if ya don't mind, Ignacio," Pa said.

"Yes, the healing waters will help him," Ignacio agreed. "Make him feel new. Then we put him in a sweat and let him sweat the white man's poisons from his spirit."

"Yeah," Stoney agreed. "I didn't think about a sweat. That'd fix him right up."

"Leave horses," Ignacio said. He waved his arm toward a pole corral that had been built on one of the flats close to the river.

"Me and Chris will do the horses," Stoney said. "You take Matthew over to the springs."

Pa nodded and handed his reins over to Stoney. I handed mine to Chris and lifted Bucklin down from the saddle. The Indian dogs had all lost interest and returned to the warmth of the fires. We walked toward the plume of steam comin' from the pot hole.

As we got close, I could detect a pungent smell. It smelled like a combination of sulfur, burnin' hair, salt, and somethin' else nasty.

"They still smell like nothing I've ever come across before," Pa said to no one in particular.

"Smell like elk guts, but make you all better," Ignacio said to me.

We stopped short as we got to the bowl in the rock and Bucklin whined. There was mammoth bubbles breaking the surface of the blue-green water, like some giant monster was burping down deep. There were thick mineral deposits gathered all the way around the rock bowl, and not a single thing was growin' for a long ways around the hot spring.

"Best place is down over that slope," Pa said. "The water runs down the rock into the river. There's a little basin down over the slope that's about four feet deep."

I walked over and looked down. The basin was there, and the river was just below it.

"Shed your clothes, boy," Pa said. "I want to get you healed up. We got places to go and things to see."

I peeled down to my short pants and made my way down to the little bowl. There was minerals plastered all over the rock around the narrow, shallow stream that come out of the big spring. I got down to the level of the tub-shaped hole and stopped. There was steam comin' from the green water, and the smell was enough to make a possum puke.

"You ain't gonna get healed up standin' there lookin' at it," Pa said.

"Looks kinda hot," I said.

"Probably is," Pa agreed. "You'll get used to it."

I walked around the edge and found a spot where I could get in a little at a time. I stepped in, and dang near backed out. It was hot enough to boil an egg. I might have quit, but I'd heard Chris and Stoney come up, and I knew they'd all have somethin' to say if I didn't bear down and get it done. I stepped in deeper and felt my heart start poundin'. I'd had a few hot baths in my time, but this was times again hotter than that. I got in to my waist and then squatted down 'til the water was up to my neck. I stayed down as long as I could stand it, then stood up. The air felt like it was comin' right off an ice block, and my skin was red as a pickled fish. I looked myself over where I could see, and I was shocked to see how many black and blue marks I had on me. I'd taken a purty fair poundin'.

I ducked down again, waited a spell, then stood up again. My legs and tail seemed to take it better than my upper body. I kept doin' that for what seemed like forever, then Pa had me crawl out. I was weak as a newborn calf, and felt tired all over.

"Sweat is over there," Ignacio said.

I looked where he pointed and saw a little cone-shaped hut that was banked with dirt. I figured a full-sized man would never fit in.

"My woman has heated the rocks in the fire," Ignacio said. "It is ready."

Pa and Stoney walked me over to the little hut, folded me up a couple times over, and stuffed me inside. It was cold in the hut, but they soon started puttin' hot rocks in with me and pourin' a little water over 'em.

"The steam quits comin' off them rocks, ya pour a little water on 'em. The sweat will do ya good," Stoney said.

They closed the door and the only light I had was a little bit that come in around the door. I started sweatin' a little, so I poured some more water over the rocks. Five minutes later I was sweatin' rivers. They left me in 'til the rocks started to cool, then walked me back over to the springs.

We did that turn and again for the rest of the day. By night-fall I could barely walk, and I was so tired I hardly knew where I was. They got me into one of the lodges and under the blankets with my dog snugged in next to me. I slept the night through without stirrin' except some mighty stirrin' dreams about Lee. They started in on me again the next day, and Ignacio gave me some kinda drink that made me see double and triple.

By the third day I was some better, and by the fourth day I figured I was as good as I was gonna get. I started out not particular believin' in the healin' waters, but now I was a man that figured the stories for true. Without soakin' in the springs, I'd a been a month healin' up. I was still black and blue, but the soreness was gone, and I felt like a new man. Four days was all it took. I was a believer. I surely was.

Stoney and Chris had been huntin' and got a nice buck just up the river from the camp. That night the Utes built a big council fire, and we had quite a feed. The moon come over the mountain big and yeller just as the Utes started the dancin'. 'Fore the night was over, Pa and Stoney had danced the bear dance with the Ute gals. Me and Chris watched and laughed. Bucklin had made friends with the Utes, since he'd whipped most of their dogs, sometimes two or three at a time. I hadn't seen the fights, but Buck didn't have a scratch on him, other than one ear that was a mite chewed. He'd proved he could take care of himself. I'd quit worryin' about him.

The moon got high up in the sky, and the light was so strong that you could see some of the trees on the side of the mountain. The stars looked like they was close enough I could near touch 'em. I surely wished Lee was sittin' on the log beside me with my arm around her. I guessed I wasn't much of a dreamer, but it seemed I was surely spending a lot of time lookin' at the moon and thinkin' about a certain gal that was way back East somewheres.

I looked up high on the top of the range, and higher than the trees could grow, there was a stack of snow. Wouldn't be long before it would be deep and cold up where Pa wanted to go.

I could tell Pa had the treasure fever, and so did Stoney. They'd talked of nothin' but Captain Stewart's gold since we'd got to the springs. They'd tried to talk with the Utes, but the Injuns had little to say about the story. Even if they knew where the creek was, they wasn't gonna tell. They'd learned that if one white man found gold, there'd be a thousand to follow after. They didn't mind a white man now and again, but they knew they'd lose their land if gold was found.

As I crawled into my blankets, I got to thinkin' about the story of Captain Stewart's gold, and I reckoned I must be as bad as the old men. I always was a sucker for stories of buried treasure, and more so now since we'd found some old Spanish gold a while back. I was fair itchin' to get on Sin and ride the high country.

Chapter Six

"**M**y client says the job must be done this weekend," Degan said. "Edna Wilkes has to be out of circulation by Monday."

"We been watchin' her," the skinny crook said. "We'll have a chance on her before Monday." He paused a moment and then looked at the headmaster. "We got one little problem . . ."

"We can't have a problem. This has to go without a hitch," Degan said with some heat.

"It's not serious," the weaselly man said quickly. "There's a younger girl showed up at the house this evening . . ."

"If you catch them together take them both," Degan said with some satisfaction. "Make sure you have enough men to do the job. I want them both in the hospital. In fact if the younger one were to wind up dead, well . . ."

"Two of them means it'll cost you more."

"I don't care," the headmaster replied. "Just do it."

"You got it, Boss," the skinny man said.

Degan nodded, pushed away from the bar, and walked from the tavern without another word. He would have to get word to that Marilyn Beck woman. If indeed Lewara Conall became a victim of the gang . . . well, the five thousand in gold would be a very nice addition to his retirement fund.

The skinny man watched the schoolmaster leave and then waved a finger at a man standing in the shadows near the wall. The man walked into the light and stopped for a moment, looking about carefully. He walked over to the skinny man and sat down on the stool that Degan had just vacated.

"Get Perkins, Smith, and Ranney. We got a job to do," Weasel said. The man nodded and left through the back door.

"Gosh, Aunt Edna, this is nice," Lee said as she settled back on the cushions of the closed cab. "School has been so boring. We seem to be going over the same material we covered months ago."

"Repetition causes the lesson to be well learned," Edna replied with a smile. "That's what my mother used to tell your mother and me."

"I'm glad it's almost over," Lee said as she adjusted a pin in her hair. "I feel like I'm wasting time."

"It seems that way now, but what you learn now will benefit you the rest of your life. What do you plan on doing when you graduate?" Edna asked, changing the subject.

"I've been thinking I'd like to go back to Colorado, but I don't want to leave you," Lee replied.

"I don't want you to leave, but I am not going to hold you here if you'd rather be out West," Edna said carefully.

"Well, I have a little time yet . . ." Lee began.

"Yes," Edna agreed. "In the meantime we will enjoy what time we have together."

"What is the play?" Lee asked. She pulled back the curtain on the window and looked into the night.

"Othello," Edna replied. "It's not my favorite Shakespeare, but it will be better than staying at the house."

The cab turned a corner at a street intersection and the iron-rimmed wheels became much noisier on the cobblestone street. Clayton had taken the evening off, which had necessitated the use of a public cab to transport them to the theater.

"This driver must know a shortcut," Edna observed. "I don't remember this street."

They proceeded a few blocks, and Lee could see the alarm mounting in Edna's face. Suddenly the cab stopped. Edna moved the curtain aside a crack. They were situated mid-block, and the street was nearly pitch black with the inadequate gas lamps located only on the intersection corners. The interior of the cab was dimly lit with a small candle lantern.

"Don't panic," Edna whispered to Lee, "but I don't like this situation."

Lee nodded and didn't look the least bit panicked.

"Driver, why are we stopping here?" Edna inquired in a loud voice. There was no answer from the driver's platform. Edna reached under her long dress and pulled a small pistol from a holster strapped to her thigh.

Lee smiled at her aunt and also produced a pistol from the folds of her wrap.

"Comes a time now and again when a woman needs to be prepared for the worst," Lee said. "It's instruction I didn't learn in the academy. It was hard-learned in a much rougher school."

Edna nodded and pulled the hammer back on her Smith and Wesson. "I'm going to open the door and see if we have company," she whispered. She swung the door of the cab open and immediately stepped down to the street with Lee close behind her. They could see the shadows of several men coming at them from both directions. The driver was gone.

"They mean to harm us," Edna whispered. In reply she heard the hammer of Lee's pistol being cocked. "We are armed, gentlemen," Edna said in a loud voice. It echoed from store front to store front on the nearly empty street. They saw the men hesitate a moment, and then a raspy voice replied, "I think you're lyin'."

"If you think she's lyin', mister, you just take five more steps, and I'm gonna make you start leakin'." Lee's voice was trembling, but her resolve was apparent.

"I think you're bluffin', and we got a job to do," the raspy voice again came from the darkness. There was a sound of running feet and both women raised their weapons and fired almost simultaneously. The shots were loud in the quiet night, and a man started screaming. Edna fired again and another man that had almost reached her fell onto his face. The men were gone as quickly and silently as they had arrived. They left two of their number lying on the cobblestones. The one lying in front of Edna was obviously dead. The one on Lee's side was groaning and trying to crawl away. They heard voices, and two of the Boston Watch came running around the lighted corner a half block away. They had their sidearms in their hands, and one of them was carrying a lantern.

The policemen ran up to the two women and the larger one opened the shutter on the lantern.

"What happened here?" he demanded. He raised the lantern and shined it into their faces. "Mrs. Wilkes . . . ?"

"It's me, Clancy," she said. The relief in her voice was evident. "We were set upon by several men. This is what they left behind," she said motioning to the two lying on the street. She quickly told the large policeman how they had come to be on the dark and lonely street. He nodded, stepped back from them a few feet, and began to blow loudly on a silver whistle. In less than five minutes there were a number of the Boston Watch assembled around the scene.

"Mulvey, I 'spect this cab is stolen. Load these ladies up in it and drive 'em home," Clancy said. "Jolly, you go with him, and both of ya stay there until I come to get ya."

Suddenly, Clayton was at Edna's side. "Edna . . . ?"

"I'm fine, Clayton, and so is Lee."

"Uncle John?" Lee said. Edna looked past Clayton at a man standing just inside the circle of light cast by the lantern.

"Lee, are you . . . ?"

"I'm fine, but this gent's been used a bit," she said, directing his attention to the wounded man who was still groaning. Clancy walked over to the man and shined the light full on his face. Lee gasped as she recognized him. It was the little weasel-faced man that had been at the school speaking with headmaster Degan.

"Degan is in jail and the academy is adjourned, at least for now," John O'Malley said. Two days had passed since the incident with the outlaws. "Clancy found a journal in Degan's desk that explained a number of beatings and cuttings that have occurred over the past few years. Also, the little outlaw that Lee shot, Morgan I think his name is, has confessed to most of the incidents. Degan is still not talking, but when he learns what the judge has in store for him, it might loosen his tongue about who he was representing." He paused a moment and then turned to Lee. "Do you know anyone who would wish you harm?" he asked her.

Lee looked curiously at him. "I can't think of a person," she replied. "Why do you ask?"

"It seems there was an entry in Degan's ledger that referred directly to you. Something about a woman and five thousand dollars in gold paid to him if something happened to you."

"I can't imagine . . ." Lee began.

"Maybe it was just wishful thinking on his part," he said cheerfully, trying to ease her mind.

John walked to the bay window that overlooked the street in front of Edna's home. It was the first time they'd seen him since the incident, and Lee had made the formal introductions when he'd arrived a few moments before. Edna thought John O'Malley a fine figure of a man. She guessed him something over six-foot with big arms and chest. His hair was salt and pepper and cut short. He had a carefully trimmed handle-bar mustache, and a scar that stood livid on his right cheek. She thought it looked like a scar that a sword might leave. He was an altogether attractive man with a calm manner.

John was quiet a moment, looking outside at the police watch that was still mounted at Edna's home, and then turned to face the two women. "In the meantime, Mrs. Wilkes, Clayton has informed me that you have a business problem that involves my rail line on the west side."

Edna was seated on a small couch, watching him carefully and thinking him direct, which she liked. "I am Edna to you, sir, and I do indeed have a problem."

John O'Malley smiled at her and walked across the room. "Please, I am John, Edna. Uncle John to some," he said teasingly, looking at Lee. He took a seat on an overstuffed chair four feet to the side of the couch.

"It begins this way," Edna said. She told the story in a straightforward manner, relating to him the mistakes that she'd made and the apparent consequences. The telling took nearly half an hour.

When she fell quiet, John looked intently at her, and then toward Lee. "I think we can arrive at a solution, but it will turn the tables on these men, and I suspect it will make you even more unpopular in Boston than you say you are now."

"I've decided to sell my holdings here and move my base of operations back West," Edna said. She realized as she said it that she'd been contemplating, in the back of her mind, such a move ever since her husband had died. It seemed natural now that she'd spoken it. She'd always been more comfortable in the western cities in any case.

"My civil engineer has informed me the property Wingate is trying to acquire is not suitable for my rail roadbed. He feels the water table is too close to the surface. I've decided to realign and place it on the property that lies immediately west of Wingate's place, if I can buy it from the current owner."

"That's my land . . . and I'm sure we can arrive at a price that benefits both of us," Edna said with a smile.

"Well, isn't that a coincidence," he said, returning her smile.

"I'm sorry you are going to lose money, Mr. Wingate, but I still can't see why it's my problem," Edna said sweetly. They were seated around a large oak table in a walnut-paneled conference room. The Chamber had twelve-foot ceilings and was in the very center of the Bank of Boston building.

"I've paid for the land. I closed the deal early. I have title to the property," the city councilman said. "I had assurances from people close to O'Malley that my property was where he planned to run the railroad."

"It is my understanding that O'Malley's engineer found the water table was too close to the surface on the land you acquired, Mr. Wingate. Instead, he has made me a very generous offer for my section." Edna waited a moment, allowing this piece of information and its ramifications to sink in. She saw Wingate's face turn pasty white and then red. She looked over at Jensen as his eyes dropped to the floor.

"He intends to realign the roadbed so that it very nearly cuts my land in half, and he wants to purchase the entire parcel instead of just a right-of-way. Apparently he has some plans for development . . ."

Wingate jumped to his feet, knocking his chair over in the process. "He can't do that! Every penny I have is wrapped up in that property. I stand to lose it all."

Edna also stood and looked Wingate directly in the eye across the table. "It seems to me that you moved a few days too early, Mr. Wingate. You should have waited to close on the land until which time Mr. O'Malley had offered to at least buy a right-of-way."

"I couldn't wait," he nearly yelled. "If the idiot that owned the land knew O'Malley was planning a railroad on it, he'd've jacked up the price."

"You took a normal risk of business based on your information and you lost. It's that simple," Edna said.

"I can't lose," Wingate yelled. "I won't . . ." He stared around the table. There was a deadly look in his eye.

"Mr. Wingate," Edna said in a sharp voice. "Let me advise you that I will not tolerate your yelling at me or threatening me in any way. If you persist, you will not enjoy the consequences."

That stopped him dead in his tracks. Everyone in town had heard how Edna and her young niece had reacted when attacked by a group of thugs on a dark side street.

Wingate had beads of sweat dripping from his brow even though the room was cool. His color was poor and Edna thought he might be going to have a heart attack. She didn't really care.

"I'd like to know how you got O'Malley to change his location . . ." Wingate began, but Edna cut him off.

"Mr. Wingate, I am sorry you are losing money on this deal. In fact, I am feeling so badly about it that I will buy your piece of ground if you are of a mind to sell." She saw the light of hope come up in the councilman's eyes. "I'll give you fifty dollars an acre, cash money," she said bluntly.

Wingate sagged against the table. He saw how she had manipulated him to this very point. It was half the money he had offered her for her section of land, and many, many thousands less than he'd paid less than twenty-four hours before.

"Let me know this week, Mr. Wingate. I am planning on leaving town for an extended period of time," Edna said. She looked at the two men that had planned to defraud her, and on whom, with the help of John O'Malley, she had neatly turned the tables. They were defeated, and strangely she felt no great satisfaction in the fact that she was the instrument of their failure. She even felt a little sorry for them.

She left the building and stepped up into her covered coach with a hand from Clayton. John O'Malley and Lee were sitting behind the curtains waiting for her.

"How did that go?" John asked curiously.

"Just as we expected," Edna replied. "I almost felt sorry for them."

"Well, don't," he said. "They wouldn't feel sorry for you if the roles were reversed."

"I know, but I seem to have lost my appetite for the intrigue," Edna said softly.

They fell quiet for a moment as Clayton started the carriage down the street toward home.

Edna turned to Lee and took her by the hand. "Let's go to the house and begin packing. I want to smell some sagebrush and see some mountains."

"I'm ready," Lee agreed simply. She had in mind to see more than just sagebrush and mountains. She was going to find Matthew.

Chapter Seven

Iwas just tyin' my blanket roll on behind my saddle when I heard 'em down the canyon makin' their way along the river toward us. There was one leather-lung feller who knew each mule in his team by name and managed to introduce us to 'em while he was still a ways back down the canyon. We were packed and ready to ride the high-lonesome, but we waited until they pulled up in a small cloud of dust. There was a dozen wagons full of furniture, plows, men, women, and kids. A feller got down from the lead wagon and hurried over to us.

"I got a man in my wagon we found back down the trail at Newton Spring. He's badly wounded."

We hustled over to his wagon as he threw back the rear fly.

"Rosebud Charlie," Pa exclaimed. He climbed up into the wagon with Stoney close behind.

"Matthew, go get Ignacio and tell him we got a hurt friend here. We surely gonna need some of his fixin's."

I turned and nearly ran into Ignacio as he walked up to the wagon.

"You know Rosebud Charlie?" I asked the big Ute.

"I know. Post down . . ." Ignacio pointed with his lips back down the canyon.

59

"He's in that wagon over there, shot up. Can you get . . ."

"I get my woman. She has plants." Ignacio turned and quickly made his way back to his lodge.

"We passed a building at South Fork that'd been burnt and was still smoking when we pulled past it," the man from the wagon said.,

"That'd be Rosie's trading post," Pa remarked. "You see any sign of his woman?"

"We buried her, but we didn't hang around long." the man offered. "We figured it was Indians, and we wanted to get some distance."

"Where'd you say you found him?" Stoney asked.

"Newton Spring, just after you hit the flat below Wolf Creek Pass," the man replied.

"That's a fer piece from South Fork," Stoney said.

"Takes a hard man to make that many miles bein' shot up like he is," Pa said.

"He's come awake a time or two when my woman tended him," the man said. "Mentioned he had to find Matthew."

"I reckon that'd be me," I said. "He tell you why he had to find me?" The man shook his head and looked back into the wagon where Rosie lay.

Ignacio's woman showed up with a buckskin bag and crawled up into the wagon. Pa and Stoney got down and let her have some room. Ignacio stood beside me watchin' what was goin' on.

The man from the wagon showed some savvy. He climbed back onto the platform, rummaged around for a few minutes, then stepped down with a flour bag in his hand. He started handin' out biscuits and honey to the Utes that was standin' around close. It was the same thing ol' Brig and the Mormons had done up in Utah. His policy had always been to feed the Injuns 'stead of fightin' 'em.

"My name's Nathan Dustin," the man said, "lately of Missouri."

Pa nor Stoney said anything. They just stood watchin' and waitin' for him to get on with it.

"We're headin' for a place west of here," he said, "and we're wondering if we're on the right track."

"Ain't much west of here," Pa replied without much excitement in his voice. He didn't like immigrants much.

"My brother, Seth, has established in a valley west of here. They even started a little town named Animas City, and when he wrote me last, he said that there were ten families located in the valley with cabins up. I got the letter right here," Nathan said, pulling a much-handled piece of paper from his pocket and started readin' out loud.

" 'Nathan, this is as close to heaven as you will find on earth. The mountains rise above us, but the weather is temperate and the soil deep and sweet. We have planted over three hundred acres of mixed vegetables, alfalfa, and grain among the lot of us, and are hoping to plant another hundred yet this year.' " The letter went on for two pages and at the end invited Nathan to join Seth.

"If you decide to come, please bring enough staples to last for a year for your family, and include a minister in your company as the women are hungering for the word of God," Seth had written.

Nathan must have taken Seth at his word, 'cause he'd brought a sky pilot with him, and the man of the cloth started prayin' for deliverance as soon as he'd walked up to us. I 'spect he'd seen how many Ute lodges there was along the river and figured he was about to meet his maker. It was in my mind that he'd better be for watchin' Pa instead of the Utes. Pa could only take so much out-loud preachin' 'fore he'd pop his belt. It wasn't that he didn't hold with religion, but he could only stand it in small doses. Even Buck seemed to take offense at the skinny, long-nosed reverend. He'd walk by him slow and growl, actin' like he wanted to take a piece of his leg and bury it somewhere.

Stoney and Pa was standin' together lookin' thoughtful after

Nathan had finished readin'. "There's a place over by the La Platas, a little valley that the Animas river drains. I'd reckon that's where they'd be," Stoney said.

Pa was noddin' his head. "That's got to be it. Mighty purty place, but high up for farmin'. Be a better place to raise stock than farm. Probably don't have but three months between frosts, four at the most."

"Are we on the right track?" Nathan repeated his question.

"You're on as much a road as there is," Pa replied.

"You mean it gets worse than what we've already been on?" one of the women asked.

"It ain't no worse," Stoney said. "Wolf Creek Pass was the worst you'll see, but it's still a fer piece of country from here, and the road ain't really a road. It's just a trail that follows the creeks." A kind of collective groan come out of the folks in the wagons.

"What worries me most is you're late in the season, and there's still some high country 'tween here and there," Pa said. "Once it starts snowin' it just don't quit 'til spring, and we're overdue for snow."

"You'd be better off turnin' around and winterin' over in Cherry Creek," Stoney said.

"We considered it," Nathan replied, "but some of us have every dollar wrapped up right here in these wagons. When our foodstuffs are gone, we can't buy any more. We have to go on."

"Even if ya knew the country, I'd give ya less than an even chance of makin' it," Pa said, takin' a glance at the sky and then over at the preacher who was still prayin'. He'd worked himself around to asking for forgiveness for the heathen, and he was lookin' straight at Pa as he prayed.

All the rest of the people in the company had gathered around us, maybe twenty or thirty people total countin' the kids, and were listenin' to what was bein' said. There was a bunch a long faces among 'em. They'd all supposed they were a lot closer to the end than Pa said they was.

"How long you calculate it will take us to get there from here, mister?" the leather-lung mule-skinner asked. He was a big, florid-faced man with an easy smile. "Name's Sam Draper," he added. "I used to freight on the Santa Fe trail, but got sick of it. I'm tryin' to get a new start."

Pa looked at Stoney, and then at the wagons sittin' just down the way.

"Ya don't have any breakdowns, and the weather holds . . ." Pa started.

"Maybe ten days," Stoney finished. "Might be a little less than that."

One woman took hold of her man to keep from fallin' down, and most of the faces got even longer. They'd come a far distance already, and it must've seemed to most of 'em that they just wasn't ever gonna get there.

"Reverend, I wonder if we could get you to pray to yourself just a minute so we can discuss this situation," Nathan said to the preacher. The prayin' cut off short like it'd been chopped with an ax. I was glad, 'cause I'd been reachin' for my short gun to take care of the preacher myself.

"We don't have many choices, folks," Nathan said to the gathered company. "We've agreed that we can't go back. We obviously can't stay here . . ." he said this as he looked around at the Injuns and the lodges close about, "so that means go on."

"What the heck are we standin' here jawin' about it then. Let's quit prayin' and lookin' for help from other folks and get on with it." The woman that was speakin' was probably near on to Pa's age. Her hair was gray, her face was lined with years, but there was somethin' about her that grabbed your attention. She was a strikin' woman both in looks and stature, and they was all listenin' to her. "We been together for quite a spell now, and we've come through some sore trials. This is the last part, and it may be the roughest tribulation we've had so far, but nothin' worth havin' ever come easy." She turned away and walked back to her wagon.

"I reckon Frone is right. If we drop this wounded gent off here, we can get on with it," Sam agreed, and he also walked over to his wagon. That seemed to settle it and the group broke up, each headin' for their teams and wagons.

Ignacio's woman stepped out of the wagon and waved him over. She spoke rapidly to him in Ute for several seconds, and then he turned toward us.

"She says that she has wrapped the wounds with snake root and done all she can. She will give you some plants to make a drink for him. She thinks he will still die," Ignacio said. "He cannot stay here," the Ute chief added. "We are going into the valley at Los Pinos before the snows come."

"You fellas wouldn't consider goin' with us as guides would you?" Nathan asked, lookin' at Pa. "We could leave Mr. Rosebud right where he is in my wagon. It might be the best thing for him anyway."

"We got a place we got to go . . ." Stoney started to say, but was interrupted by Pa.

"Hold on a minute, Stoney," Pa said. "It's a shorter ride for Rosie to go with these folks than to go with the Utes, and if he lives through the trip, he's gonna want some people around that he knows. 'Sides, I want to know what happened at the Forks." I also noticed he was still lookin' toward Frone's wagon. "We ain't doin' much that can't wait 'til spring," Pa added, "and these folks be needin' help. My vote is we give 'em a hand."

The look on Stoney's face was enough to make me want to bust out laughin'.

"I guess it ain't gonna hurt us much if we lend 'em a hand," I said. I knew Chris wouldn't have no problem with it. Stoney just turned to his horse mutterin' and cussin', settled his Hawken deeper in the boot, pulled on his cinch, and mounted up. He was goin', but it was plain it weren't his idea of a good time.

"We're with ya, Nathan, but you got to promise that you'll get control of that preacher. If'n he goes to baptize on me or somethin', I'm gonna skin him slow and feed him to the wolves."

The preacher was standin' close enough that he heard, and he turned pasty white. Nathan laughed thinkin' Pa was foolin', but I weren't so sure.

"We're gettin' close to being at the end," Pa said as we topped out on a long climb and stopped to let the animals take a breather. It seemed to me that we'd been building road the whole week since we'd left the Utes. The trail we'd traveled followed mostly creek drainages and was full of boulders and downed trees. Pa had set the pace slow for the mules, but we kept at it steady from first light 'til full dark. The teams were well broke and in nice shape. The wagons were lighter than they'd been when the folks had left home, and the feed along the way had been good. We'd made decent time considerin' the condition of the road and the kinda country we was in.

Rosebud Charlie had actually got better during the ride. He was sleepin' a lot and eatin' nothing but jerky broth and juice made from dried apples, but he was improved. Since it was me he was askin' after, I talked to him first when he come full awake on our second day out.

"It was Bull Burdett and his cronies," Rosie'd told me. "They come front and back at the same time. They killed Sky while she was cooking supper. I managed to touch off both barrels of the Greener before they got me, and I did for a couple of 'em. They fired the place after I was down. I managed to get out and crawl up on one of my mules. The only thing I managed to save was my shotgun." He pointed beside him and I could see his ten-gauge shotgun was laying just under the fold of the covers. "They shot the hell out of things, set fire to the place, and rode back toward Del Norte laughin' like they was goin' to a dance. I rode 'til I couldn't keep a seat on the mule, and when I woke up, I was in Nathan's wagon. They been almighty good to me, and I owe 'em a debt."

"Why'd you tell these folks you was huntin' for me?" I asked him.

"They killed my Sky," Rosie said simply. "I can't never look her people in the face again if I don't try and make it right."

I nodded. I knew just how he felt.

"Folks say you're the best man with a gun there's ever been," Rosie said, "and I been told that you never let a friend down or break your word. I count you and your clan as my friends. I wanted you coverin' my back."

"You get well, and I promise ya we'll get things even, Rosie. I'll cover your back. Soon as you can ride and we get these folks settled in their valley, we'll be goin' on the hunt."

He'd gone to sleep then, and he'd been gettin' better right along durin' the time we'd been on the road. Nothin' makes a man heal faster then knowin' he's got a thing to do.

"Another long day, two at the most, ought to get us there." Pa's voice brought me back to where we was.

The folks in the wagon company were gettin' drawn up some, but they was still game. The end was nearly in sight, and you could tell that everyone was more than ready for the trip to be over.

"There's spots on this downhill where we're gonna have to block the wheels," Pa said so everyone could hear him. "It's steep enough that the brakes ain't gonna hold to keep ya from runnin' over the teams. Nathan will lead off, and the rest will foller along."

Stoney and Chris rode over the edge followed by Nathan and the other wagons. Pa waited for Frone, who was drivin' the last wagon. I'd noticed for bein' the supposed leader, Pa was spendin' a lot of time ridin' at the rear of the column. Turned out that Frone was a widow and Nathan's aunt. She'd decided to come along and take care of her nephews as they settled in Animas City. I gathered that the two boys were all the family she had left. Pa had surely taken notice of her.

Frone drove her span of Missouri mules over the edge following the narrow track that passed for a road. It was washed out, with deep ruts that caused the wagons to jump and jolt. No question that it was a rough ride, and it was hard on wagons, animals, and people. The slope was sharp downhill, but manageable in most places.

We went on for most of the day, takin' only a short break at noon, and only had to block the wheels twice. Late afternoon we came to a long ledge of rock and everyone pulled up. I looked over the edge and caught my breath. It was steep, and the face of the grade was covered with boulders. It didn't look like to me there was any way to get a wagon down to the trees below.

"Everybody get their ropes out," Stoney hollered. "We're gonna have to belay off this big spruce and ease the wagons down with block and tackle."

"We'll lead the teams down separate, and the men will walk each wagon down to keep 'em from tippin' over," Pa yelled over the noise of the wagons and teams.

It was a sight to see. Folks pullin' together, even laughin'. Sam Draper, the mule-skinner, was an accomplished swearin' man, but never directed his rough language at any of the people. He cussed the spruce tree as he helped rig the ropes. He cussed the wagons as they lined them up to start them down, and he cussed the mules, each by name, as they were unhooked from the wagons. Every time he had a spasm of cussin', he'd turn to the ladies and apologize. He never forgot to say he was sorry, but it never slowed him down neither.

It was clear the preacher had made about as much impression on Sam as he had with Pa, and the preacher and Sam stayed well away from each other. Sam was a happy, loud, and friendly feller and the preacher was narrow between the eyes, unforgiving, and nasty-minded. I wasn't real sure that anybody in the company could really abide him. His name was Reverend Willard Gates. He was over forty, greasy-haired, middlin' dirty of clothes and body, and he insisted on preachin' to the folks every night after supper. His preachin' was a real ordeal since he worked mostly on how adulterous our generation was, how sinful man was by nature, and how we was all gonna burn in hell. It didn't do much to raise folks' spirits.

We rigged a stretcher with some aspen saplin's and a couple of blankets, and carried Rosie down to the bottom. Most of the women and kids walked down as we started lettin' the wagons over the edge.

I'd've never thought it could be done 'cept I seen 'em do it. Each of the wagons was slid, pushed, pulled, and cussed down the slope, and after three hours of sweat and skinned knuckles and knees all the wagons but Frone's was into the trees below. The men went back up to the ledge and hooked the rope to the rear axle of her wagon. Sam and Pa pushed the wagon to the edge of the ledge and started it over. Nathan and three other men walked split on either side to keep the wagon from tippin' over as Sam and Pa used the block and tackle to hold it back.

Suddenly, there was a loud pop. I heard Pa yell, and Frone's wagon was on the loose. It smashed off rocks, rolled over on its side and slid all the way to the trees. Those of us that were on top made our way as fast as we could to the bottom. Frone had gone down with her team earlier and was standing over the wreckage of her wagon. Her face was grim and she walked up the side hill pickin' up her scattered belongin's.

"The hardware on the block and tackle give out, Frone. I'm real sorry," Pa said.

"Weren't nobody's fault," she said. "Things happen." She was standing over the smashed ruins of a chest of drawers gathering up her clothing. "My ma brought this chest with her when they come out of Bohemia, and her ma had it before her. Been in my family a long time." It was plain for all of us to see that losing one of her prized possessions was hurtin' her worse than she wanted to let on. None of these folks had much, and they held dear those things they had managed to bring with 'em.

"We'll gather up all the pieces, and I think I can fix it," Pa told her. "It's busted apart in the joints."

We finished gatherin' her stuff and rolled Frone's wagon back on its wheels. We started to check it over to see if we could get it runnin' again.

"Back axle is busted," Sam observed, "and left rear wheel is knocked out."

"If we got an ax, I can cut a temporary axle out of one of these spruce trees purty fast," Pa said.

"The tongue is cracked, but I think we can wire wrap it and make it work," Nathan added, as he moved around the wreck, "and I got an extra wheel."

"I think we can fix it," Stoney agreed, "but we got another problem."

We all looked at him and waited.

"We're gonna have a storm inside of two hours, and it's gonna be a bad one."

I looked at the sky and saw it had turned a lead-gray color. The temperature had dropped by maybe fifteen degrees over the past hour. To make it worse we was only a couple hours from full dark.

"The rest of ya get hooked up and get down off this hill," Pa said. "Leave me an ax, the wire, and the wheel. I'll get Frone's wagon fixed an' foller after as quick as I can."

"I'm stayin'," Frone said. Her voice was hard, and it was plain she surely meant it. "It's my wagon and my belongin's. Besides, it's gonna take two sets of hands to do the fixin'."

"We can't just leave you here . . ." Nathan started.

"We ain't got time to argue. I got work to do," Pa said. He turned to me.

"Matthew, you, Stoney, and Chris get these folks into the valley. Keep goin' 'til you get there, even if you have to push through the night. We're still above ten thousand feet here and we don't want happenin' here like what happened with the Donners."

All of us knew what had happened with the Donner party

up in the Sierras. They'd got caught in an early blizzard and ended up eatin' each other. It made our situation more real to all of us.

"We'll get 'em down and come on back," I told him.

"Just get 'em down. I'll foller along directly."

"Let's move out," I heard Stoney holler. I mounted Sin, made sure Buck was with me, and turned my back on the man I loved most in the world. It was a hard thing to do knowin' that if we got a five-day blizzard I might not see him alive again. It was a hard thing.

Chapter Eight

"Clayton, we need a wagon, a sound team, and a couple of good saddle horses. You know what I like, and there looks to be some excellent stock about," Edna said.

"Price?" he asked.

"Whatever it takes," Edna replied. "I expect we'll have them for a long while. I doubt I'll ever go back East." Clayton nodded and moved toward the livery.

"Isn't it grand?" Lee said, surveying the bustling Denver street.

"It is exciting," Edna acknowledged. "I think there is a world of opportunity here. It's a raw place, but it will soon have refinements."

Edna looked about her and felt transported in both time and place. Denver now looked surprisingly like San Francisco had many years before when she'd first begun.

Both women turned back toward the train station to watch the progress of their luggage.

"Take the bags over to the new hotel," John O'Malley said to one of the two porters who were pushing a large, four-wheeled cart full of steamer trunks, carpetbags, and wooden crates. "Tell the manager that John O'Malley is back in town and will be needing the entire top floor."

Edna looked with surprise at John and smiled. "That's a bit presumptuous, isn't it?" she said in a teasing tone.

John returned her smile and took her arm. "Not at all. I own the place." He laughed at the look on Edna's face as they began to walk toward the large, pineboard and batten building at the end of the block. "More correctly, I put up the money and my son Thomas hired a crew and built the Mountain Palace while I was back in the East working with the railroads. Thomas is back East now, working on some of our business arrangements."

"The name Mountain Palace implies a lot of things," Edna said.

"All of which I hope to make happen before I'm finished with it. I want to make it the best hotel between Kansas City and San Francisco.

"That shouldn't be hard," Edna noted. "As I recall there's not much between Kansas City and San Francisco."

John chuckled and turned to Lee. "I can see that I'll be hard-pressed to stay ahead of this lady."

Lee smiled back, but didn't comment. She listened as the attractive couple bantered back and forth as they walked toward the hotel. John and Edna had become close on the long train trip from Boston.

"Mrs. Wilkes!" The raised male voice caused them to stop and turn. A short, bowlegged man was hurrying toward them from the direction of the train station with his arm raised.

"I'm sorry to approach you on the street," he said as he came panting up to them, "but I'm heading into the mountains, and I wanted you to hold our contract until I get back."

"I'll be happy to, Mr. Feenan," Edna replied.

"One half of anything I find is yours, Mrs. Wilkes. I know it's there, and I'll surely report back by spring if not before."

"Take care of yourself, Mr. Feenan, and I'll look forward to your report," she replied with a smile.

Owen Feenan waved and hurried off.

"That's money you'll never see again, Edna," John said.

"Probably, but it wasn't much, at least in the relative sense. Five hundred dollars means a lot to a prospector, and I can afford it."

"I've grubstaked a few myself," John acknowledged, "and Feenan is at least honest."

They made their way to the hotel and entered the lobby. The smell of fresh-sawn pine filled the air and was strangely refreshing.

"John, it's good to have you back. The boys are taking your things up to the top floor." The man speaking was wearing a white shirt with a highly decorated vest. What hair he had was parted carefully in the middle of his head. He had an impressive mustache hanging under his nose and was of medium height with the start of a belly pushing at his vest.

"It's good to be back, Lyle. I had all of Boston I could stand." He turned to Edna and Lee and formally introduced them to the manager and then guided them to the stairs.

"Don't let his appearance fool you," John said quietly as they ascended the two flights of stairs to the third floor. "Lyle Hansen can be one of the meanest men you've ever seen if he gets riled. He's an excellent hand with either a gun or knife, and a good man to have on your side in a fight."

"Many men in the West are not what they seem," Edna agreed.

"I'm sorry, Edna," John said. "I keep forgetting you've been out here before."

"Not at all, John. I appreciate your insights."

They reached the landing on the third floor and John showed them each their respective suite of rooms.

"Goodness, John. I must say I'm impressed," Edna said as she observed the comfortable furnishings.

"It'll get better as soon as we get some of our shipments from the coast. I have special lighting coming as well as some other nice trappings," John replied. "There are two maids assigned to this floor, so you shouldn't want for anything. My rooms are at the end of the hall," he said, pointing. "As a matter of fact, I believe I'll go wash some of the dust off before supper."

"Agreed," Edna said, "and then I'll take us all to supper in about an hour. Let's meet right here."

The three doors closed almost in unison, and Lee flopped down on the bed. She was tired, her clothes, face, and hair dusty and travel-stained. She stood, walked to the window, and pulled aside the lace curtains. The street below was full of people, horses, wagons, and buggies. She noticed a woman standing on the boardwalk on the opposite side of the street. The woman looked up, and Lee got a good look at her face. She was an older woman with an enormous bust that certainly drew attention. She seemed to be the only person standing immobile in a moving river of people, and she was paying particular attention to the hotel. Lee shrugged and pulled the curtain.

"Mr. Miller, I've just had a very bad experience with a banker in Boston, so I'm finding it hard to place much trust in men in your profession."

"I completely understand, Mrs. Wilkes, but I must tell you that out here a man is only in business as long as his word is good. My bank is only a year old, so my list of references is short, but it does represent most of the prominent business people in Denver."

"Your name came to me from John O'Malley, who helped me greatly in Boston, and whom I trust completely."

"John is one of my biggest clients and my dearest friend," Miller said. "We have known each other for fifteen years, and he is, in fact, the reason I relocated from Kansas City to Denver."

"Which brings us to the reason I am here," Edna said. "I have a rather substantial amount of money that I need to get into a bank, and I need someone I can trust completely to help me make investments in enterprises that are both safe and have the potential to earn money."

"How much are we talking about?" the banker asked.

Edna took a pen from a holder on the scarred desk, and Miller provided her with a piece of paper. She scratched some figures on the paper and turned it so he could read what she had written. A look of surprise and concern passed over his distinguished face. She suspected that the amount she had brought with her from Boston would make her his largest depositor.

"Mrs. Wilkes, whether it be my establishment or one of my competitors, you must get that into a vault immediately."

"I agree, and I've decided that the First National Bank of Denver, your bank, is where I shall deposit it," she said, making the decision like she made many of her business judgments on instinct and gut-level feeling. "The money is in Federal notes, gold and silver coin, and several assorted bank bills. I'd like to convert the Eastern bank bills into either gold and silver, or your bank bills."

"I'll be happy to convert whatever you want, Mrs. Wilkes, and I promise you won't be sorry you trusted me."

"No, I'm sure I won't, Mr. Miller. The money is currently in John's safe at the Mountain Palace. I would suggest a couple of guards and a couple of trusted employees to move it over here."

"Of course," Miller agreed. "I would also advise that we keep the information as quiet as possible. Discreetness is always a good business practice," he added.

Edna sighed with relief. Miller was obviously an accomplished banker and an astute businessman.

"As far as business opportunities, I know an individual that's just opened up a saddle shop," the banker continued. "He's from Texas originally and a very talented leather worker. He makes some of the most beautiful saddles I've ever seen. The problem is that he doesn't yet have a reputation out here. I don't think it will take him long, but in the meantime he needs a loan to carry him over . . ."

"It sounds like my kind of venture," Edna agreed. "Go ahead and set it up."

"The standard interest is . . ." Miller began to fill her in on the details of the transaction. Edna felt the old thrill of excitement she always felt as business began to take shape. She already loved Denver.

"I sent a letter from Boston as soon as I knew we were coming west," Lee said, "and I thought I might send a telegraph message over to Garland in case one of the boys showed up there."

"Why don't we just head on over to the ranch before the snow sets in?" John asked her.

"I don't want to leave Aunt Edna here alone," Lee replied. "I'd hoped that maybe we'd get a reply back from my Boston letter, but the post office here has gotten nothing for me at general delivery."

"They certainly got it at the ranch. The mail has been pretty dependable going that direction," John observed.

"Maybe he just doesn't want to see me again," Lee said, looking toward the mountains.

"I hardly think that's the case," John replied with a smile. "I suspect they are either busy getting ready for winter, or Matt might not even be at the ranch. Brother Tirley's not much of one for staying put, and he'd surely take Matthew along if he went traveling."

"Maybe that's it," Lee said.

"I'll go over to the saloon and see if anyone's heading that direction. If one of the miners happens to be going back into the hills, he could take a message to the ranch and let them know we're in Denver," John said.

"That might just work," Lee agreed. "I'll meet you back over at the hotel for supper. Aunt Edna should be done at the bank by now."

"For supper then?" John asked.

"About six-thirty," Lee agreed. They parted with John O'Malley heading across the street to the saloon. Lee began walking down the new boardwalk toward the Rainbow City

Café, at which, in another life, she had been head cook, bottle washer, and money counter. Thinking back to those days brought a pang of homesickness to her. She desperately wanted to see Matt.

As she walked, she became aware of a group of men that had come out of the mercantile in front of her. They were obviously drunk, and one of them, a giant of a man with a badly scarred face and filthy clothes, took notice of her.

"What we got here?" he asked no one in particular leering at her.

Lee was not about to be intimidated although she did feel a thrill of fear course through her. She reached her hand into the hidden pocket of her dress and grasped the little top break pistol.

The man took two quick steps and blocked the walk so she couldn't pass.

"Hi there, Missy," he said in a thickly slurred voice. "How about a little kiss for old Bull?"

He was completely disgusting, and Lee felt her stomach turn over. She tried to make her way around him, but he grabbed her by the left arm. Like a striking snake Lee's hand leaped from her pocket, and she pushed the pistol barrel up under the man's chin with some force.

"Mister, I'm not a saloon girl, and you'd better learn that out here if you mess with a good woman, they'll string you up by your dirty neck. Now, let go of my arm or I'm gonna make you have a real nasty toothache." Lee's voice was as steady as her resolve. Apparently Bull believed her because he dropped his hand from her arm and stepped away. She walked around him and took a dozen quick steps before she turned to see what the men were doing. Most of them were just watching her, but the big man was rubbing the spot where she'd marked him with her pistol.

"This ain't over, Missy," he said in a quiet voice. "Nobody treats Bull Burdett like that and gets away with it."

Lee turned, walked quickly to the Rainbow City front door,

and stepped in. The friendly familiarity of the interior made her feel safer. She'd made an enemy, and a bad one at that. She'd have to be careful.

She looked out the window of the café and saw the older woman she'd noticed across the street from the hotel, walking briskly toward the man named Bull. The woman engaged in conversation with the big man for a few moments, and then they walked away together. Lee had a strange feeling that she might be the topic of their conversation.

"I've never seen a storm like this," Edna said looking from the window of the hotel. The snow had been falling and the wind howling for the better part of three days. They were very nearly snowed in, and only a few people moved between the buildings. It was cold, and the hotel staff was hard-pressed to keep enough coal in the stoves to even provide a measure of warmth.

"It'll do this for another day, maybe two, then the sun will come out and it will warm up some," Lyle Hansen said. "Won't be spring-time warm, but it'll get up into the thirties and it'll feel like spring."

A man came lurching in from outside, throwing the door wide and kicking snow in.

"Close the door," Lyle bellowed. "We're havin' enough trouble keepin' warm in here."

"You want it closed, you close it," the man said belligerently. Lyle took five quick steps, grabbed the man by the front of the coat, and lifted him off his feet. The man squealed in pain since Lyle had grabbed a good share of his chest along with his coat and shirt. Lyle spun around toward the open door with the man's feet kicking in the air and chucked him out into a pile of snow.

"You come back in here you'd best be real humble and polite or I'll rip your head off and . . ."

He stopped, looked at Edna, and kicked the door shut. "I'm

sorry you had to see that, Ma'am, but some idiots have no manners."

Edna smiled at Lyle and patted him on the shoulder. "I've seen and heard worse, Lyle, believe me, but I do appreciate your concern."

Lyle walked over to the potbellied stove, threw the door open, and tossed in a couple more big pieces of coal. The stove pipe was glowing red, but there was still a chill in the lobby.

John O'Malley came pushing in through the door carrying armloads of groceries, looking over his shoulder at the man who was just extricating himself from the snow bank. He looked at Lyle and grinned. "I saw him come flying out the door . . ." John said, his tone questioning.

"He was drunk and impolite," Lyle said.

"Ah, enough said." John smiled at Edna and carried the food to the registration desk. "Thomas and Joshua are bringing everything else. We bought all the foodstuffs that were left at all three of the mercantiles. I suspect it will be something like a week or ten days before they get the train through with more supplies, but we should have enough to last us until then."

Lee was coming down the stairs, and she heard what John had said. "I can't imagine anything stopping a train," she remarked.

"Out at the edge of town there are snowdrifts that reach the eaves on a two-story house. The rail crews are going to have to dig, and it will be particularly bad in the cuts. I've seen them use dynamite to clear the cuts."

Lee stepped onto the landing and walked across to the window that looked out onto the deserted street. The wind moaned around the eaves, and the snow rattled off the windows. She reached out and touched the frost that was on the inside of the glass.

"He's out there. I know he is," she said, mostly to herself. She'd had the feeling since the storm started that there was a particular danger in the blizzard for Matt, and she hadn't been able to shake it.

"We won't be able to find him now until spring." Uncle John had walked up quietly beside her. "I doubt if they even open the wagon road into the San Luis considering the depth of the snow."

She shook her head and fought back tears. Spring was a long time away.

Chapter Nine

The storm hit us like a giant fist. The wind came slashin', slappin', breakin' trees off and rippin' covers off the wagons. Close on the wind came snow. It was like someone above had a giant bucket brigade dumpin' snow by buckets and tubs. We pulled on our heavy coats, tied the covers, put our heads down, and rode into the teeth of the gale. I picked Buck off the ground and put him on the saddle. He seemed happy to crawl inside my coat. Stoney and Chris took the lead, and I followed up the rear. After an hour the blizzard got so bad we couldn't see each other.

"Get yer ropes out and tie your teams to the wagon ahead of you," Stoney hollered above the wind. "We got to stay together."

It took us a half-hour to get set up and then we was movin' again. My mind was on Frone and Pa. The blizzard was worse than I'd expected, and I knew they was in trouble. The only thing in their favor was Pa had been through it before. He'd spent many a winter in the high country and seen more snow piled up than most folks. If anybody could make it, Pa could.

We kept at it hour after hour. Puttin' one foot ahead of the other, heads down, trustin' in Stoney and Chris to take us to the valley. The wind came in fits and gusts, and it was so dark

81

I could barely make out the wagon tailgate two feet ahead of me. My feet got so cold that I knew I was close to frostbite, and I took turns with my hands puttin' 'em between me and Bucklin to try and warm up. Fact was, he was about the only warm spot on me. I heard a kid cryin', and I knew all the folks ahead of me had to be scared and cold. All of a sudden, I near ran into the wagon ahead of me. We'd stopped. I pushed Sin around the wagon and rode through the knee-deep snow to the front of the column. Stoney and Chris was down off their horses looking ahead into the storm. I stepped down, set Buck on his feet, and walked over to my friends.

"We lost the trail a spell back," Stoney said. "We're headin' about right, but the trees are gonna get so close we can't get the wagons through."

"It wasn't much of a road to begin with," I said.

"We are thinking that we should unhook the teams, leave the wagons, lead the teams and walk into the valley, amigo," Chris said. "There are cabins there and shelter, but if it's too far the children will suffer, and the small ones might not make it."

"You fort up and get a fire goin'. I'll ride ahead and see if I can find the settlement. How far out you think we are?" I asked Stoney.

"I'd say no more than an hour or two. It's late, and we've been keepin' on steady. If you move downhill, you're gonna hit the river. You get to the river you're just gonna have to make your best call on upstream or downstream."

"What's your take on it?" I asked

"I'd be inclined to go downstream, but I was wrong, once." Stoney smiled. "You do the best ya can, Matthew. We trust ya."

I loaded Buck back on the saddle, crawled up behind him, and pointed downhill. It didn't seem as steep as it had, but the trees were thicker. The forest cut the wind and held the snow back, but the wind was screaming high over my head.

It was cold. I figured maybe it was fifteen or twenty degrees, but the wind worked to make it colder. I was sufferin'. I hated bein' cold, and the time had long passed that I could feel my feet. Sin was tired and stumbled from time to time, but he was game. I knew he had the heart to go 'til he tipped over dead. I rode downhill for what seemed like forever. After a while the trees started to thin, and the snow got deeper. Out in the open I wasn't protected from the wind, and it was blowin' so hard that Sin was havin' a hard time makin' his way ahead.

All of a sudden it came to my mind that I was in trouble. I was surely frostbit, I was so tired I could barely keep my eyes open, and I had no idea where I was or where I was headin'. While I was thinkin' I was in trouble, Sin stumbled and went to his knees. I rolled off and lay on my back with Bucklin on my chest. I was laying in four foot of snow and the wind was whistlin' over my head but not touchin' me. I was warm with my dog snuggled up to me, and I was sorely tempted to just stay where I was and sleep through the storm.

Then it hit me. There was folks back behind me that depended on me to bring 'em in safe. I couldn't give up. I struggled to my feet, sat Buck down, and checked Sin. He seemed alright, but his head was down. I'd only seen him like this once before, and I knew he was near onto his last legs. I took the reins in my hand and started moving downhill again on my own hind legs, breakin' trail for my animals. I kept puttin' one foot ahead of the other, my mind blank, my feet and hands frozen, knowin' I couldn't quit. I kept at it until I stumbled over a downed tree and fell flat on my face. Buck come up and tried to crawl under my coat again. He was crusted with ice, and I pushed him away. I struggled for maybe five minutes to get to my feet and finally grabbed a stirrup and pulled myself up. I grabbed Buck, lifted him to the saddle, and climbed onto Sin. I let him have his head, and he started movin'.

I don't know how long we went on that way, Sin movin' slow but steady, and me barely hangin' onto the saddle horn.

There finally come a time when I realized we'd quit movin'. I lifted my head, but couldn't see anything. I kicked Sin to get him movin', but he only flinched and didn't move a step. We was done. I knew it plain as anything. I'd give it my best shot, but now they was gonna find the three of us in the spring when thaw come to the country. At least I was goin' out with my two best friends. I'd got to the point where I just didn't care any more.

I slipped from the saddle and went straight to my knees. Buck slipped away from me, and I pitched forward. I hit my head hard on a log and seen stars for a spell. The only thing that was really botherin' me was that I was never gonna see my Lee again. I knew we'd've had a wonderful life together full of laughin' and kids. I shook my head and felt above me with numb hands. I'd hit my head on a log. A log meant fuel, and I had some matches somewhere. If I could get a fire goin' . . . I fumbled and felt around, but I couldn't find my matches anywhere. I reached up again, got hold of the log, and pulled myself up. I weren't thinkin' straight and the world seemed to have drawn in on me. I struggled to my feet and felt the log. There was more than one, and they was stacked one on another. It come to me slow, but finally I hit on the idea that if they was stacked, it didn't happen by accident.

I started hollerin'. If there was really somebody close about, I didn't know if they could hear me over the wind, but I was too done in to move. I screamed, hollered, screeched, and yelled 'til I was out of air and 'bout to pitch over on my face again. Buck got so excited he started barkin'. I was about to give up when I seen a light come around the corner of the logs.

"What the heck," I heard somebody say, then I was down on my face again.

"Get that horse over to the barn, Jessie, and rub him down good. He's been hard-used."

I could hear 'em, and I knew I was 'sposed to be tellin' 'em somethin', but I couldn't get it out. I tried to talk but the words was stuck in my throat. They walked me into a room lit by candles. There was a giant stone fireplace in one end of the room, and there was a woman throwin' wood on it by the armful. As the fire flared the room lit up and the warm started workin' on my face. It hurt somethin' terrible, and I still wasn't havin' much luck talkin'. I tried but it sounded more like a sick bullfrog than a person.

"My dog," I finally managed.

"He's layin' on the floor under the table, meltin' all over," the woman said with a smile.

The door opened and a man come in with a half bushel of flying snow.

"Seth, he's frozen nearly solid. We got to get his clothes off and get him under some blankets," the woman said.

The name Seth sparked somethin' in me, and I started tryin' to talk again.

"People," I managed to stammer, "Nathan, up the hill." I stopped for a minute and sucked in some air. "In the timber."

The woman stopped cold and looked at Seth. "My God, Seth. Get the men turned out. You got to go get them."

Seth moved like somebody had lit a fire in his drawers, and he was hollerin' before he got out the door.

"Come over and sit by the fire," she said to me. "Soon as we get your clothes thawed, we'll try and get you under some blankets. My name is Sadie Dustin. I'm Seth's wife."

Sadie helped me stumble over to a chair made out of lodgepole pine, and I fell into it. I was startin' to drip on the plank floor and knew I shouldn't, but there was nothin' I could do about it. My face was burnin', my hands hurt so bad I wanted to bawl, and I still couldn't feel my feet. I was shakin' so hard that the chair was rattlin' under me. I knew I had to get up and help the folks off the hill, but I couldn't seem to raise my carcass out of the chair.

I sit in the chair for maybe ten minutes, then Sadie come over with a blanket and put it on my shoulders.

"Soon as you can, you get out of those wet clothes, and I need to see your feet."

I nodded my head weakly and worked at gettin' my boots off. I finally got it done, but it took all I had. In the meantime she'd heated a tub of water to lukewarm and she pushed it over to me.

"Put your feet in the water, and we'll see how bad your toes are frozen."

I still couldn't feel my feet, and I couldn't bend over to get my socks off. Sadie finally peeled 'em off, and helped me lift my feet into the water. I bawled like a baby. I been shot, beat, stomped, run over by a horse, stabbed, and even half hung, but nothin' ever hurt me as bad as my feet in that water. I didn't want to bawl in front of Sadie, but there was just no help for it.

Sadie fed me some hot cereal, poured some hot tea down me, and I was finally able to stand up and shuck out of my clothes. The blanket was small but covered most of me, and after awhile I was in a bed with Buck up tight against me. I slept but it was bad sleep. The wind was screamin' outside, and I kept thinkin' I could hear Pa callin' my name, and Lee cryin' somethin' awful.

"It was very bad," Chris said, "but maybe not as bad as you had. We burned up Señor Sam's wagon to keep warm, and we lost one mule, but all of the peoples made it. There are maybe fifteen cabins here and they are all in the cabins."

"Still snowin'?" I asked.

"It is, but the wind is not so bad now."

We were both thinkin' the same thing. We still had two people out there in the blizzard.

"Your feet are very bad, amigo."

My feet were on the outside of the blankets because I couldn't stand to have anything touch 'em. They was bright red, all but my little toe on my right foot. It was chalk-white and cold to the touch. Stoney had been in earlier in the morning and pronounced that I would probably lose my little toe. I weren't lookin' forward to that, but it was still better than what had almost happened.

I was weak as a newborn rabbit. I could barely hobble around and do them necessary things, let alone gettin' up and out. Chris checked on Sin and reckoned him sound, but still needin' some rest. I knew the feelin'.

Sadie kept feedin' me chuck full about every two hours, and I slept most of the day through. The night come on with a howlin' wind again and more snow. The drifts had already piled high against the cabins and still didn't show any signs of lettin' up. The next day brought more snow, and the next even more. I'd never seen the like, and Stoney said it was the worst he'd ever seen in all his days. With every inch that fell I knew that Pa and Frone's chances got worse. I was worried sick, but there was nothin' I could do about it.

Stoney looked at my foot on the morning of the third day we'd been snowed in. "We got to take it off, Matthew, or you're gonna get gangrene and you'll lose your leg, or maybe even die," My little toe had turned black, and I could see that what Stoney said was true. I watched him as he heated up his knife blade to help slow the bleedin' and then they cut it off. By middle of the afternoon, it was throbbin' each time my heart beat, but I figured I'd live.

The mornin' of the fourth day the snow quit and a light wind blew the clouds away. I hobbled to the window and looked out. There was snow piled clear over the roof of the neighboring cabin, and the men had dug tunnels under the snow so they could feed the animals. It was purty in the bright sun, but made me understand how small a man really is. Sometimes you could fight and fight and still not win against nature.

I'd tried to put my boots on, but my feet were so swollen I couldn't get close. Chris went out to the barn and gathered up the Ute moccasins I carried in my saddlebags, and I was able to get 'em on. Buck had managed to circulate from cabin to cabin with Stoney and had made friends with everybody, 'cept the pastor, who was still preachin' gloom, sin, and damnation. He was wearin' thin on everybody, particular since we was all kinda livin' close together, and he smelled like a dead civet cat.

I practiced on my legs most of the day, and come evenin' I started gatherin' my truck up. Stoney looked at me and rubbed his whiskers.

"You goin' somewhere, boy?"

"I'm gonna head out in the mornin' and see if I can get to Pa and Frone," I replied.

"Snow's twenty feet deep in some spots, and soft. How you figure on doin' it?"

"I reckon if I stay to the timber, the snow won't be so deep," I replied.

"Gonna get below zero tonight, and probably colder tomorrow night. Don't take long fer a man to freeze solid in that kinda cold." He cleared his throat and rubbed his beard again. "Don't think that all the rest of us ain't doin' considerable ponderin' over the two we left up on the side hill, but it ain't gonna make it any better if'n more of us die trying to bring 'em in. If I know your Pa, they're doin' fine. They had food, and they probably got into the timber before the storm hit, so they got a fire with lots of wood about. Let's give it a little time."

I didn't say much. I wanted in the worse way to head up the hill, but I knew Stoney was right. I'd nearly croaked myself, and it hadn't been below zero.

It got almighty cold during the night, and by morning we was growin' frost on the inside cabin logs away from the fire. The sun come out, and by afternoon it warmed enough to start meltin' the snow on the top. Come night, as soon as the sun slipped behind the mountains, the temperature really dropped off. We'd all takin' to sleepin' on the floor of Seth and Sadie's cabin, and even with a roarin' fire the cabin was still mighty cold just a few feet removed from the fireplace. We crawled into the blankets early just to warm up. About two in the mornin' I heard a tremendous pop and jumped out of bed grabbin' for my short gun.

"Trees are blowin' up," Stoney said. "The trees are freezin' clear to their hearts, and then they blow up. I only seen it this cold one time before, and that was way up north." He crawled back under the blankets and then looked out at me.

"Get some sleep, Matt. We're gonna go get your pa in the mornin'. There'll be a crust on the snow that'll surely carry a man."

I didn't sleep much the rest of the night, and come first light I was out and gatherin' up my stuff. Stoney had already gone out, and he come stompin' back in swingin' his arms and blowin' wind.

"Crust on the snow has to be ten inches deep," he said. "Any place the sun hit on yesterday will be like travelin' on a highway. It'll still be soft under the trees, but there might even be enough crust to carry a man in the timber."

"I guess we'll find out purty quick," I said.

Sadie cooked up a big breakfast of venison and fresh bread with gooseberry jam. When we'd finished, we pulled on our coats. I'd already put on two extra pairs of socks in my moccasins. My feet were still mighty tender, and Stoney had promised me I'd feel the cold worse now I'd been froze. Chris was gonna stay in town just in case somethin' happened and they had to come after me and Stoney. Buck seemed to be happy to be out of the cabin, and it'd warmed up some as it got lighter. It was my first time to really see the whole valley, and I had to admit it was a right purty place. The cabins that lay close about all had a curl of smoke headin' for the sky, and the snow made the place look pure and clean. Buck had found easy travelin' on the snow crust, and he'd went over to the timber at the edge of the river. Suddenly, I heard him cut loose with his battle roar. I looked over and he was standin' stiff-legged lookin' into the trees. I figured he come up with a bear that had got up for a stretch, and I started workin' my way

toward him. As I watched Buck, he started wigglin' and wag-
gin' all over and run into the timber. I stepped up my pace,
even though it made my feet hurt. I'd never seen him act that
way, and it had me almighty curious. I got almost to the timber
when I heard a ruckus comin' out of the trees, and I seen the
two-tone buckskin mule that Frone thought so much of. What
Buck seen was Pa and Frone crossin' the river ice, ridin' two
of her mules and leadin' the other two.

"We had to leave the wagon back up on the side hill, but
Frone figures what we managed to pack on the mules will get
her by 'til we can get back up there," Pa hollered down at me
and Stoney. I never been so glad to see anybody in all my
born life.

"If you're gonna get snowed in with somebody, it's mighty
handy if he turns out to be an old mountain man," Frone said.
"He built us a lean-to on the side of the wagon, banked it with
snow, made a fireplace outa rocks, and had us snug as could
be not two hours after the storm hit."

Pa was glowin' like a June-born firefly. Nothin' like a little
emergency to make friends out of near strangers, and it looked
like to me that Pa and Frone had gotten purty friendly during
their little emergency.

"There's only one problem with bein' snowed in with a
mountain man," Frone continued. "You get dang sick of listenin' to his stories. I was scared to death that we was gonna
be snowed in all winter on that side hill. I weren't scared about
starvin' or freezin', but I was some worried that Tirley would
plumb talk me to death by spring."

I laughed with everybody else. There was more than a little
truth in what she said.

It was the second night after they'd come down from the
hill. We were lucky in that two families had got fed up with
the valley come fall and had taken out for California. They'd
left two cabins empty. The rest of the families had been spread
out with the townsfolk so Frone took over the smaller cabin,

and the five of us took up the other one. We was in our cabin. The sun had went down near to two hours past, and we was sittin' 'round the fire smelling the tobacco smoke from Stoney's pipe and havin' quiet talk.

The door swung open and we all turned to look. It was the preacher, and he was all het up.

"Frone Riggins, it ain't seemly for a single woman to be alone in a cabin with four men." He near yelled it, he was so fired up.

"Since when you been keepin track of me, preacher man?" she asked in a quiet tone.

"Some of the women of the settlement are purty upset by your carryin' on," he said. "It just ain't seemly."

Frone reached down to the belt at her waist and pulled a narrow-bladed knife from a sheath that I hadn't noticed before. She picked up a pine stick from the floor and began to whittle on it. It was plain to see that the knife was sharp.

"Preacher, in case you haven't looked around the room, I ain't alone with five men. There's six men in here, and one of 'em is my nephew, Seth. If you'll look a little closer, over in the dark corner by the fireplace is my niece, so I'd say you be misinformed. Another thing . . ." Frone paused a minute to gather her breath. "Them women of the settlement wouldn't be getting all in a lather unless there was someone with a nasty mind talkin' about me. I 'spect that someone is you, and if'n I find out it's true, well . . ." she didn't say nothin' more, but she cut the pine stick in half with a violent motion and grinned right at the scrawny sky pilot. He went out the door like the devil hisself was on his heels.

"Gonna be a long winter with that little pissant hangin' 'round," Stoney remarked. What he said turned out to be true. It was a dang long winter.

Chapter Ten

"Looks like winter's finally over," Edna said as a warm spring breeze tossed her hair.

"I thought last January that there was so much snow it would never melt, but now it's nearly gone," Lee remarked.

"Sure made a mess of the streets," Uncle John observed. "That guy is never gonna get that wagon unstuck."

They were standing on the boardwalk in front of the Mountain Palace Hotel looking at a wagon buried to the axles in front of the mercantile. The owner had unhooked the team and was trying to lead them out of the quagmire that was the street. He was struggling in mud over his knees and the team nearly ran over him as he fought to pull his legs loose.

"The frost went out all at once," Lyle Hansen said from behind them. "It'll be two weeks before the streets will be decent." He turned and walked back into the hotel followed by the rest.

"I hear Bull Burdett killed a man over at the Diamond Saloon last night," Lyle remarked as he walked behind the hotel counter. "Seems he's quite a hand with a gun."

"I heard he started to work with a short gun after he'd taken a bad beating from someone in Del Norte. He plans to find him and kill him," John said.

Lyle looked up sharply. "I figured you knew the whole of that story since the man that whipped him is related to you."

John looked at the hotel manager curiously. "I hadn't heard who it was, only that it happened."

"Matthew O'Malley, the gunfighter, was the man that thrashed Burdett. Ain't he relation of yours?" Lyle asked.

They heard a gasp and turned to look at Lee.

"Matthew was in Del Norte last fall?" she said.

"That's the story," Lyle confirmed. "Seems he whipped Burdett and then a week later over to South Fork cut the lip off a feller who was working himself up to draw on Matt."

"There's a man that hangs with Burdett that's missing half of his upper lip. I've seen him several times," John said. He smiled and looked at Lee. "Sounds like Matthew is still busy making friends."

"Lyle, have you heard where Matt went from South Fork?" Lee asked.

"All I heard was he disappeared headin' west with two old mountain men and a Mex that's about his age. If I'd a known you had an interest, I'd've asked a little closer."

"That'd be Stone-Cold Phillips, Tirley, and Chris Silva with Matt," John said. "They told me they were going on a trek out west."

"So, Matthew beat Bull Burdett," Edna remarked. "Your young man must be something else," she said to Lee.

"He's not patient when it comes to bullies like Burdett," Lee acknowledged.

She looked through the open door of the hotel. The sun was shining brightly, and the breeze was pushing white puffy clouds across the sky. "I wonder where he is now," she said, mostly to herself.

"It's the durndest thing I've ever seen," John said.

"That's just the way it was layin' in the shaft," Owen Feenan replied. "I ain't found anybody that seen the likes of it. I figured to give it to Miss Edna just the way it is."

"Must be nearly a pound of pure silver," Lyle said.

"There's tons and tons of it," Feenan replied, "and as soon as folks down here find out what I got, there's gonna be a rush on."

"Lyle, would you round up Thomas and have him meet me here at the hotel?" John asked. "I want him to see this."

"Where is Miss Edna?" Feenan asked.

"She went over to the bank but should be back any minute." John replied. Just as he spoke Edna and Lee came in through the door.

"That new place down the street makes the sixth store that's gone up in the last two weeks," Edna remarked to John. "The town is getting crowded."

"Look what Feenan found up in the hills, Edna," John said.

Edna hurried over and looked at the silver lying on the countertop.

"Good grief," she remarked in surprise, "it's shaped just like a plume on a lady's hat."

"Solid silver, Miss Edna," Feenan said, "shaped just like a feather. I found it three days ago in my shaft. There's tons of pure silver in the vein I uncovered, and half of it is yours."

"I don't know what to say, Mr. Feenan . . ." Edna said.

"If you hadn't grubstaked me, I'd've never been able to get into the mountains last fall, and somebody else would've found the vein ahead of me. The hills is crawlin' with prospectors now, but we got us a vein of the richest lode silver that's ever been seen. You helped me find it."

Just then a tall man with broad shoulders and black hair came in through the open door of the hotel.

"Thomas, take a look at this," John said. Thomas O'Malley walked over to the counter and looked at the chunk of silver shaped in the form of a large feather.

"Feenan made a strike, and Edna is a full partner in the mine. Where's there's one strike there'll be at least three more big ones, and a wealth of smaller ones. I say we go build us a town," John said excitedly.

"Can you do that?" Edna asked. "Can you just go and start up a town?"

"Under the terms of the Townsite Act of 1844, the United States Congress says that settlers can stake out three hundred and twenty acres for the princely sum of a dollar and a quarter an acre paid to the government land office. We then have the right to lay out the entire town in lots measuring one hundred and twenty-five feet by twenty-five. We can then turn about and sell the lots for whatever the traffic will bear. It's all perfectly legal," John O'Malley explained. "In fact I'll go over today and file with the land office."

"Silver Plume," Lee said. "Let's call it Silver Plume in memory of the original strike."

"That's a great name," Tom agreed. "Has a ring to it, and it'll stick." His voice was deep and quiet. Lee looked closely at him and felt her heart turn over. He looked enough like Matthew to be his brother instead of his cousin. His jaw was square, his cheekbones high, and his eyes were the same brilliant sky-blue as Matt's.

"I guess I'd better introduce everyone," John said. "Thomas came in on the afternoon train yesterday, and I sent him down to the springs to check on the progress of our spur. He just got back this morning. Thomas, this is Edna Wilkes, Lewara Conall, Owen Feenan, and you know Lyle, of course."

"I'm pleased and honored to meet you ladies," Tom said. "I've heard a lot about both of you. Mr. Feenan, congratulations. It looks like a major strike."

"Miss Edna, this here silver feather is yours to keep," Feenan said. "Now I got to get back to the hills and get to work."

"We have work to do as well," John agreed. "I want to open a general mercantile at the Silver Plume site no later than one week from today, and we have a townsite to lay out." There was an edge of suppressed excitement in his voice that was contagious. Lee felt a surge of exhilaration sweep over her. Maybe that was why she liked the O'Malley clan. They made things happen.

"Oh, by the way," John said. "Since it looks like we are about to get very busy, I might as well announce now that Edna and I are engaged to be married."

Lee gasped, then smiled. It was a surprise, but then again it wasn't. John and Edna seemed to naturally go together. Lee was happy for them.

"I have one bottle of champagne left," Lyle said. "I'll see if I can find some ice, and we'll have a party tonight to celebrate."

"Get it lined up, Lyle. We'll celebrate tonight, and tomorrow we'll get ready to go build the city of Silver Plume," John said. He wrapped his arm around Edna and they walked up the stairs laughing and holding each other.

"Most everyone, except dad, calls me Tom," Thomas O'Malley said to Lee and swept off his hat.

She smiled. "I'm Lee," she replied.

"I know. Dad's told me a lot about you."

"He has?" she asked. "I hope some of it was good."

"He greatly admires you," Tom said, "and he wants you and Matt to get together. He says you belong with each other."

"Do you know Matt well?" Lee asked.

"Never met him," Tom replied, "but what I know of him, I like. He's two years older than me, and he's made his own way for most of his life."

"Do you think your father is doing the right thing by starting a town at Silver Plume?" Lee asked, changing the subject.

"My dad nearly always does the right thing. He has an instinct for it." His tone revealed a great respect for his father. He cleared his throat and looked away from Lee. "Dad told me yesterday that he wants to find Matthew this spring and bring him home. After meeting you, I'm not sure I want Matt found right away."

Lee smiled. "I thank you, sir, but it will do you no good.

As your father said, Matthew and I are meant to be together. I know it."

Tom smiled back at her and took her arm. "Well, let's be friends anyhow. The wildflowers are blooming, and the colors are magnificent. There's quite a display at the edge of town if you'd care to take a short walk."

Lyle watched them as they walked out the front door, and then turned to look up the stairs where he could hear John and Edna talking quietly on the landing. He shook his head and smiled. "Ah, a man has to love springtime," he said to himself.

"Good grief," Lee exclaimed. "I've never seen such a show. There must be acres and acres of them."

"I spotted them yesterday," Tom replied. "The mountain wildflowers don't last long, but while they're blooming, it's quite spectacular."

"After the winter we've had, I needed to see a bit of color," Lee said quietly. "It gives a person a feeling of hope."

"Spring always does that for me as well," Tom acknowledged. He turned and looked back toward the busy streets they had just left. "We're living in exciting times. There's so much happening across the entire nation, and I see a world of opportunity just waiting for those bold enough to grasp it."

"That sounds just like your cousin, Owen O'Malley. He's always looking to the future," Lee said.

"I think I'm going to like my cousins," Tom replied, looking again toward the field of spring flowers.

"I know you will," Lee agreed.

They stood quietly for a moment letting the warm spring breeze wash around them.

"We'd best be going back," Lee suggested.

"I suppose," Tom agreed. "It sounds like Dad and Edna have big plans for tonight, and they include us."

Lee turned, and as she did a shot rang out from the direction of town. They both heard the whine of a bullet passing close to them. Tom pushed Lee to the ground, and a Smith and Wesson Russian appeared as if by magic from under his coat.

"Stay down," he cautioned her. They were less than a hundred yards from the nearest building, and he ran quickly in that direction. After a few minutes he motioned to her, and she joined him at the edge of town.

"That bullet very nearly hit us," Tom said.

"Was it aimed at us?" Lee asked, pushing a strand of auburn hair out of her eyes.

"I don't know," he replied. "There's always shooting going on, so it may have been a stray shot."

Lee hoped he was right, but she remembered clearly the older woman she'd seen a number of times that seemed so interested in her. She also remembered the offhand comment from Uncle John about a woman named Beck back in Boston. Were they connected? Had she been the target of the seemingly stray bullet?

A shiver ran down her back, and she took Tom's arm.

"Can you believe so much could happen in just two weeks?" Edna asked, turning to John. They were standing on the dirtway that passed for a street in the new town of Silver Plume.

"What I can't believe is that there's so many people camped in two square miles of mountain and creek," John replied.

"The word sure got around in a hurry," Edna agreed. "Lee has three men working in the tent making meals with her and they can't keep up."

"Thomas says they can't haul the hardware up from the valley fast enough to keep up with the demand, and he has six wagons working the trail. Feenan said there was another big strike made today up toward the top, and his vein is getting richer the deeper they drive the shaft. He's in nearly a hundred feet, and he hired three new miners today."

"It's so loud, and in an odd way, exciting," Edna said.

"It's exciting, and as long as the price of silver stays good, there'll be a lot of money made here," John said. "But you and I both know that any economy based on one commodity can boom one day and bust the next."

"I know, and I've advised Feenan to diversify, but he's hit it so big he's having trouble seeing it might end one day," Edna said.

"Not might, but will. It always ends. Sometimes sooner than later," John observed. They fell quiet as they watched the miners and prospectors working on the mountainside that rose in front them.

"I sent Lyle west toward Utah to see if he could get a line on Matthew and Tirley," John said. "I figured if I didn't send him, Lee was gonna rent a horse and take off on her own."

"What about the hotel?" Edna asked.

"I sold it."

"You sold it?" Edna exclaimed, surprised.

"Once we get married, I didn't figure I'd have time to keep track of you and a hotel at the same time," John said with a smile.

Edna laughed and turned to him. "I hear there's going to be one heck of a celebration on the fourth of July here in Silver Plume. Why don't we add to the festivities and get married then?"

"Somehow getting married to Edna Wilkes and Independence Day don't seem to be compatible terms," John said, laughing again.

"Not getting cold feet are you, Johnny Boy?" Edna asked him.

John took Edna into his arms and kissed her gently. "July fourth is a month away. It seems a long time to wait for my dreams to come true."

"Why, John O'Malley, I do believe there is a bit of the poet in you, or perhaps blarney." They both laughed and then turned as they heard Lee's voice behind them on the narrow plank walk. Lee had set up a cook tent, hired some men, and served up meals twelve hours a day for a dollar a head.

"You'll never guess what I heard happened in Denver," Lee said. She was fairly bubbling with excitement. "I guess the good folks got sick of Bull Burdett and the rest of the bad element, and they ran them out two steps ahead of a rope."

"A vigilance committee?" John asked.

"That's the way I understand it," Lee replied. "Bull killed another man in a gunfight, except this time the man had a family and didn't carry a gun. It sounds like the mob that went after him was over hundred men, and they had ropes with them. They planned on stringing him up." She didn't sound particularly upset at the prospect.

"Good grief, Lee, they would never approve of your attitude at the academy," Edna observed. Lee laughed. "No, I don't suppose they would, but if anyone ever deserved to swing, it's Bull Burdett."

"I wonder where he'll head now?" Edna asked.

"Farther west would be my guess. Some little town on the other side of the divide where he can walk hard-heeled, and people will be scared enough of him to do his bidding," John said grimly.

Chapter Eleven

"We gonna head back over to Pahgosa?" Stoney asked Pa.

"I reckon sooner or later," Pa acknowledged. "We still got a creek full of gold to find up there."

"Looks to me that the snow's mostly gone," I observed. I'd been thinkin' that I'd been in one place long enough. Sin horse was probably figurin' I forgot how to ride.

"I promised Frone I'd build a shed out back of her cabin, but I reckon it can wait 'til we get back," Pa said looking over his shoulder in the direction of Frone's cabin.

"She's got ya doin' a passel of chores lately," Stoney observed.

"There's a lot needs doin', and she's got no one to do fer her," Pa said, completely missin' Stoney's taunt.

"She's got two nephews that are plum able-bodied," Stoney said.

"Sam said he'd help her if she needed it as well," Rosie added.

"They got families to take care of . . ." Pa stopped talkin', abruptly realizing he was makin' excuses. "Okay," he said suddenly, "let's leave out at first light."

"I'll get my goods together and be ready," Stoney said,

tryin' to hide a smile, "and Rosie told me yesterday he's ready."

"I'll let Chris know. He'll be glad. He never was much for farmin', and he's been tryin' to help," I said, lookin' down across the valley at the furrows that had recently been turned.

"Nope, his family's more inclined toward horses with a few cows throwed in here and there," Stoney agreed.

"Matthew, how come you ain't been wearin' your short gun lately?" Pa asked me, changin' the subject.

"It gets in my way when I'm workin'," I replied.

"It's yer call, but I recollect a time when trouble come on us fast, and there weren't no time to go huntin' a gun."

"You're right, Pa. I hadn't give it much thought," I agreed. I remembered, not long past, when I'd swore I'd never be without a gun close at hand. Trouble had a way of comin' on a fella sudden, and it was best to be prepared for the worst. I walked to the front door of the cabin, nearly fell over Bucklin, who'd taken to nappin' on the step, and pulled my gunbelt off the peg just inside the front door. I buckled it on and looked down toward the new log church we'd put up a few weeks ago. There was a commotion in the small yard in front of the buildin' and it looked like Chris Silva was in the middle of it.

"I seen ya lookin' at my daughter, Mex. I'm gonna make you pay for that," the red-faced man's voice was raised, and he had a finger stuck in Chris' chest. He was a medium-large fella by the name of Kevin Bishop, standing a head taller than Silva, and a farmer that we knew with no particular favor. He was packin' a short gun in his belt, as most of us did. Thing was, when he braced Chris Silva, he'd took on a load of trouble, and he was too stupid to even know it. Silva's eyes was narrowed down, and I knew Bishop was only a half step from meetin' his maker. The hawk-nosed preacher-man was standin' behind the farmer eggin' him on.

"This is no affair of yours, O'Malley," Bishop said as I walked up.

"This man's my partner, and that makes it my affair, Bishop," I said. "Also, I figured I might warn ya that I only know one man faster with a gun or knife than me, and you're facin' up to him right now." I turned my attention to Chris. "You kill him, Pard, you dig the hole. He's kinda big, and I'm plum sick of buryin' people that make ya mad." I looked over at Bishop and the preacher and then back to Chris. "You line 'em up right and you might get both of 'em with one shot. You can say the preacher was an accident, and I'd be right happy to dig the hole for him."

Bishop's face turned white and he took a quick step back. "I never asked for no gun trouble, O'Malley."

"Your fight is with me, señor," Chris said in a quiet, deadly tone, "not my compadre, and it is a very small thing to die for, me speaking to your daughter."

Bishop's face had turned white as fresh-washed underwear, and he took another couple of steps back. "I just didn't want her gettin' cozy with a . . ." he let the sentence die, and Chris took a step forward his hand on his pistol.

"Looks like we wore out our welcome," I said to Silva. "We're good enough men to pull them and their families through hard times, but when the sun's shinin' they want to get shed of us."

I saw the tension drain from Chris' shoulders, and figured he weren't gonna kill Bishop right then, even though the man richly deserved it.

"Looks to me like first light ain't quick enough fer leavin'," Pa said from behind me. I turned and saw that he, Stoney, and Rosie were standin' behind us. "Let's gather up the animals and head up the trail. I had about all this city livin' I can stand," Pa added.

An hour later we were on the trail foggin' dust out of Animas City. We stopped once as we reached the last ridge. I could just barely see Frone's cabin, and there was a lone figure standin' out on the step lookin' our direction. She'd started settin' store by Pa's company, and I knew it pained both of 'em when we left.

"We find the gold, we'll come back," Stoney said.

"Maybe," Pa said. He swung his horse's head around and we headed back east for Pahgosa with Bucklin leadin' the way.

"You go over the top, and the water runs east. She ends up in the Atlantic Ocean. Water on this side runs to the Pacific. That's why Lewis and Clark, or somebody, called these here mountains the spine of America," Pa said. He clamped his pipe between his teeth like he was invitin' argument.

"It had to be them two," Stoney agreed. "Them boys was the only ones that come this far west ahead of us."

"Now, that ain't rightly true," Pa objected. "My pap said he went from sea to sea when he was just a lad, and his pap before him done the same thing."

"Mighta done," Stoney agreed. "There was some long hunters back then what seen country no one's seen yet to this day."

We'd topped out just under the high peaks of the San Juans above Pahgosa Springs in the late afternoon. Pa had knowed right where he wanted to go. He led us to a spot where he'd camped before. It was nestled up against the base of the rock that formed the last thousand feet of the mountain peaks. The rock face formed an overhang. It wasn't a real cave, but it gave shelter with room for both us and our animals. We built a fair-sized fire to warm the rock up and sat about fixin' supper. We'd eaten just as the sun was goin' behind the mountains across the valley.

We was about as high up as a man can get and still be on the ground. The river valley lay a long ways below us, and there was still a touch of winter chill in the air where we was sittin'.

I looked to the south and saw the lightnin' blaze against the thunderheads buildin' over the tops of the mountains. The last of the evenin' sun was shinin' red on 'em just right so we could see the wind blowin' 'em back on themselves and pilin' 'em even higher. It was a purty sight.

"It won't make it to us," Stoney said quietly. "They'll build like that fer a spell and then head east."

It was still and peaceful. We'd kicked back and were listenin' to the old men tell stories as they smoked their pipes. Rosie was cleanin' his shotgun and drinking coffee from his beat-up tin cup. He was always with us, but he was quiet. He'd been plumb quiet all winter.

"How'd ol' Stewart come about to find this here gold you been talkin' 'bout?" Stoney asked.

"I was just gettin' wound up to tell ya that," Pa said, settlin' a little deeper into the blanket he had wrapped around his shoulders. "You remember what this country was like back in '58," he said, lookin' at Stoney.

"She was rough," Stoney replied. "The Utes was meaner than a two-headed rattlesnake, and if they didn't kill ya there was a fair chance the country would."

Pa nodded in agreement as he tossed a piece of cedar on the fire. "It was mean and nasty right enough, and Stewart had only four men with him. He'd made up his mind to cut through, not wastin' any time. He made it to this here spot with a fast ride, takin' just two days from Garland," Pa said wavin' his hand at the small valley that lay slightly below and just to the west of us. "When they got here, it was late and he decided to build a quick camp, make supper, sleep 'til the moon come up, and get on down the trail."

"Sounds like a good plan," Stoney nodded in agreement.

"He reckoned it was. Anyhow, while he was at Garland, a Mexican kid named José somethin' or other begged to come along on the trip to California. He said his pa was beatin' him and plannin' on sellin' him for a slave to the Utes. Stewart felt sorry for the kid and told him he could come along if he had his own horse. He told the kid he could be the chore boy around the camp."

"Always nice to have," I remarked, tryin' to add somethin

to the conversation. I could tell by the look on Pa's face that he'd as soon I'd keep my comments to myself. It was his story, and he'd tolerate Stoney buttin' in time to time, but not his own kid.

"José somethin' went down to the crick to get a pan full of water to cook with, and while he was bent over scoopin' the water up, he seen a funny lookin' rock in the bottom of the crick. He picked the rock out a the black sand and took both the water and the rock up to the Captain. Stewart took a look at the rock and went right back down to the crick with Jose to have him show where he found it. Stewart took five or six more rocks that looked the same and stuck 'em in a little bag, then went back up to the camp." Pa stopped a minute lookin' into the fire. He opened the top button of his shirt, pulled out his medicine bag, opened the drawstring, and fished somethin' out. He held the gold nugget up that he'd showed me back in the barn at the ranch.

"This here's one of them rocks," he said holdin' it between his thumb and forefinger. "Stewart knew me fer a mountain man and figured I might know the spot where he'd found it. He told me the story while we was restin' up after a little skirmish we'd had with Jeb Stuart and his rebs at Brandy Station." I looked across the fire and saw that Pa had all of Stoney's attention, and Chris' eyes was lit up like a kid at Christmas. Rosie was looking back over the mountain, probably thinkin' about what happened at his place, but I could tell he was listenin' to Pa's story.

"I'd a stayed and scooped up everything I could find in the bottom of that little crick," Stoney observed.

"Stewart mighta, but when he went back down to take another look, he found a moccasin track in the edge mud. He knew right then there was Injuns about."

"He just left it?" I asked, surprised.

"Just like he found it except for the nuggets he'd picked up," Pa said. "He reckoned that he knew right where to come back to when there wasn't quite so many people watchin'.

Like most good trail men he'd took note of the landmarks. He also figured that all the gold in Colorado wasn't gonna do him no good if'n he was dead."

"Good point," Stoney agreed.

"Did he come back, señor?" Chris asked in his quiet voice.

"Well, the war come on, which is where I met him, case I ain't told ya that part, and then he got assigned to one of them big forts in Kansas. He come back, but it wasn't 'til ten years had come and gone."

"He did not find it when he came back?" Chris asked.

"He found a shoein' kit they'd left behind. One of the pack animals had slipped a shoe. They fixed it by the light of the fire, then forgot the kit when they packed up. He found what he thought was the stone fire rings of their camp, but no sign of the little crick.

"So what happened to it?" I asked Pa.

"Some folks think the Captain was lost when he come across it, and that's why nobody can find it again," Pa said. "I know him and there ain't been a day since he was born that he didn't know right where he was." Pa took his pipe out of his mouth and blew a smoke ring toward the fire. "I figure it's more likely the Utes hid it."

Chris looked at Pa and smiled a little. "How is it the Utes could hide a creek, señor?"

"I'm glad you asked that question, 'cause I watched 'em do it, and not far from where we're sittin' right now. I didn't have a clear idea of what they was doin' then, but I've studied on it since, and I think they was hidin' Captain Stewart's little creek."

"You watched 'em doin' it?" Stoney asked in a surprised tone.

"I never told nobody 'cause it was just an idea of mine, but over the years the more I thought about it . . ." he paused a minute for effect. "I'd come out on a trek with Carson and Tobin late in '58. Probably not long after Stewart had come through here. The farmin' was done at home, the boys was in school and big enough to do the chores, so I told Ma I'd be home in a month, and I takin' out. I'd a hankerin' to see some of my old country, so after I left my partners at Bent's Fort, I come on over into the San Juans." Pa stopped a minute, studied his white clay pipe, and then started on again. "I'm purty sure I saw the Utes hidin' Stewart's creek. I was high up on the slopes. I'd come through that tight, keyhole pass up where the La Platas drop off onto this side. I cut across the top of Cherry Creek Canyon and was makin' my way fer right here. I figured if I hurried, I could get to the cave and spend the night without stirrin' the Utes up." He stopped a minute and looked over at me. "The Utes and me weren't exactly friends at the time. We'd had us a little disagreement over a cache of furs, and I called a feud down on 'em." He paused, lettin' that piece of information settle in. "Anyhow, I was ridin' careful 'cause I knew the Utes was wishful of takin' my hair, even though it'd been years since I'd been in the country. I seen their smoke from up high and snuck down to see what they was about. That's when I saw 'em doin' it."

"What'd ya see 'em doin'?" Stoney asked. "You beat around the bush long enough to scare all the birds out, and you still haven't got to the point."

"I'm gettin' to there, just don't rush me," Pa replied. He took a puff on his pipe, just to irk Stoney, and continued.

"I was layin' tight under a big serviceberry bush, and the Utes was fair workin' themselves into a sweat. I thought that was a mite strange since I'd never known a Ute to work at somethin' like that. I mean they was good providers for their folk. They be good hunters, and their women's good at making clothes and such, but this here time they was diggin'. Utes consider diggin' to be white man's work. They just never had no use fer it, but they was doin' it that day."

"I don't recollect ever seein' a Ute dig now that you bring it up," Stoney agreed. "That'd surely draw a man's attention."

"It did. I was mighty curious, so I hunkered down and watched. Looked to me like they'd already been workin' fer a couple of days. They had this here little meadow purty well churned up, and they'd cut down some quakie trees."

"You mean livin' trees,?" Stoney asked.

"Yep, still had the leaves on 'em."

"They be diggin and cuttin' down live trees," Stoney said. "That just ain't natural fer 'em. Not at all."

"My thought exactly. I could tell they was up to somethin'. They was laying all them cut quakies in a line, throwin' the trimmed limbs on top of the trunks, then pitchin' dirt and sod on top of the whole mess."

"That's just what they was doin'," Stoney agreed. "They was hidin' that creek. That's the only thing that can explain it."

"That's what I figured out. Stewart told me once that it weren't much of a crick anyhow. You could step across it easy, and it kinda disappeared after it started down the hill from the valley. I'd bet we ain't sittin' more than a mile from Stewart's gold right now," Pa said.

We fell silent for a few minutes, listenin' to the fire pop and dreamin' of treasure.

"I never had much care about havin' a lot of money," Stoney said, "but it would be kinda nice to have a little put by 'case I live to be an old man."

While Pa'd been stretchin' his story out, it had gotten full dark. The fire popped again, and the sparks went straight up into the night sky. There was at least a million stars hangin' close over our heads. Pa still had the nugget in his hand where we could all see it.

"His name was José Martinez," Chris said all of a sudden.

We all looked at him, wonderin' where that outburst had came from.

"The Mexican boy that came with Señor Stewart. His name was José Martinez."

"Now how would you be knowin' that?" Stoney asked.

"He was my older cousin. My mother's first cousin was José's father. He was a very mean man. The soldiers killed him after he'd stolen a case of whiskey from the fort. He was a disgrace to the family." We sat there for several minutes digestin' what Chris had said. "I too have heard this story of Señor Stewart, but from the Mexican side," he added.

Pa looked at Chris kinda sharp. Probably wonderin' if he was gonna argue the fine points of the story Pa had told. Pa'd been knowed to embellish the truth when it come to some of his stories.

"It is just as Señor Tirley has said," Chris said, and Pa relaxed. "José tried to find the little stream two or three times, but he never could. He died trying to find it."

"The Utes get him?" Stoney asked.

"No, the Anglos at Del Norte."

We was all quiet. Sometimes, like now, I felt a little bad about even bein' a white man.

"They said he had stolen the horse he was riding. It was my father's horse which José had borrowed. They said that no Mex could be riding a horse of that quality unless he had stolen it. They hung him. My father and I rode to Del Norte with thirty vaqueros from our ranch. We brought Jose home to lie beside his father."

"You had thirty hands and you didn't wipe out that nest of snakes at Del Norte?" Pa asked.

"I was just a boy, and my father said that if we killed them, no matter what the cause, the army would attack us."

"Purty good chance your pa was right," Stoney agreed.

"My father gave me this. It had been José's."

Chris fished a nugget out of his pocket that could've been a twin to the one Pa had in his hand.

"Well I'll be a . . ." Pa started to say, and then stopped obviously speechless, which was the first time I'd ever seen that happen.

Bucklin stood up, stretched, and then walked over to where the firelight met with the black of the night. He looked into the darkness for a moment and then come back over to me. I rubbed him behind the ears and started thinkin' about crawlin' into the blankets. Suddenly, I felt the big dog tense. He was staring into the night and started growlin' deep in his gut. "Pa," I said, turning to look across the fire.

"Let's get out the light," Pa said, but Chris and Stoney had already faded into the darkness. I reckoned they'd gone to the horses. We was friends, of a sort, with the Utes, but that didn't mean that they all liked us, nor that they wouldn't try and steal one or more of our horses.

I grabbed my Henry and slid behind a big spruce tree at the edge of the light cast by the fire.

We stayed hid for maybe a quarter of an hour without movin'. My eyes had adjusted to the dark, so I started workin' my way around the little clearing that lay in front of the cave where we'd sheltered. Buck was still alert and lookin' back down the trail. If somebody followed us up from below, they'd likely try to come at us on foot and probably along the trail since it was clear of trees. I heard a soft footfall and felt my hair start to come up a little. I didn't much believe in haunts and such, but a man never knew for sure. I heard another step, and then the sound of labored breathin'. It surely didn't sound like a human-made sound, and I remembered the stories Pa had used to tell us boys about the banshee. I eased the hammer back on the Henry and took a silent step forward. I didn't know if the banshee could be stopped by a bullet, but if he come at me I was surely gonna find out.

Suddenly, there was a groan that started down low on the scale and worked its way up. It didn't end in a scream like I thought it would, but was cut off short. Buck was crowded up close against my leg and he was silent. I'd learned that he either went quiet right before he attacked or give out that almighty roar of his. He was ready to fight. Me, I was mighty tempted to turn tail and run back to where the rest of the boys was.

There was another groan, softer than the first, and then the sound of something hittin' the ground hard.

"Don't sound human to me." Pa's voice came from beside

me, and I near wet myself, he scared me so bad. He had a habit of turnin' Injun when we was out in the bush, and I surely hadn't heard him move up beside me. Buck probably had, but since he knew Pa he'd paid no mind.

"Let's ease down there and see what we got," he said in a whisper. The moon was hangin' low in the sky and just startin' to throw some light. Pa stepped out with me close behind. We traveled a hundred yards when we spotted a horse standin' in the trail. There was a body layin' beside the horse on the ground.

"Cover me," Pa said. He moved quickly, and I stepped to one side so I could see everything. Pa stopped close by the horse and spoke to it in a soft voice. I could see the glint of his tomahawk in his hand. He liked the 'hawk instead of a gun when it came to up close work. He bent over the still form on the ground and rolled him over.

"Matt," he said. His voice was urgent. I ran down to him ready for anything.

"It's a white man and he's got at least one bullet in him," Pa said as I came up. Buck went behind the horse and continued to stare off down the trail. "We got to get him to the fire."

I helped Pa boost the man onto his saddle face down, and we led the horse up the hill toward our camp. Chris, Stoney, and Rosie came out of the dark as we gained the fire.

"I don't recognize him, but he's been shot," Pa explained.

Chris built up the fire as we stretched the man out on Pa's bedroll. He was a smallish man, probably in his late thirties, and had the look of prosperity about him. His clothes, horse, and saddle were of a better grade than most cowboys could afford.

"Jason Wheeler," Rosie said. "He's a cattle buyer that sells mostly to the army. He spent some time down at my tradin' post the past couple of years. He's a good man, and honest." Pa stripped off Wheeler's jacket and then his shirt. He had a bullet high in his chest on the right side and as we rolled him over we found another one in his back on his left side. It was more of a flesh wound, but the bullet had dug out a couple of pounds of skin and muscle. Wheeler was white as a new-washed sheet, and looked like he was nearly bled out. His breathin' was hoarse, labored, and loud. He was a mighty sick man, and he didn't look to me like he was gonna get much better 'less he got to a doctor. Buck come up to me and whined. Something almighty bad had happened down in the valley and the big dog seemed to know it.

Chapter Twelve

"We're going back to Boston for our honeymoon," Edna said. "I want to finish selling my properties there, and John has several business deals to close. He sold the last building lot on Main Street yesterday and sold the rest of the Silver Plume town plat to Feenan this morning, so there's nothing much left for us to do here. I expect that we'll be gone two or three months." They were standing on the main street of Silver Plume after greeting what seemed like hundreds of people that had turned out to their open-air wedding reception. Since they were two of the most prominent citizens of the community, everyone both in town and in the hills had turned out to wish them well and eat the free food.

"Two or three months seems like such a long time, Aunt Edna," Lee said. "I'll miss you both so much . . ."

"You can go with us," Edna said.

"No, I think I'll go down to the Storm King Ranch," Lee replied. "It's not that I wouldn't enjoy going east with you and Uncle John, but it is your honeymoon . . ."

"We've been married almost two hours, Lee. We're old married folks now." Edna replied with a laugh.

"I know, but still I'd like to see the ranch again and talk with the boys. Surely they've heard something from Matt."

"Well, it's your decision. What are you going to do with your restaurant?"

"It's really nothing more than wagon covers over a wooden frame," Lee laughed. "That's why I called it The Eatin' House. To call it a restaurant seemed a stretch."

"No matter what you call it you've built a clientele, and the benches are always full," Edna replied.

"I have made a good bit of money in the past few months, but it's been a ton of work. I'm ready for something different." Lee looked down the street toward her business. There was a line of men in rough mining clothes stretching nearly a block waiting to get in. The main street of Silver Plume now boasted newly painted signs on several raw pine, false-fronted buildings. The canvas-covered temporary structures were being replaced quickly as the new buildings went up. The population was said to be nearing a thousand men and nearly a hundred women. The noise of building, mining, and living began before first light and continued through the night.

"I had an offer from a man with a restaurant in Denver. He wants to expand into the mining camps, and his offer is more than fair," Lee said, still looking down the street.

"This is probably a good time to sell. You don't have much invested, and you never know how long the boom will last," Edna observed. "It's a particularly good time if you want to do something else."

"You know I do, Aunt Edna," Lee said turning to look at the older woman. "I went to Boston to learn to be a lady . . ."

"I understand, Lee," Edna interrupted. "You need to find him, and I don't blame you. John expected to hear from Lyle before now, but there's been no word."

"I need to go to the ranch," Lee repeated. "The people there are as much my family as you and Uncle John, and they may have heard something."

"We leave in the morning for Boston. You're certainly capable of taking care of yourself, but I will miss you," Edna said.

"When you and Uncle John get back to Colorado, why don't you come out to the ranch. It's a beautiful place, and I want you to meet that branch of the O'Malley family."

"You can count on it," Edna replied. "Now, If you'll help me pack . . ."

"I'd be happy to, Aunt Edna, and then I'm going to find the man from Denver and sell out. By tomorrow I'll be on my way home."

"Oh, that brings something to mind. I wonder if you would mind if Clayton goes with you? He won't go to Boston with John and me, and you might be able to use his help," Edna said.

"Of course he's welcome, and I think Thomas might be going as well. He wants to meet the cousins."

"It's settled then," Edna said. "Sounds like we'll all be leaving our little town." She looked down the street and back at Lee. "Maybe it's for the best. The boom towns grow a little stale after a year or so. They're not quite a city and manage to hold but little of the romance of their beginnings. I know. I've seen a number of them come and go." She watched as a horse and wagon hurried down the street with a load of fresh-sawn lumber. "The towns are no better or no worse than the people that build them. Some of them live for a while, then die. Perhaps this one will have a long life."

"Hurry back," Lee hollered after the carriage, which seemed strangely out of place on the dirt main street of Silver Plume. Edna raised a hand, waving at her niece as she and John began their journey to Boston.

"I'm really going to miss them," Lee said, wiping a tear from her cheek. She couldn't remember the last time she'd cried.

"They'll be back before you know it," Tom said.

"I know," she said, watching the carriage move out of sight, "but Boston is so far away, and so much can happen."

"They'll be fine," Tom assured her. "When do you want to head for the San Luis Valley?" he asked, changing the subject.

"As soon as we can get ready," she replied. "I've sold The Eatin' House, and there's nothing here for me in Silver Plume."

"I agree," Tom said. "We've disposed of our properties, and I'm ready to see new country. I'm also anxious to meet my cousins."

"Tomorrow morning?" Lee asked.

"Agreed," Tom said with a smile. "I'll tell Clayton."

"I'll meet you in front of the restaurant at daylight," Lee said.

"First thing," he agreed.

Lee turned toward her room a block up the street with sound of hammers keeping pace with her as she walked. The energy of the little community was nearly tangible, and she was proud to have been a part of it.

She began to hurry as twilight started to fall along the mountain ridges. As she moved along Lee failed to notice someone keeping her pace and staying to the shadows behind her. As she opened the door to her little tarpaper-covered cabin, she felt the cold muzzle of a pistol shoved against the back of her neck, and she gasped.

"Go on in, quickly," a woman's voice harshly said. Lee stepped in with the woman following on her heels. The door closed behind them. A hand in her back pushed Lee toward the back wall, and she turned to face the woman who had attacked her. It was the older woman that she had seen a number of times during the past few months.

"I've waited a long time for this," the woman said. "I've followed you from Boston, to Denver, and then to this hole. I finally have you."

"Who are you?" Lee asked.

"Marilyn Beck, and I'm going to kill you just the same way you killed my sons."

"Falcon . . ." Lee exclaimed.

"Yes, Falcon and Macon both. I know you had a hand in killing them."

Lee took a step back and looked at the rock-steady pistol in the older woman's hand. She realized she was as close to death as she'd ever been. Her hand was in her pocket and she carefully grasped the breaktop pistol she always had hidden on her person.

"I . . ." Lee began. She was instantly cut off by Marilyn Beck.

"Shut up," Beck said, through clenched teeth. "You keep your mouth shut until I tell you to speak." There was a small scraping noise outside. The enraged woman took a glance out the small window, but the gun didn't waver.

Marilyn Beck uttered an unladylike oath and backed quickly toward the back door. "I'll get you," she hissed. "You're not going to know when or where, but I'll be back, and you'll die." She reached behind her with her free hand, opened the door, and disappeared.

Lee looked at the still open door, with the darkness gathering outside and heard footsteps on the wooden walk at her front door. A knock came and Tom O'Malley's voice.

"Lee, I forgot to ask you about the horses," he said through the door.

Lee's hands and knees were shaking as reaction set in, and she loosened her grip on the small pistol.

"Come in, Tom," she said. "You may have just saved my life."

"I don't recall ever seeing you wear a gun openly," Lee said as Tom mounted his horse. She and Clayton were seated in a large spring wagon that contained nearly everything they owned. Clayton had the lines in his hands and was holding the team steady.

"We haven't been where it seemed prudent for a merchant to wear a short gun in plain view. From what you've said we might be heading places where an O'Malley might need a gun close at hand," Tom replied.

"Well, the O'Malley name does certainly cause a reaction

in the San Luis Valley. Some of it's good and some not so good," Lee smiled. "That and in light of what happened last night with Marilyn Beck, it's probably prudent to have guns close at hand. We don't know who she might have recruited to help her."

Tom nodded and looked into the back of the wagon. "We have everything we're going to need, Clayton?"

"Far as I can tell," Clayton replied.

"Let's get on the road then," Tom said as he took the slack out of his reins.

"O'Malley?"

The deep voice came from behind them, and they turned to look at the speaker. He was a tall, thin man with a square jaw riding a beautiful gray horse. There was a badge on his chest.

"I'm Tom O'Malley."

"My name's Joe Bush, United States Marshal."

"What can I do for you, Marshal?"

"I was told you was headin' toward the San Juans," the tall marshal said.

"We are. The O'Malley ranch up near Saguache," Tom replied.

"Mind if I ride along?" Bush asked. "The Utes are working themselves up a bit, and it'd be safer for all of us."

Tom looked at the marshal and smiled. "Mr. Bush, why do I have this feeling you're not telling me everything?"

" 'Cause I'm not." Joe Bush smiled back. "I'm huntin' a man I got a warrant for, and I hear there's an O'Malley that's come crossways of him up to Del Norte."

"That'd be Matthew and Bull Burdett," Lee said.

"You're hunting Bull Burdett?" Tom asked.

"That's what the warrant says," Bush said. "Killed an un-armed potato farmer east of Denver. Judge wants to have a conversation with him. A serious conversation that'll probably include a rope."

"You'll have to kill him to take him," Clayton said.

"Might be," Bush replied. "Wouldn't be the first."

"We were just getting ready to head out, and you're welcome to ride along, Marshal," Lee said. "What makes you think the O'Malleys are going to know where Burdett is?"

"Burdett swore an oath that he's gonna kill Matt O'Malley. Him and his gang are trackin' him now. I figure I find Matt, I find Burdett. I also heard over at Fort Collins that Burdett had recruited Dee Skinner from down in Texas. I'm thinkin' that Matt O'Malley may be needin' some help."

"That's not real encouraging," Tom said.

"There's another little chore the judge wants me to do. He wants me to swear Matt in and pin this on him." The tall man held a U.S. Marshal's badge in his hand. "We marshals always take up for each other if it gets real serious. I know I'd want Matt to help me if the situation was reversed."

The fire popped as Clayton threw on a couple of more pieces of cedar. The summer moon hung directly over their heads in the sky, and not far away a coyote yipped and howled.

"That was mighty fine eatin', Miss Lee," Joe Bush said. "I haven't had but maybe four or five meals over the last year that I didn't stir over a fire myself and didn't have beans as the main course."

Lee laughed, as did Tom and Clayton. The past two days they'd come to appreciate the company of the tall lawman. He pulled his own weight and had a quiet sense of humor.

" 'Lo, the fire," a voice hollered from the darkness. Clayt moved out of the light of the fire and Marshal Bush pulled his shotgun over close to his hand.

"Come on in if you're friendly," Tom hollered back.

A man rode his horse up to the picket and stepped down from the saddle with a grunt. He wrapped the reins around the picket rope next to the rest of the horses and walked into the light.

"Lyle Hansen!" Lee exclaimed. "We thought you'd been eaten by a grizzly."

"Ah, you folks are a sight for sore eyes," Lyle said. "I feel like I been pulled through a knothole in a board fence by a twenty-mule team hookup. I've rode near a million miles and none of it on flat ground the past month. I'd surely rather be back in Denver runnin' the Mountain Palace."

"Did you find him?" Lee asked.

"I found where he's been," Lyle replied. "I was always 'bout three steps behind them. They spent the winter at a little town over west called Animas City, where they made some mighty fine friends and a couple of enemies. Last the town-folks seen 'em they were comin' back east. I met up with some Utes around Pahgosa, and they pointed me up toward the high country. All I found up there was a coffee pot with a bullet hole in it. I ain't been able to find hide nor hair of any of 'em for ten days."

"You hear anything of Bull Burdett or Dee Skinner?" Joe Bush asked quietly.

"This is U.S. Marshal Joe Bush, Lyle. He's hunting Burdett." Tom made the introduction.

"Heard a bunch about him, but didn't come across him or any of his gang. Bull himself killed the man what run the ferry over on the Colorado because the man wanted the two bits from Bull that he charged everybody else."

"Sounds like he's still doin' what he does best," the marshal observed.

"Grab your bedroll and settle in," Tom suggested. "We even left some supper we'd share with you."

"Sounds good to me. I'm plumb weary," Lyle agreed.

He tended his horse, then came back to the fire with his bedroll. He looked down at Lee, and rubbed the three days of beard on his dusty face.

"I swung a purty wide loop, Lee. It's like they fell right off the face of the earth."

Lee handed him a plate of biscuits and meat and poured him a steaming cup of coffee.

"There is one good thing," he said around a mouthful of

biscuit. "I didn't come across any fresh graves." He chewed thoughtfully for a few minutes and then spoke again. "I'd say they're still out there somewhere, and I got a feelin' that they might have headed north. It's purty wild country that direction with almost no people 'cept Injuns. Be easy to miss four men, particular when two of 'em spent most of their lives in the hills."

"I guess no news is good news," Lee said quietly.

"There's something else," Lyle said looking at the lawman. "Burdett is voicin' around that Matthew is a dead man next time they cross paths. He's surely huntin' Matthew, and sooner or later they gonna meet up."

"Matt can take care of himself," Lee said.

"He can handle one or maybe even three or four, but Burdett been attractin' every no good skunk in three states and five territories, plus he's got that scum Skinner ridin' with 'em. Skinner will cozy down behind a rock or a tree and wait 'til Matt rides by. He's a sure-thing killer and takes no more chances than he has to. Burdett's got maybe thirty men with him now, and I doubt if Matt even has any idea he's bein' hunted."

Lee felt a chill come over her even though the night was warm. "We have to find him, Lyle."

"I'm of the same mind," Lyle agreed. "My plan was to get to Denver, report what I'd been doin', resupply, and hit the road again."

"Edna and Uncle John got married and are taking a honeymoon trip to Boston as we speak," Lee said. "We're heading for the Storm King to see if the brothers have heard anything of Matthew."

"John told me he was thinkin' of askin' Edna to marry, but I didn't think they'd be this quick about it," Lyle replied.

"Dad said he didn't see any sense in waiting," Tom offered. "He said neither one of them was getting any younger, and my brothers and I agreed. My mother's been gone for nearly twenty years. It'll be good for Dad to have a woman around to steady him."

"From what I saw of Edna, she'll surely steady him up some," Lyle agreed. "She's all woman with a good head on her shoulders." He fell silent a moment and then looked around the fire at them. "I reckon if you don't mind I'll just trip along with you all. Sounds to me like there's a fight shapin' up, and I'd really hate to miss out on it."

"It's my thought that when my cousins hear there's a gang of men hunting Matthew, they'll certainly want a piece of the action," Tom said. "We O'Malleys are notorious for our feuds, and it's said that if you take one of us on, you've got the entire clan. The tradition of family unity runs all the way back to Grania and her boys, or so the story goes."

"Ol' Bull may of taken on a bigger bite of meat than he can chew," Lyle remarked. "It's not only family that sticks up with the O'Malleys. They make friends and stand by them. I can tell you a dozen men that'd join us right now if they was knowin' an O'Malley was facin' up to trouble."

"I expect we could raise a hundred men if we needed them," Tom agreed. He paused a moment, looking seriously at Lyle. "I hope we don't need them."

"Well, if Burdett is huntin' a fight and Matthew, he'll find both sooner or later," Lyle said.

"I'm scared for him," Lee said. "If he knew he was being hunted it's one thing, but what if Burdett or especially Dee Skinner takes him from ambush?"

"Ain't much chance of that happenin' from what I know of Matt and the people he's travelin' with," Lyle said. "They're almighty savvy, and they leave no more trail than a chipmunk."

"There's still a chance it could happen," Lee said, looking into the fire. Nobody argued with her.

Chapter Thirteen

"We got to stop the bleedin' or he's done for," Pa said.
Chris ran to his saddle and threw open the flap on one of his saddlebags. "Here is a shirt my mother made me." He threw it across to Pa, who caught it and immediately began to tear it into strips. It was white and looked soft. Probably cotton. I took a step away from the fire and turned to look toward the trail.

"Good idea, Matt," Pa said. "Somebody might be followin' him."

I ghosted my way back down to the aspen grove and took up a spot where I could see back toward the river valley below us. Buck stood beside me at attention. It was cold and still. I could see my breath makin' a fog in front of my face. I'd not taken the time to throw on my jacket and waitin' for any length of time was gonna get right chilly. Suddenly, I heard a man cough way down below. It was a quiet cough, but sound carried a long ways on the mountain. Buck started to growl, and I put a hand on his neck. I hustled up to the fire, belted on my short gun, slung on my coat, and looked over at Pa. "We're gonna have company," I said.

"How long?"

"Hour, maybe less."

"We got him bound up, and he come around fer a minute, so we managed to get some water down him." He looked down at Wheeler. "We got to get him off this hill. He's lung shot, and there ain't much more we can do fer him here."

"Animas City?" Stoney said.

" 'Bout our only choice," Pa agreed. "The Injun agent was a doctor of sorts back in the states." He turned to me. "Give us some space and time, Matthew. Make 'em cautious enough that they don't set out trailin' us 'til daylight."

I nodded by way of reply. I knew what needed doin'.

"Let's get movin' " Pa said to the rest of the men.

"I wish to stay with Matthew," Chris said. There was no argument in his voice. He simply stated a fact.

"So do I, Chris, but it'll take all of us to get Wheeler off this mountain." Pa looked quietly across the fire at me. "Matthew will do just fine."

Chris picked up his saddle and moved over to his paint horse. Stoney was already packin'. Pa lingered a minute.

"You go straight across this meadow west, and it narrows down toward the rim. There's a trail that goes down to the river. Cross the river and head west on the south side. You ought to catch us by daylight. Soon as you catch up, we'll start makin' tracks that even a 'Pache couldn't find."

"Take Buck with you," I said. "I got to move fast after I open the ball, and I'm 'fraid I'll lose him in the mix."

Pa nodded. "It's a half mile 'cross the meadow. I'll tie your horse just inside where the dark timber starts. Stay away from the quakies. You'll show up against the white trunks as bright as the moon is."

I reckoned that was a fine piece of advice, and somethin' I might not a thought of. "I'll see ya come daylight," I said.

"Make sure ya do," Pa replied. He turned, grabbed his saddle, and moved toward the horses.

"You stay with Pa, Buck," I said to the big dog. He looked in the direction I pointed and trotted over to the horses. I checked the loads in the Henry and moved into the darkness.

I heard the rest of the wood being thrown onto the fire, but didn't look. I had to get my eyes adjusted. They'd build the fire up to make it look like we was still in camp.

I moved a couple hundred yards away from camp and stopped. I waited 'til my breath was comin' even and my heartbeat had slowed. I closed my eyes and tried to make myself a part of the night. Mankind ain't a night animal. We build houses to keep out the dark when we're home, or if in the wilds we at least build fires. The Injuns refuse to fight at night, least most of 'em. They figure if they get kilt their spirit will wander forever in the darkness. It's always been that way. I bet Adam even hated the night, and maybe lived in a tree 'til he got his house built. I could work in the dark, particular with a moon, but it was still a risky thing.

I got back to where we'd found Wheeler, then worked my way down the trail slow 'til I found what I was lookin' for. I'd remembered a small clearing, maybe sixty yards wide, that broke out of the spruce trees. The trail from the bottom cut right through the middle of it, and the men below would be exposed for several minutes. I picked me a comfortable spot under the hangin' branches of a giant fir tree on my side of the clearin'. There was no way they'd ever pick my form out in the shadow of the tree. I hunkered down and waited, my breath makin' tiny clouds in front of my face. If it weren't for the fact I was facin' up to trouble I'd a been taken by the beauty stretched out in front of me. I started thinkin' about Lee. It always happened on starry, moonlit nights, and I wondered if I'd ever see her again.

Maybe a half hour passed when the first one came out. He come on slow, lookin' to the ground, and then lookin' across the clearin' He was maybe seventy-five yards from me and downhill. A tricky shot at best. He got about a ten-yard lead, then two more gents come out of the timber ridin' side by side. Purty soon there was a whole passel of folks makin' their way up the trail. The lead guy pulled up about halfway across the clearin'. The rest of the men pulled up even with him and stopped.

"He leastways got this far," I heard the first man say. He was ridin' what looked to be a buckskin horse, though it was hard to tell in the moonlight. "I found his track back at that little seep." I could hear him like he was standin' next to me.

"Let's get him found 'fore he dies," a man answered. "He knows where the money is. Can't tell us if he's dead."

The man turned the buckskin around facin' me and started him walkin' up the trail. I placed the front sight squarely on the lead man's chest and changed my mind. I didn't like shootin' a man from hidin', and I had no idea who these people were. They might be the law for all I knew, although I doubted it. Anyhow, I had a thought of how I could make even more confusion if I could make the shot. I knew right where the Henry was lined up, and I aimed at the haunch of the buckskin horse. If I could just burn him with a bullet it ought to stir things up a mite. I let out my breath and took up the slack in the trigger. When the Henry spoke, it took me by surprise, just like it did the man ridin' the buckskin horse when it started pitchin' like a half-broke mustang. As soon as the buckskin started kickin', he ran into the horse behind him, and he in turn started jumpin'. I didn't stick around to see the rest of it. There was a couple shots directed up the trail that come nowhere near me.

I ran, stayin' to the shadows of the tall pines, back toward the meadow on the west. I ran 'til my breath was comin' in jerks, and I had a stitch in my side, then I slowed to a quick walk. I saw the glow of our fire and figured next they'd come lookin' that direction. They'd come on a mite slower now, not knowin' exactly what they was up against. I stayed well below the fire and made my way to the little meadow on the west side. I walked up the hill 'til I was about the same elevation as our camp and turned to look. I was maybe a couple a hundred feet away. The fire had burnt down, but the red coals was still plainly visible. I found me a spruce next to a rock and settled in to wait again. I could still hear quite a ruckus back down the trail where the gang of men was. It was gonna be a long night for all of us.

It took 'em another hour to get up to the fire. By then most of the coals were gone and there was only a thin wisp of smoke to mark our camp.

"Whoever it was is gone now, and it's likely they took Wheeler with 'em," a man said.

"Let's bed down here 'til daylight, and then take after 'em. We get into a shootin' war in the dark and we'll just as likely shoot each other." I recognized the voice and knew that the gang of men riding up to the fire pit weren't lawmen. The man talkin' was Bull Burdett. I kinda regretted that I hadn't been shootin' for the men while I was back down the trail in the moonlight. This whole group meant trouble, and they was surely gonna be on our trail come first light. I needed a way to slow 'em down.

One of the men threw an armload of wood on the fire, and after a few minutes it burst into flame lightin' up nearly the whole meadow. Another man brought out a big blue coffeepot and sat it on the rocks at the edge of the fire. In less than five minutes I could smell the boiling coffee and see members of the gang spreadin' out blankets and chewin' on jerked meat. They was just makin' themselves right to home in our campin' spot. The feller who had put the coffeepot down walked up to it, reached down to grab the handle, and jerked back swearin' as it burned him. It give me an idea. I figured I needed to let 'em know that chasin' us wasn't gonna be as easy as they thought, and I needed somethin' to slow 'em down. Most of the pack had pulled up and either sat or squatted down close to the fire. I could see my buddy Bull sittin' just about across the fire from the coffeepot. If I could just do it right . . .

I eased my Henry to my shoulder and took a fine aim right at the base of the big pot. I sucked a deep breath, let a little of it out, held it, and begin to squeeze the trigger. The rifle barked, and the coffeepot blew across the fire and into Bull Burdett's lap almost in the same instant. I reckoned the pot held somethin' over a gallon of boilin' coffee, and most of it ended up on Burdett. He was screamin' like a girl that seen a spider, and I was makin' tracks for where I figured Sin was tied. They'd be careful about gettin' comfortable around the fire the rest of the night.

I was lopin' along kinda lookin' over my shoulder from time to time, when all of a sudden my left foot stomped through somethin' soft, and I fell full on my face. I sat up and checked myself over and found that I'd turned my ankle. I crawled over to the hole I'd made, looked in, and realized I could hear water runnin'. I reached down through the rotted tree and felt the water movin' past my hand. If I wasn't mistaken, I'd just located the little creek that Pa had watched the Utes hide.

"I got him," I heard a man yell close at hand. The moon was right overhead, and I could see him plain as daylight. He was pointin' a rifle at my brisket, and it surely looked like he planned on shootin'. I palmed my pistol and shot him before he'd even realized I moved. Suddenly, there was five or six of them right there in front of me and close. I shot until my pistol was empty, and then I began to scatter bullets across the meadow with the Henry. By the time I'd finished there weren't a man in sight. I'd either shot 'em all, or they'd run. I picked myself up, loaded my guns, and started hobblin' to where I figured Sin was waitin' for me.

He was tied right where Pa said he'd be, and he was ready to go. I stuck the Henry in the boot, crawled up into the saddle and pointed down the trail toward the valley

"He ain't as bad as he looks," the agent said. His name was Curly Thomas, and he'd been an agent for ten years. He'd been assigned to the Utes the previous fall and had picked Animas Valley for the temporary location of the agency. He'd built a small adobe cabin a mile south of town. The townsfolk weren't real happy with the Utes comin' around all the time, and Curly agreed. He'd located a spot about twenty miles east on the Pine River for the permanent agency, but hadn't made the move yet.

"My grandpap soldiered with a guy named Solomon Van Resselaer that took one through the lungs at the Battle of Fallen Timbers," Curly continued. "He not only lived to tell about it, but twenty years later, durin' the war of 1812, he was shot five times in one volley. He lived through that as well and died when he was seventy-eight years old. It always surprises me how much abuse the human animal can take and live through it."

Curly lifted the bandages off the wounds and bent his head, listening. "He suckin' a little extra air, but it ain't whistlin', so it might've already started to close. We'll keep it bandaged tight and hope for the best."

"Can we leave him here with you?" Pa asked the agent.

"Yep. I got nothing better to do besides wonder where the Utes is camped for the summer. Besides, I know Wheeler and his family. Known them for quite a while. They're good folks. He's sold me beef here and at two other agencies I've headed up over the past ten years. He's always been honest." He stopped a minute and looked at the wounded man. "You know what happened?"

"Near as we can tell he was shot for the money he was supposed to be carryin'," I said. "I overheard a piece of a conversation."

"That might be," Curly responded. "He packed a good bit of money time to time to buy stock. You know who shot him?"

"Got a purty good idea," I replied. "From what I seen, I'd say it was Bull Burdett."

Curly Thomas got pasty white around the gills and his mouth dropped open.

"Why don't you boys stick around a while," he suggested. "I can handle a gun, but I ain't up to someone like Burdett.

Might be that he'll track Wheeler right to here, and I'd be obliged to try and protect him."

"We'll be here a day or two just in case," I replied for all of us. "More than one of us has a score to settle with Burdett."

"Maybe we ought to fort up a little," Stoney suggested. "They might try and tree us."

"This buildin' shapes up to be the best place to fight from if it comes to that," Pa said. "Adobe don't burn, it'll stop a bullet, and the roof is sod."

"Got shutters with shootin' holes cut in 'em just in case the Utes decided to sport with the agent some time," Curly offered.

"We been in worse spots," Pa said, lookin' at Stoney.

"That we have," Stoney agreed, with a chuckle.

"I'll go out and keep a watch," I said, pickin' up my Henry.

I walked over to the door, pulled it open, stepped out, and walked right into trouble. Sittin' his horse and grinnin' down at me was the half-lip man that I'd shaved a few months earlier, and he had five of his cronies with him. They all had their guns in their hands with the hammers back. Right that minute, for some reason, I remembered I hadn't told Pa about findin' Captain Stewart's little creek up above Pahgosa.

Chapter Fourteen

"**M**y goodness, Lee, you've turned into a perfect lady," Owen O'Malley said with a smile.

"Thank you," she said, her face turning red.

"You are absolutely beautiful," Patty, Owen's wife, agreed. "Matthew will be surprised."

"So you haven't heard from them?" Lee asked, changing the subject.

"They left here soon as the first hay was put up last year," Owen O'Malley said. "We haven't heard from them, but we have heard about them."

"Soliders came through here just before the snow hit in the high country and told us about the fight Matt had in Del Norte. They was talkin' about it clear over to Denver," Wedge added. "I'd a surely loved to have seen it."

"We heard they wintered in a little town on the Animas River," Mike O'Malley said, "and a rider came through a month ago and said he'd seen them on the trail heading for Pahgosa."

"They didn't say when they would be coming back?" Lee asked.

"Nope. Tirley just said they was goin' trekkin'," Wedge offered. "We did kinda think they might come back this fall."

"From what you say, Matt and the boys may have what amounts to a troop of well armed men hunting them, and they don't even know it," Dan O'Malley said, his former military experience showing. "At the very least we have to get word to them."

The big front room of the main cabin was full of people. All the brothers O'Malley except Matt were gathered, as were a half-dozen close friends of the family. Lee, Lyle, Clayton, Tom, and Marshal Joe Bush rounded out the group.

"I 'spect that would fall to me," Bush said. "I got orders to find Matt anyhow."

"Two of us, I think," Dan agreed. "We still need to get the work done on the ranch, so all of us can't go."

"I got orders to find him as well," Lyle Hansen said from the back of the room.

"Three of us then, but that's all for now," Dan said. "We'll send word back so you all will know what's going on. If we need help, you'll be the first to know it."

Lyle had moved up to stand beside the Marshal, and Dan turned to them. "We'll each take a pack animal with enough supplies to last for a few weeks. I doubt if it'll take that long, but we need to be prepared."

"When do you want to leave, Captain?" Joe Bush said, using Dan's former military rank. Bush himself had been a sergeant major in the Grand Army of the Republic, and he knew well Captain Dan O'Malley's reputation earned during the war.

"I reckon first light," Dan replied. "We still have some daylight remaining today so we can get ready." He turned toward Lee and smiled at her. "Don't worry, we'll find him."

Lee surely hoped so. She had a feeling time was running out.

"I talked to a couple of the settlers at Animas City when I took the first trip. They told me the boys had headed back this direction huntin' for gold Tirley knew about in the mountains above the springs," Lyle said. "They've surely been here, and not all that long ago, but they headed back west, or so the Utes think. One of the braves said there was some shootin' up on the mountain late one night, and they think it was Matt and the fellas." He stopped for a moment and looked over at the Indian camp. "You know how they are. They don't like mixin' in the white man's business. They know more, but they ain't gonna tell us."

The three men were standing beside the stinking, steaming water of Pahgosa Springs, and Lyle had just spoken to a small encampment of Southern Utes on the far side of the river. "When I was out here before," Lyle continued, "I rode up to the meadow the Injuns told me about, and the only signs I could find was a spot where a campfire had burned, and a big coffeepot with a bullet hole in it laying alongside the pit. There'd been several riders up there since the snow went out according to the tracks, but I couldn't tell much about where they'd gone." He stopped, dug around in his vest pocket for a moment, and finally brought out an empty brass cartridge. "I did find a spot where there was a bunch of empty shell casings from a Henry rifle piled up, and it seemed to me Matt carried a Henry. I didn't say anything about that back at the ranch 'cause I didn't want to worry Lee."

"Sounds like they may have run into some trouble," Joe said quietly.

"So we know they came back this direction from Animas City," Dan said, "and we know they left from here and took the trail leading to the keyhole pass. The last we can learn of them is the Utes think there was a fight up on the mountain, and no one's seen or heard about Matt, Tirley, or any of the rest since." Dan looked up to the mountains towering over them, and then back to the men he rode with. "I don't like the way it shapes up."

"I 'spect we should go up toward the pass and see if three sets of eyes can pick up sign of where they might have gone," Joe suggested.

"I didn't spend much time up high," Lyle agreed. "I'm a purty fair hand when it comes to a fight, but there's folks around that can read a trail sign a lot better than me."

"We'll camp here tonight and head out in the morning. Maybe we can figure out how they got down off the mountain without coming back past the Utes."

"I found a spot under the trees up the slope for a camp," Bush said. "I 'spect we'd best stay away from the Utes. They seem peaceful, but it don't take much to get 'em stirred up."

"Probably a good plan," Dan agreed.

They rode up the slope and dismounted in a small clearing that was surrounded by ponderosa pines. They soon had a fire going and the smell of frying bacon permeated the air. Lyle had offered to cook, and he didn't get an argument from the other two.

"Either of you know anything about this Bull Burdett who seems to be hunting Matt?" Dan asked.

Joe was sitting on a convenient rock, cleaning his sawed-off shotgun. He looked up at Dan and then back down at the gun. "He come out from the East two years ago," Joe volunteered. "From what I've been able to piece together he was on one of the fighting fire companies in New York for a spell, and then he knifed a man for spilling his drink in some dive along the waterfront. Turned out the man he killed was the master of a ship who had come in to see if his crew was misbehaving. The captain was a well-liked man, and as soon as the crew found out he'd been killed they started hunting Burdett with a promise to hang him from the yardarm of their ship. Burdett took out, but not before he'd robbed a bank so he'd have some traveling money." Joe sighted down the barrels of the Greener, slid two shells back into the chambers, and snapped the action shut. "He landed in Chicago and tried to establish himself as a legitimate business man, but some woman problems put him on the road again. He figured the gold camps would be a good place to settle in, and that's how he ended up out here."

"You know a good bit about him," Dan said.

"I made a study on him," Joe replied. "I always try and find out as much as I can about a man before I hunt him. Men are creatures of habit. They can change their names, even change their looks, but they rarely change their habits. If I know their tendencies then, I know the man."

"Makes sense," Dan agreed.

"These taters are about done," Lyle said, "and the bacon is burnt about as much as it's gonna get."

They broke out their plates, and Lyle was just dishing up from the skillets when they heard horses approaching. Joe set his plate on a rock, picked up the shotgun, and stepped back behind the screen of trees. Lyle set his plate beside Joe's and went on the other side of the clearing behind a big tree. Dan stood calmly by the fire, changed his plate from his right hand to his left, and hitched his pistol into a more convenient position.

Courtesy dictated friendly folks stopped away from the fire and asked permission to come in. The three men approaching ignored good manners and rode right up to Dan in a small cloud of dust.

"We was plannin' on campin' here," a red-haired, greasy-faced individual said in a voice that was too loud.

"I expect there's room for all of us, but I'm not sure I care for your attitude or your manners," Dan replied quietly.

"What if I told you we don't care if you like our manners, and we're campin' here whether you like it or not." The man stopped a moment, looked over his shoulder at his buddies with a nasty smile on his face, and then turned back toward Dan. "I reckon you'll be the one movin', or maybe we'll just shoot you and chuck you out in the trees for the coyotes."

Dan set his plate down, carefully watching the red-headed man as he did so. "Mister, I'm bound to tell you there's two other men with me, and they aren't strangers to trouble. One of them has a Greener loaded with buckshot, and the other has a Winchester. I'd guess they have them pointed in your direction about now."

"Aw, don't be feedin' me that lip," the redhead said. "You're up here alone."

"I don't think he is, Wiley," one of the men behind him said. "There's three plates of food dished up, and there's six horses."

Wiley looked down at the food, and then quickly out to the trees surrounding the camp. He caught sight of Lyle's rifle barrel pointed directly at his chest from behind the tree. He swallowed and looked back at Dan.

"You'll hear from us again," he said. "This ain't over."

"Why not now?" Dan pushed. "No sense dragging it out for another time and place."

"Wiley, if you move on this, you're by yourself," the man behind him said. Then he pushed his horse back a few steps and looked toward the trees. "Whoever's out there, we're out of this," he said in a loud voice. Sweat was breaking out on Wiley's forehead, and his hand was close to his gun.

Marshal Bush stepped from the cover of the trees and pointed the shotgun at Wiley. "You Wiley Hudson?" he asked. Joe had found it prudent over the years not to wear his star on the outside of his vest, so Wiley had no idea he was a lawman.

"That's my name," the redhead replied belligerently.

Joe rolled his vest back so his star was visible and took a step forward. "Wiley Hudson, I have a warrant for your arrest for the murder of . . ."

Joe didn't get any further as Wiley's hand streaked down for his gun. The bandit really didn't have a chance. Marshal Bush was an expert with his shotgun, and as Wiley tried to draw his pistol, Joe cut loose the double barrels of his Greener shotgun. Wiley was blown from the saddle and landed on the ground, limp as a half sack of feed. Dan had his pistol out and pointed at the remaining two men.

"We ain't even friends of his," one of the men said quickly.

They had their hands on the pommels of their saddles where they could be seen.

"Where'd you pick him up then?" Dan asked.

"We was all in a saloon in Denver, and the word went around there was a big job out West. A gun job. It sounded easier than punchin' cows in Kansas, so we all hooked up." The man paused a moment, looked at his partner, then back to Dan. "Me and Foley here had already talked about cuttin' loose from Wiley. He was a hard man to get along with."

"Looks like the marshal cured that," Dan said, looking at the dead man.

Lyle came from behind the tree and walked over beside Dan. "You mind me askin' what kind of gun work you boys were figurin' on?" he asked.

"Bull Burdett has been spreadin' the word there's a war brewin' out here, and he's payin' fifty bucks a month for gun handlers. He also said there'd be a bonus at the end if everything went right."

"Well, my suggestion to you boys is you head east and don't come back out here for at least ten years. I 'spect if we see either of you ever again, we're just gonna have to shoot you," Lyle said.

"You let us go, mister, and I guarantee we'll never come west of the Kansas border again. I seen all of Colorado I can stand."

"Take this carcass with ya and get goin'," Lyle said, pointing at the dead man. "I'd make it quick if I was you. Our supper's gettin' cold and that surely gets my back up."

The two men climbed quickly down from their horses, slung the dead Wiley over his recently emptied saddle, and left like there was a fire under their tails. The three friends watched them go, and then turned their attention to their supper and coffee.

"I don't like the sound of Burdett gathering more men to him," Dan said. "It has to be somethin' to do with Matt."

"Where would Burdett get money to pay a bunch of gunnies? When he left Denver he didn't have two pennies to rub together."

"Looks like he found himself a backer," Joe said.

"Sounds to me like we'd better find those boys as quick as we can," Dan said. "They have no idea what's coming at them."

"I'm going," Lee said. "I can't bear to just sit here and wait."

"Where will you go?" Patty asked.

"I think to Animas City," Lee replied. "That seems to be the natural jumping-off spot for anything west."

"I've known you a long time," Patty said, "and I know there's no arguing with you once your mind is set, but I think you're walking into something very dangerous."

"Maybe, but I can take care of myself." Lee paused a moment and looked at her friends gathered in the front room of the main cabin. Dan, Joe, and Lyle had been gone a week, and the time had been moving slowly for all of them.

"Mike, if you can get along without me, I think I'll ride along with her," Tom O'Malley said to his cousin. "That is, if she'll have me."

"I'd appreciate the company," Lee said, and Mike nodded his head in agreement.

"I've got some good horses over in the corral," Mike said, "if you don't mind riding astride, Lee. You can't make any time on the roads west of here in a wagon. They're too rough."

"I'll ride," Lee said. "I brought some pants along." She stood and walked toward the back of the cabin where her room was located. "I'll go change right now, and we can leave within the hour," she said over her shoulder.

Tom stood and picked up his rifle from the corner of the room. "Guess we'll need to borrow a couple of saddles," he said to Mike. "I've got mine, but Clayton will need one. I know Edna asked him to keep an eye on Lee. He'll be going with us."

"We've got a small one Patty uses when she rides, and I have an old army saddle out in the barn that's still in good shape."

The two men went out the front door toward the barn. Patty watched them go, and then turned to her brother.

"Wedge, I just don't think this is a good idea," she said.

"Probably not, but she's bound to go, and you know there's no stoppin' her. I feel better about it since Tom and Clayton are goin', but still . . ."

"I wish we could all go," Patty finished for him. He nodded his head and watched the horses being saddled through the open front door.

Lee came into the room wearing pants and a tucked-in man's shirt. "I'm gonna start passing the word for the clan to gather," Wedge told her as she shoved clothes into her over-sized saddlebags, "and if we don't have good news from you inside of a few weeks we're headin' out."

Lee nodded agreement. "If something's going to happen it will surely be soon, and if you haven't heard from us . . ." she let the sentence drop.

An hour later Lee, Tom, and Clayton rode towards La Garrida Canyon and points west. When they were out of sight, Wedge looked around at the few people left at the Storm King Ranch, and then directly at Mike O'Malley. "I'm gonna go over to Saguache and send out some telegrams in case we need more help."

Mike nodded his head in agreement and watched the dust settle on the road west. He sighed and headed for the barn, this time with Wedge. It was shaping up to a fight, and it looked like the O'Malleys were badly outnumbered.

"Well, there's nothing new about that," Mike said to himself.

Chapter Fifteen

They were certain sure they had me. Their guns were in their fists, and they were all pointin' right at me.

"I been waitin' fer this for quite a spell," Half-Lip said with a nasty grin.

They expected beggin', or at least talkin', but I couldn't see any sense in it. They was set on a killin' whether we talked or not. I just shucked my old Army and let her rip, and as my first shot roared, I let my feet fall out from under me. They didn't expect it, and I heard the bullets hit the adobe over my head.

I shot Half-Lip first 'cause he was right in front of me. They was shootin' at me, but as soon as I started the ball rollin' the horses they was sittin' on jerked heads and kicked feet. I could hear bullets hittin' around me, and I heard someone start shootin' from behind me. Half-Lip hit the dust, dead before he landed. Another man fell off his horse, and I nailed him as he tried to stand. There was a tremendous blast from beside me, and I reckoned Rosie had cut the Greener loose. Another man hit the dirt, and I shifted my aim to one of the two that was still sittin' in the saddle. Stoney popped him with his Hawkin and blew him fifteen feet backwards. The bandit that was left jerked his horse's head around and laid the spur to

141

him. I saw a flash of brown and black from the corner of my eye, and Buck cut loose with his battle roar. He grabbed the man by the calf of the leg and drug him from the saddle. The man jumped to his feet and Buck backed off, waitin' for word from me. Rosie cut loose with his ten gauge as the man tried to get his gun turned. The impact of the buckshot threw him into the cedars. His horse ran ten yards and stopped.

"They was some of the ones that killed my Sky." Rosie's voice was ice-cold, and the look in his eyes gave me the shivers.

Suddenly, it was so quiet I could hear a chickadee squeakin' in a pine tree at the edge of the clearin'.

"We best see to a couple of them horses. Looks like Rosie put some buckshot into 'em," Stoney said.

The Injun agent came out, took a glance at the dead men layin' in his yard, and then went to the injured horses. "Easy now," he said in a quiet voice as he walked up. He checked first one and then the other. "They ain't bad," he said. "They'll be sore for a couple of weeks, but they'll heal. More than I can say for these polecats layin' here," he said, pointin' at Half-Lip.

"Well, Matthew, you made yourself a mess. You better get to cleanin' it up," Pa said.

"I didn't do it all by myself," I said.

"If it wouldn't a been for us helpin' out, we'd be cleaning you up out of the grass," Stoney said with a grin.

"It is true, amigo." Chris chimed in. "There was one more of them than you had bullets."

"There's four shovels over in the shed," the agent said, "and I think there's a couple more in the house so we can all work at it."

There was considerable grumblin', but we went a ways out into the cedars, got 'em planted, and scattered some loose dirt on the blood spots.

"Where you think the rest of the gang is?" the agent asked as we leaned on our shovels.

"Hard tellin', but they'll miss these here boys. They'll surely be comin' 'round sooner or later," Pa said.

"Let's go up to the station and get somethin' to drink," the agent said, wiping the sweat from his forehead.

"That's the best idea anybody's had all day," Pa agreed. We stacked the shovels back in the shed and walked to the adobe station.

As we drew near, we could hear a voice callin' feebly from inside. When we walked through the door, Mr. Wheeler spoke up.

"I thought there for a minute everybody was dead and I was going to have to nurse myself," he said in a weak voice. He fell back on the bed and took a deep breath. "You boys sure do make a lot of noise."

"I 'spect it was a little noisy in here fer a minute or two," Pa agreed.

"Was it some of Burdett's people?" Mr. Wheeler asked.

"It was," I said.

"It was him that shot me," Wheeler said. "They'd found out I'd been given several thousand dollars by a California syndicate to buy cattle in Kansas. I caught wind that Burdett's gang might be tracking me while I was still in Nevada. I headed north trying to throw them off the track." He stopped a minute and sucked wind with a wheeze, then took off again. "I went up toward Colter's Hell, and then headed south and west again. I figured they'd think I was heading for South Pass, when I was really planning on coming down to Wolf Creek. I thought I'd lost them, but somewhere close to Steamboat I caught a glimpse of some smoke. A little later in the day I thought I saw someone a mile or so behind me when I looked down from a ridge." He held up a minute, lookin' toward the open front door. "I hid the money," he said. He breathed a minute, and then asked for some water. Curly Thomas handed him the dipper and he drained it. He looked at us one by one and then started talkin' again.

"The only reason I'm telling you all this is I know and trust a couple of you. Stoney I've heard about for years, and everybody knows who Matt is. I figure anybody that rides with them have to be good folks, and I need help. Even if I live through this, I'm not going anywhere for a good long time. I'm responsible for other people's money, and I gave my word. I need someone to go recover the money from where it's hidden."

"I reckon you got it marked some way so you could find it later?" Pa asked.

"It's marked, but in a tough place. I heard about it from an old fella years ago," Wheeler said. "I sent a map to myself from Yampa to the new Indian agency at Animas City."

"You're at the Animas agency now," Curly said, "but the mail ain't in yet. Due in today, 'bout anytime."

"What would have happened if you'd been killed?" I asked.

"I sent a letter to the bank at San Francisco at the same time I sent the map here. I told the bank president if they hadn't heard from me by Christmas, to come to the Animas agency and get the map so they could recover their money." Mr. Wheeler closed his eyes and took another deep breath. He was gettin' weak, and I supposed we better lay off the talkin' for a while.

"I reckon we'll probably go and get it for ya," I said.

"We'll wait around here for a spell and see if Burdett or any more of his buddies show up and see if the mail gets here," Pa said. "You rest up, and we'll figure it out when you get to feelin' better."

We drifted back outside, all but Curly who was stirrin' somethin' up on the stove, and Stoney lit his pipe. He got it heated up and puffed 'til there was a cloud hangin' around his head. "I don't know exactly how it happens, but you boys do get yourselves in the damnest fixes," he said.

"I reckon it won't hurt us to help a good man keep his word," Pa said. "It ain't like our dance card is full."

"That might not be all the way true, Pa," I said. "I think I might've found your little gold creek up above Pahgosa when I had my run in with Burdett and company."

"Why in tarnation didn't ya say somethin'?" Pa asked.

"I been a touch busy, Pa," I replied.

We heard a horse comin' at a good pace down the road so we spread out a little and waited. A man came ridin' into the agency yard from the cedars, and he didn't look like an outlaw. He pulled up when he seen us spread out, and I figured we might look more like outlaws than he did.

"We're friendly," Stoney called out.

The man rode slowly up to us and stepped down from the saddle.

"You smell as much gunpowder as I have, and it tends to make a fella a mite suspicious," he said.

"I 'spose we ain't the purtiest group you ever seen," Stoney agreed, "but we're friendly most of the time."

"Well, I got the mail here . . ."

"Curly, mail's in," I hollered.

Curly came out and gathered the two sacks from the carrier and gave him one to take out. "Your fresh horse is around back of the barn. Same one you left last time you was in."

"Thanks, Curly. I surely like that chestnut better than this one. He's a good pacer," the carrier said. He grabbed the reins of his horse and headed back of the barn.

"It's here," Curly said, holdin' up a letter. "Wheeler's letter to hisself."

Curly handed me the letter, and I looked at it front and back.

"I don't feel right openin' up another man's mail," I protested, tryin' to hand it back.

"I don't want to know what it says," Curly said. "If I don't know what's in it, I won't be tempted to tell nobody." He turned and went into the house with the rest of the mail.

"I reckon it's up to you, Matthew," Pa said.

I opened the envelope and shook the paper out. It looked

to be a rough map of the western slope of the Rockies. I handed it to Pa.

"Well, looks to me like he covered some mighty tall country, and from the spot he left the mark, he surely put it in one of the roughest places a man could find. It's right in the shadow of Sleepy Cat Peak. I'd be right curious who Mr. Wheeler heard about this spot from. I reckon there ain't ten white men that know about it."

"High lonesome country that is," Stoney agreed. "Around eleven thousand, plus a few."

"Meek and me come through there in '32 and again in '39," Pa said. "Some mighty purty spots, but dangerous. The Shoshones was wanderin' around up there, and I'd called down a feud on the Utes. They was huntin' us purty heavy, and Ol' Joe finally split off from me, figurin' I was gonna get my hair lifted 'bout any time."

"It's purty plain that we cain't just up and leave Curly and Wheeler. Sure as we do, Burdett and his gang's gonna show up here, and them two is no match for Burdett," Stoney said.

"How 'bout Chris and I go after Wheeler's money, and you three stay here in case Burdett or some of his buddies show up," I suggested.

"I don't know . . ." Pa started.

"It only makes sense, Pa," I argued. "Two of us can make the trip faster, and we can surely take care of ourselves."

"He's right, Tirley," Rosie agreed. "Since some of Burdett's gang showed up here, the chances are purty good the rest of 'em are close about. Some of us got to stay here with Wheeler and Curly."

Curly came out on the porch and looked at us. "Chris Silva, you got a letter, and from the look of the envelope it's follered ya around since March."

Chris walked over, took the worn envelope from Curly, and carefully opened it. I seen a change come over him, and then he looked up at me. "My brother has been killed and my father badly hurt," he said softly. "They don't know if he will live. He might even be dead now."

"Who . . ." I started.

"Not who, amigo. They were caught in a slide in La Garrida," he replied.

"Take my gray," I said. "The ride you're gonna make is certain sure gonna use up your horse." He nodded and walked to the agency to gather up his truck. A half-hour later I was wavin' at him as he rode down the road. He knew what we was facin' up to, and I couldn't go with him, no matter how much I wanted.

Pa was quiet for a spell and then looked at me.

"I'm goin', Pa, and there ain't much you can say to stop me," I said.

He nodded. "I reckon you got to do it." He turned and looked at the mountains. "Ya ride up the side of Hesperus Mountain, through Windy Gap, and along the ridge top you'll hit a trail. It ain't much, but as you go north it gets better. When ya get on the west side of Sleepy Cat, maybe ten or eleven days' ride from here, you'll hit another trail. Ya foller it up to the top and over to the other side. You'll find a cliff face down from the top on the east side, maybe five hundred yards. Follow it north maybe a half mile, and there's a crack that'll let you down to the bottom. Look just right when you hit the bottom and you'll see a little rock cabin nestled up against the cliff. That little cabin's been there longer than anyone knows. It was old when me and Meek found it, and we reckoned we was the first white men to have ever seen it, 'sides the one that built it. It ain't Injun built, leastways no Injun we ever found built like that, and we knew most of 'em. Anyhow, according to Wheeler the money's under one of the flagstones in the floor." He stopped, looked at me, and rubbed his chin. "I want a favor 'fore ya head north." He stopped again and looked off toward the top of the mountains, then carried on. "I want you to ride over to Animas City. Just ride in, look things over, and ride back over here and let us know what's happenin'. I'm a mite worried about Frone."

"You expectin' trouble over there?" I asked.

"Well, with Burdett around ya never know, and she's there mostly alone. I kinda got attached to her last winter, and I just need to know if she's makin' it alright," Pa replied.

I nodded my head. "I'll just ride over to Frone's and take a peek."

There was smoke hangin' over the Animas Valley as I rode in. It was comin' on to sundown, and folks was stokin' up the cook stoves to fix supper. I rode right down Main Street with Buck trailin' along and was surprised by the number of new cabins in the little settlement. Frone's cabin lay off the edge of town, and I could see a curl of smoke comin' from her chimney. I pulled up in front of her place and stepped down from the saddle. She heard Sin blow and stepped to the open door to see what company she had. I saw her face light up as she recognized me.

"Well, land sakes," she said. "Look what the dog drug in from the barnyard."

"Howdy, Miss Frone," I said. "I was kinda ridin' through and thought I'd see how you was carryin' on."

"I'm doin' just fine," she said with a big smile. "The boys helped me dig up a garden spot, I traded for some turkeys from some Navajos, and three of the younger lads are gatherin' wood for me. By the time the snow flies again, I'll be purty well fixed."

"How's the town doin'?" I asked curiously. "Looks like more folks have moved in."

"We've had a spat of folks come in from both the east and the south. Must be nearly sixty souls in the valley now."

"What's bringin' 'em in?" I asked.

"They found a little gold in the river, so that brought a few in, and some of the others was just lookin' for a piece of ground. Sam's even built a store." Frone turned and looked into the cabin and then back at me. "I got some biscuits on, and there's plenty of beans in the pot. You might as well pull up to the table."

"I'd be right honored," I said, rememberin' her feather-light biscuits. "Is the basin still 'round back?"

"Right where it was last winter," she said, "and hurry up. I not only got biscuits on, but Nathan found a bee tree a week back, and we got fresh comb honey." She paused a minute, lookin' at Buck. "Might as well bring that ugly dog in with ya when ya come. We can't let him starve on the front step."

I was fair slobberin' down my chin thinkin' about eatin' some of Frone's fixin's again. I took Sin 'round back, washed up in the basin, and went into the cabin. The air was heavy with the smell of venison, biscuits, and peach pie. I ate 'til I couldn't eat no more, and then ate most of the pie. I was purely contented when we got done and kicked back from the table.

"That was surely the finest eatin' I've had since we was here last winter," I told her.

Buck gave a satisfied groan from under the table. We'd slipped enough food under the table to fill him up.

"So what's yer Pa been up to, Matthew?" Frone asked me.

I related to her all that had happened since we'd left, and I saw a look of concern come over her face.

"You mean to tell me there's a wounded man expectin' your Pa to nurse him back to health?" she asked me.

"I guess that's a true story, more or less," I agreed. "Stoney's there, along with Rosebud Charlie, and Curly Thomas."

"Still don't sound to me like the man has much of chance with that crew carin' for him." She stood up from the table and began to gather up the dishes. I moved to help her.

"We'll clean up and then take us a ride down to the agency," she said. "I'll see to Mr. Wheeler until he can do fer himself." She was quiet a minute and then looked at me. "Matthew, you go over to Nathan's place and tell him I'm goin' down to help. Ask him to tend my stock 'til I get back."

"Yes, Ma'am, I'd be pleased to," I agreed. I picked up my Henry and headed for the door.

"You expectin' trouble?" Frone asked, lookin' at the big rifle in my hand.

"We didn't leave here with particular good feelin's with certain folks, so it don't hurt to be ready."

I was bein' watched. I'd not seen another human being, nor any sign for that matter, for nearly five days. I'd left the Animas agency the morning after I'd had supper with Frone, and I'd been travelin' north since. I'd not seen another human being, but I was surely bein' watched. I'd kept an eyeball on Sin and Buck, since they always picked up on a critter or man long 'fore I did. They'd not given any indication of trouble, and I hadn't seen anything to make me think I was bein' followed, but I was. I knew it.

I was high up in about as lonesome a country as I'd ever seen. I'd struck the little trail middle of the first day out from Animas City, high up on the side of the mountain. The trail weren't much at first but it was there, and I'd stayed with it now for most of three days. I figured it was an old game trail, but I reckoned the Injuns used it as well. The longer I followed it north the wider and deeper it got. It weren't a road by any means, but it was a good trail. It run north and south and just under the spine of the Continental Divide. I'd come across a passel of grizzly tracks, seen maybe a thousand head of elk, more deer than I could count, and even a bull moose.

I'd been ridin' all day without much of a break and was gettin' mighty wore down. We'd not been travelin' fast, but there weren't much air at the altitude we was trekkin', and it made it hard to breathe.

I'd been scoutin' for a camp for more than an hour, and I'd finally laid an eyeball on what I was lookin' for. There weren't many trees 'cause we was above the timberline, and shelter of any kind was scarce. Even though it was middle of summer, it got downright cold at night, so I wanted some kind of wind-break.

It was there in front of me. A rock outcrop come down from the ridge that was maybe ten feet high and run part-way down the west side of the mountain. It'd block whatever wind might come up, and there was a little trickle of water runnin' along the base. It was made to order, and I stepped down from the saddle with a sigh of relief. The sun was headin' down, and it was gettin' cool. I scraped together some small dead bushes and pulled a bag of pine knots down from behind my saddle. I'd picked up pine knots when I was still down in the forest 'cause I knew there wouldn't be much wood up high. The knots was full of pitch, started easy, and burned a long time. I didn't plan on keepin' warm with the fire, but I did dearly want some coffee. I figured with two or three knots I could heat my coffee, and maybe even burn some bacon and beans.

I had to coax, beg, and even swear a little to get the fire goin' 'cause of the thin air. The bacon and the beans didn't cook so good, but the coffee was fine. I ate, cleaned up the skillet, and rubbed Sin down with a piece of sacking I carried with me. I finished and put him on a picket where he could reach the water. Buck was already curled up and snorin', and I didn't figure on bein' far behind him. I rolled out my bed and moved my saddle so I could use it for my head. The fire was nearly gone with just a tiny shaft of smoke risin' up to the night sky. I moved the half-full coffeepot to sit just at the edge of the coals, took off my gun, my boots, and my hat, and crawled under the canvas of my bedroll.

Sin blew through his lips, and I was out of my bed with my gun in my hand. I'd fallen asleep, and from the looks of the Big Dipper, I'd been asleep for a couple of hours. The only sound I could hear was the coffee steamin' on the few remain' coals glowin' dull red in my fire pit. Sin blew again, and I knew there was either a man or a critter just down the hill from me. Buck had moved up close to me and a gut-grumblin' growl started from him. I put my hand on his back and waited.

"I could smell your coffee clear down the mountain, and it's been a torrable long spell since I had any coffee," a voice called out.

"Come on in, if you're friendly. Fact, you can come on in even if you ain't friendly. I got a Colt centered on your brisket, and I ain't all that happy with ya for wakin' me up."

I heard some shufflin' comin' from below me on the slope, and I took the chance of kicking some of the dead brush over the coals in the fire pit. There was considerable smoke, and it seemed to take forever, but after a spell a tiny flame crackled out. As dark as it was, even the small fire seemed to give out a lot of light. I stepped back so as not to make a target and waited.

Suddenly, he was there. He looked to be older than the mountain we was standin' on. He had white hair, a white beard, and was about half the size of me. He had on a buck-skin shirt and a badger fur hat. He was carryin' a new Winchester rifle.

"I brought my cup up with me," he said in a soft voice.

"Help yourself," I said, still standing in the dark.

He walked over to the fire, took his shirttail in his hand, and lifted the pot off the fire. He poured the steaming, midnight-colored brew into a large, beat-up tin cup, blew on it for a few minutes, and then took a careful sip. He smacked his lips and grinned.

"That sure is fine," he said.

I stepped a little closer, and he looked me up and down.

"Name's Daniel Potts," he said, takin' another drink of coffee. Buck had checked him out and had gone back over to my bedroll. He was scratchin' my blankets into a pile, figurin' I was gonna talk all night. A great lot of help he was gonna be if'n I was attacked.

"Matthew O'Malley," I replied. I saw his eyes widen when I said my name.

"You favor Tirley. You any kin?" he asked.

"My pa," I replied.

"Me and Tirley covered a lot of ground together in the old days," Potts said. "We fit a few Injuns, trapped some beaver, crossed some rivers, and climbed a few mountains just to see if we could find the elephant. We seen that elephant, son, and then some. Why, I mind the time . . ."

"I've heard the stories, Mr. Potts, and I've heard of you." I wanted to cut him short, 'cause I figured he was just as windy as Pa, and I wanted to get back to my blankets. Pa had told me a good bit about Daniel Potts, and I was almost certain this little feller was him, but I had one way of knowin' fer sure.

"Pa did tell me one story about ya, Mr. Potts. He said you was missin' somethin' that most folks have."

"Well, I reckon he was right about that. Back in '29 the Blackfeet had me pinned down fer a spell, and I did lose somethin'." He swept off his badger hat, and the only hair he had was a white ring around a pale pink dome of scar tissue. "They got my hair, but thanks to your pa, I lived to tell about it. Ya satisfied it's me?"

I grinned at him and nodded. "Yes, sir, I reckon you be Mr. Potts."

"I ain't a mister, nor a sir. I'm just plain ol' Dan'l." He finished off the coffee and threw the dregs on the ground. "I got me a horse and a mule back down the hill. Ya mind if I bring 'em up?"

"Bring 'em up. I'm goin' back under the blankets," I replied. He went back down the hill, and I invited Buck to get out of my blankets. I got my bed fixed just as Dan'l Potts was bringin' up his stock.

Next thing I knew it was turnin' pink in the east, and the stars was disappearin'. I heard the fire pop and looked over.

Dan'l Potts had the coffee on and was addin' some sticks to the small flame.

"I figured to start the coffee," he said.

I nodded, threw the blankets back, and stood up. I stretched and put my hat on. I slung my gun around my hips and then stomped into my boots.

"I got a couple of fresh pine hens last night if you're sick of beans, and I make fair biscuits," Dan'l said.

"Don't let me stop ya," I said with a grin.

"If you're no better cook than Tirley, I reckon you'll let me take over," Dan'l said.

"It's all yours," I agreed. "I'll go tend my horse and get packed up."

I went over to Sin and moved the picket pin to a fresh spot. I walked back over to my saddle, pulled my good plate out of my bags, and walked over to the fire. Most times I'd just eat out of the skillet, but fixin's like Dan'l was doin' deserved my good plate. Dan'l had set a Dutch oven on the coals, and things was simmering' and steamin'. I was a man that put store by eatin', and it surely appeared that things was lookin' up.

"You want company fer a spell?" Dan'l asked. "I got no place in particular to go, and I'm kinda hungering' fer some conversation that ain't all comin' from my own mouth."

"I got a place I'm goin' and a thing needs doin'," I told him, "and there might be some folks about that'd be huntin' me." I told him the story of what I was up to, and the danger that might come on us any time. It didn't seem to bother him any.

"Me and Tirley fought back to back many a time. I reckon I can do no less with his kin. Besides, I'd like to go back south with ya and see the old coot again." He stood up and started gatherin' up his stuff. He stopped and looked at me serious-like. "I reckon you probably know it, but maybe a day's ride behind ya there's some fellers follerin' your trail. They been up close enough a time or two to catch sight of ya, but they drop back when they get too near. I kinda been watchin' things since I cut yer trail a few days back."

"How is it you didn't come in sooner?" I asked.

"Wal, I been in the hills fer most of my life, and I learned that in most cases it don't pay to mix in other folks' problems."

"So why'd you decide to side with me?"

"I jest naturally don't take to bullies, and one of them that's behind ya is the worst I ever heard tell of. I didn't know who ya was, but I figured the way Burdett was followin' ya . . . wal, you're surely outnumbered, and I was always a sucker for lost causes."

"I reckon he knows what I'm goin' after, and he figures it's gonna be a lot easier to take it from me rather than try and hunt it up himself." I grabbed the coffeepot and threw the grounds onto the few coals that remained. "How many you reckon there is trackin' me?" I asked.

"Don't know fer sure, but there's a passel of 'em. I couldn't get close enough to get a count."

We got packed up and was movin' up the trail by the time the sun was breakin' over the mountains. Dan'l told me he knew about the little stone cabin and figured we'd make it in four or five days. We headed north on the trail, but Buck stood a minute lookin' back the way we'd come the day before. His hair was bristled up, and I heard him growlin' down in his belly. I stopped Sin and looked back down the trail. I couldn't see nothin', and there wasn't any cover for miles.

"Come on, Buck," I said. He turned and went down the path ahead of us. I had a bad feelin' that trouble was comin' at us, and I didn't know how to head it off.

Chapter Sixteen

The fire snapped loudly and a million sparks rose in the night sky to join the stars. Lee looked across the flames at Tom. In so many ways he was like Matthew and yet so different. They looked enough alike to be brothers, only Matt was bigger through the chest and arms. The real differences were not so apparent. Tom was well educated with refined manners and speech. Matthew's education had been earned in the wild lands among hard men with few refinements. They both had incredible mental and physical strength, and like Tirley once said, "would make big tracks in the land."

"What do you think will happen, Tom?" she asked him.

"Looks to me like Matthew is in for the fight of his life." He paused a moment staring into the fire. "Maybe we all are." He looked up as Clayton walked into the circle of light cast by the fire.

"Horses are fine," Clayton said. He had his rifle in his hand and carried both his knife and a Smith and Wesson .44 in his belt. He squatted down and poured himself a cup of coffee from the fire-blackened pot.

"Tom's right," Clayt said, indicating he'd heard Tom's comment, "but what worries me most is Dee Skinner." He took a careful sip of the black brew and then swirled it around in his tin cup. "I met him once, a long time ago, and I've heard a lot about him since. He's a sure-thing killer. Lays in wait, stalks like a regular hunter after a deer, and never takes a chance. It's my thought that Matt can handle most of what comes at him, but he's not ready for Skinner. Matt doesn't even know he's being hunted."

"I'm curious what happened to Marilyn Beck," Tom said.

"If I never see her again, it'll be to soon," Lee said with a shiver. "I don't remember ever seeing so much hate in a person's eyes."

"You can bet she's around somewhere," Clayton remarked. "I did a little checking before we headed west. She's widowed, a long time ago. She inherited a large plantation in Georgia, sold it, and moved back East somewhere with the two boys and a daughter. She bought them most anything they wanted and paid their way out of trouble several times. Macon had to leave home first. Killed a man in a bar fight, and it was something his mother couldn't buy his way out of. Falcon followed not too long after. Marilyn still has plenty of money and likes to spread it around to get what she wants."

"What happened to the daughter?" Lee asked.

"I couldn't get a line on her. Seems she just kinda fell out of sight. If I'd had a little more time, I might've gotten more information, but we left out too quick."

"Sounds to me like you did pretty well the way it was," Tom said.

They fell silent watching the fire and listening to the horses chomp at the grass. After a few moments Tom stood, stretched, and looked to where the bedrolls were spread out.

"Guess I'll hit the blankets," he remarked. "We still have a couple of long days of riding ahead of us."

Lee and Clayt stood as well and walked to their respective bedrolls. In a matter of thirty minutes the fire had burned down to coals, and the three friends were lumps under their blankets. The horses had moved in on their pickets as the fire had burned down. They took mouthfuls of the tall grass infrequently now, their immediate hunger having been satisfied the first few hours they had been on the picket lines. All three of them had been born in the wild and raised in the mountains. They were still wild at heart and had the instincts of wild animals.

Suddenly, all three of their heads came up, and they looked intently toward the trail they had followed during the past day, even though the camp lay nearly a mile off the beaten path.

The gray blew through his lips, and the red mare took a step forward.

Clayton rolled his covers back quietly and went to the mare. He put a hand on her neck, and the starlight gleamed from the naked blade he held in his hand. He was ready. He was always ready.

Clayton had insisted he scout Animas City instead of just riding down Main Street. The closer they'd gotten to the town the more watchful he'd become. He was gone nearly an hour as Tom and Lee waited in the pine trees above the town. As it turned out, they were glad they'd taken his advice. He reported a number of hard-looking men loafing along the street, and the one saloon seemed to be doing landmark business. They had decided to skirt the town and try to find someone they could get information from without exposing themselves. Since Frone's cabin lay at the edge of town and along the natural lay of the land, they had ridden up to it entirely by accident, and Frone came out of the front door with a squirrel gun in her hand.

"Help you folks?"

"Well, hopefully," Tom started. "We're looking for some people we heard were out this direction."

"Who might that be?" Frone asked.

"Tirley and Matthew O'Malley," Tom said, waiting for a reaction.

"I got to say you do favor the rest of them no-good O'Malleys," Frone said with a half smile.

"I'm Tom O'Malley, this is Lewara Conall, and this is Clayton."

"You know them then? Tirley and Matthew?" Lee asked.

"I should say," Frone said with a smile. "They spent a powerful amount of time in this cabin during the winter. None of them boys can cook worth shucks, so I was purty popular while we was snowed in."

"Do you know where they are?" Lee asked, scarcely daring to hope the old woman did.

"Tirley, Stoney, and Rosebud Charlie are camped back yonder in the trees watching the carryin'-ons in town. Captain Dan, a U.S. Marshal by the name of Bush, and Lyle Hansen rode in a few days ago about the same way you did. My nephew Nathan was cuttin' wood out yonder, and they came on him before they went into town. He sent 'em to me. They be in the hills somewheres scoutin' the lay of the land." Frone paused a moment and looked across the little valley toward the river.

She shifted her rifle into the crook of her other arm and looked back to them. "Matthew is headin' north along the spine of the mountains. He's tryin' to help a wounded man I got here in my cabin recover some money he'd stashed up towards Wyoming somewheres. They was down at the agency, but when the toughs took over the town, the boys reckoned the gunshot feller would be better off here. The outlaws in town don't know Wheeler's here, but even if they found out the townfolks wouldn't tolerate 'em botherin' me." Frone looked at Lee with curious eyes. "I'd reckon you must be the gal Matt is always moonin' about."

"He's spoken of me?" Lee asked, her voice hopeful.

" 'Bout all he did talk about thru the winter," Frone replied. This time she smiled. Lee felt her heart leap with joy and hope.

"Better put the horses around back and get in the house 'fore some of them no-goods down in town see ya."

Clayt took the horses around back, and Lee and Tom followed Frone into her cabin. There was a blanket hung on a rope stretched wall to wall, and when Frone pushed it back, they saw a man in bed but up on one elbow with a Colt in his hand.

"They be friendly, Jason," Frone said to him. He lay back on the bed and sighed. Frone turned to Tom and Lee. "This here's Jason Wheeler. He's the feller Matt's tryin' to help." She walked to the door and looked down across the valley again, then turned to them.

"You're lucky you come up with me instead of some of the others. Burdett's men have pretty well taken over the town."

"Burdett?" Tom spoke the name quietly.

"You know him?" Frone asked.

"We know him," Lee said. Her tone of voice spoke for her.

"Yeah, well, Burdett and the scum with him's only been here a week or so, but they got most of the townfolks so scared they do whatever he says. They had themselves an election the day after they rode in and elected our no-good preacher the mayor. Burdett was elected town marshal, and the funny thing was there was about a hundred more votes cast than we got people. Burdett's taken out now, and Tirley figures he's out in the hills huntin' Matthew. He's gone, but he left plenty of his toughs here."

"No one's standing up to them?" Tom asked.

"There's some would, but Burdett has maybe thirty men here and more comin' in every day. We're mostly peace-lovin' folks, and they're leavin' us alone, for now."

"Why do you think they picked Animas City?" Lee asked, already suspecting she knew the answer.

"I think they be huntin' Wheeler's money and O'Malleys," Frone replied. She looked thoughtful a moment. "There any more of you O'Malleys out there? We're mighty thin on help if it comes down to a fight."

"We put the word out," Tom replied. "I expect we'll see a few more show up, and it usually only requires a few

O'Malleys to take care of most problems," he added with a small smile.

"I hope you're right, sonny," Frone said, " 'cause it looks like we're shapin' up to a fight."

The man's name was Finlay Kelly. He was walking on the dark side of a narrow street in Denver, Colorado. He walked another block and then looked quickly behind him as if expecting to see someone following him. He watched a moment and then turned down an alley and walked to a barn. As he entered the partially open door, he heard the startlingly loud noise of a Colt single-action being cocked. He knew it was pointed directly at him, because he knew the man that held the gun.

"It's me," Kelly said.

"So what'd you find out?" Rogan O'Malley asked. He was a large man, but gaunt and pale. He gave the impression he'd been recently ill.

"There's trouble over in a place called the Animas Valley. The clan is gatherin' for a fight," Kelly replied.

"What kind of trouble?" Rogan asked.

"Gun trouble with a man named Burdett," Kelly said in a quiet voice. "Sounds like he's gathered quite a few men around him."

A look of surprise crossed Rogan's face. "A bad one he is. Dumber than a bucket of rocks, and mean." O'Malley moved into the dim light falling through the barn door. "Who's involved from the clan?"

"Looks like Tirley's bunch," Kelly replied. "Word is Stone-Cold Phillips is with them, and maybe Rosebud Charlie."

"Good boys, and tough." Rogan took another step forward, and Kelly noticed the pistol was still in his hand. "You don't have to go with me," he said, looking intently at Kelly.

"I been mixin' with O'Malley trouble for so long I wouldn't know what else to do," Finlay said with a smile. "I got to admit, though, this Colorado country is a far cry from what I'm used to on the Texas border."

"If it weren't for that partner of mine and his stories about the wonderful cow country in Colorado, we'd all still probably be on the border," Rogan observed.

"You feelin' regretful about the move?" Kelly asked.

"Nope. After Pa died, there wasn't much left for me on the border," Rogan mused. "A three-room cabin and a section of desert ain't much to show for a man's life."

"Well, I got to say without Captain Chagrin O'Malley and his troop of Texas Rangers the Injuns and bandits would still own Texas. We civilized the place so the bankers and potato raisers could move in." Kelly looked closely at Rogan. "You still look a little pale around the gills. You gonna be alright?"

"I'm a lot better now than I was a week ago, and in another week I'll be back completely."

" 'Twas a close thing," Kelly observed.

"It was indeed," O'Malley agreed.

"There's one thing I haven't told ya," Kelly said. "The word is Dee Skinner has taken cards in the game."

Rogan visibly started, then holstered his pistol. He turned and grabbed his saddle and started toward the rear of the barn. "You go get the rest of our boys. Leave enough of them with the herd to hold them on that grass," he said over his shoulder. "I'm gonna get on the road west."

"You take a care, Rogan," Kelly said. "It ain't been a month since Skinner put two bullets in you. He still thinks he did for you. He don't know you lived through it."

"That gives me the edge," Rogan said. "I mean to kill him, or be killed in the tryin'."

"I'll get the rest of them gathered and follow after," Kelly said, moving toward the door.

"You take a care, Mr. Kelly," Rogan said. "I've gotten used to you, and I don't much want to be breakin' in a new partner."

"We'll catch up to you," Kelly said, as he walked from the door.

Rogan moved slow and careful while gathering his few possessions and saddling his horse. He put one foot in his stirrup, and swung into the saddle. He stopped a moment and drew his new Winchester from the boot. He checked to make sure it was loaded and then settled it back in the long scabbard. "I'd figured to go after Skinner even if there weren't a clan problem," he said mostly under his breath. "I can't have a man shootin' me and then suppose he got away with it."

His horse twitched his left ear, and Rogan moved him out of the barn. He pointed him down the road west.

"I got word yesterday that the O'Malleys are gatherin' at a place called Animas City. Sounds like it's over on the west slope of the San Juans in Colorado territory." The speaker was a short, square man with curly red hair. "There's family from all over beating dust that direction."

"How many can we get together?" Colin O'Malley asked, "and how quick?" He was a tall man, but slim and lithe.

"We can get ten maybe twelve," Aidan Riley, the redhead replied. He stood up and walked to the window of the large, strongly-built log cabin. "Colin, the cowboy that told me the story said he'd been down there in the Animas Valley not five days ago. He'd seen Tirley out in the hills with Stone-Cold Phillips and Rosebud Charlie. They was waitin' for one of Tirley's boys to come in from up north 'fore they started the fight. It's gonna happen, and it's gonna be soon."

Colin O'Malley walked across to the window, stood beside Aidan, and looked out across the valley he and his two brothers had settled nearly twenty years before on the edge of the South Dakota badlands. Malaon had been killed by the Sioux nearly a decade before. Conrad, his youngest brother, and he had carried on. The ranch had become prosperous, but it was not without cost in lives. Besides his brother there had been ten ranch hands killed by Indians, falls from bad horses, fights with rustlers, lightning strikes, snake bite, and a number of other fatal encounters life on the range exposed the cowboys to. Their ranch had been the first, and for many years the only, spread in South Dakota. They had fought for their land many times in the past, and he knew the generations of O'Malley that preceded him had many times gathered together for the common good. In fact, he and his brothers had been raised on the stories of the O'Malley clan and their famous fights. To his knowledge there had never been an O'Malley that failed to respond to a call for help from the family, be it direct or by rumor.

"Conrad is down at the meadow by the river," Colin said, turning away from the window and walking to the open gun rack situated on a wall. "Ride down and get him and five of the boys that are with him. Leave five to stay with the cows and calves until we get back." He pulled a rifle from the rack and checked to make sure it was fully loaded. "Send Garis over to the bald hills and get seven more hands from that crew. That will make a pretty good tribe of fighters."

Aidan moved toward the door and then turned back toward Colin. "Horses . . ."

"Jeffery and I will start gathering right now. We'll want three apiece. There's a fair piece of ground between here and Colorado, and we can't let the rest of the family beat us there."

They sat on their blankets around a nearly smokeless fire. Tirley was cleaning an old Walker Colt that looked the size of a small cannon. Rosebud Charlie was tending the fire and the coffeepot, and Stone-Cold Phillips was looking through a gap in the trees toward the valley.

"Riders comin'," Stoney said simply.

"How many and how soon?" Tirley asked.

"There's four, and I reckon they'll be up to us in a half hour or so." He stood and took a long gaze through the gap. "It looks like they might be friendly. I think Frone's with 'em."

Tirley stood, walked over beside Stoney, and watched the riders for a few minutes.

"Looks like you're right, and if I ain't mistaken there's another woman besides Frone," he observed.

"Now, how in blazes can you tell that from here?" Stoney asked testily.

"I always could see better than you, even when we was young. You wait and see if I ain't right," Tirley said with a smile.

He turned and walked over to the little creek that ran close to their camp. He took off his shirt, knelt down, and scooped up handfuls of water, splashing them on his face and neck. Stoney watched him for a minute and then quietly laughed. "Too bad you ain't got some of that skunk water the barber slaps on ya after he shaves ya."

"I'd've brought some along, but I figured you'd find it and drink it before I could get it used up," Tirley replied.

Rosie had stepped into the low brush next to the creek with his shotgun and disappeared. He'd become a quiet, cautious, angry man, and he'd vowed no one would ever take him by surprise again. Tirley and Stoney figured it would take him killin' some more of the Burdett gang to get him back to normal.

Tirley put his shirt back on and walked to the edge of the small clearing they'd camped in. Their horses were behind him in the trees where they wouldn't be easily seen or spooked. The three men had chosen their camp carefully with an eye to concealment and cover. They figured Burdett's men were hunting them after the little fracas at the agency. Another fifteen minutes passed, and the riders slowly came into the clearing. Tom O'Malley stepped down from the saddle.

"You'd be one of John's boys," Tirley said, shaking hands with him.

"I'm Tom, Uncle Tirley, and this is Clayton. He's come along for the ride."

"He's likely to get more than a ride," Stoney said dryly.

Tirley walked over to Frone's horse and helped her down, holding her close a moment longer than he probably needed to. "You're a sight for sore eyes, woman," he said with a grin.

"Wal, it's right good to see you too, Tirley," Frone replied. "Seems like it's been more than just a week since you was down at the cabin."

"How's Wheeler doin'?" Tirley asked.

"He's mendin', but it's slow. I 'spect he'll make it if he don't get an infection, or if he don't get shot again," Frone replied. "I left Nathan to watch while I brung these folks up. That purty one there is the gal that Matt has been tellin' ya about."

"You're just as purty as Matt said ya was, Lee, and there's a fella ridin' near the skyline that's gonna be plumb pleased to see ya," Tirley said, as she dismounted with help from Tom.

"Have you heard from Matthew?" Lee asked in an anxious voice.

"Nope, but you don't worry your head about Matt. He's got more savvy than a whole herd of wild Injuns. He's got a good horse under him and a fine dog beside him. He'll make out." Tirley paused a moment and looked across the mountains. "I'd reckon he's gettin' to the spot either today or tomorrow, then he'll be on his way home. Ten days, maybe less."

"Have you seen Dan, Uncle Tirley?" Tom asked.

"Dan, Lyle, and Marshal Joe Bush are all on the other side of the valley above town. They got Dan's army 'scope, and their tryin' to get a count on how many bandits we got to work with. We figure maybe there's about five apiece right now, but there's been more comin' in."

"Sounds like there's enough to go around if it comes to a fight," Tom remarked as he loosened the cinch on his saddle.

"Yeah, we'd sure hate some poor feller to get shorted and only have four of 'em to fight instead of five or six," Stoney said with a smile.

"I had the mail rider carry out a note to the boys back at the ranch. I told 'em if they didn't hurry they was surely gonna miss a good fight. That'll cut the odds some if they get here purty soon. I also told 'em not to ride right up to town. No use them gettin' the whole shebang started and ended with us sittin' up here in the hills," Tirley said.

They sat down around the fire, talked for a while back and forth, and finished off the coffee. Frone rose and brushed the pine needles from her riding pants.

"Tom and Clayton are gonna stay up with you, Tirley, and Lee will go back down to the cabin with me. You boys ain't fit company for a young girl, nor an old one neither for that matter." She laughed with the others and then turned to her horse. "We'd best get back. Nathan ain't much better at nursin' than any other man, and Jason needs the care."

"Thanks for comin' up, Frone, and maybe I'll just come callin' on ya one of these fine days," Tirley said as he helped her mount.

"You just keep yourself alive so you can," Frone said. "You'll be welcome, Mr. O'Malley. Men callers, even old catamounts like you, been a little scarce of late."

She turned her horse's head, and she and Lee followed the narrow trail down the mountain toward town. Tirley stood looking after them.

"If I didn't know better, Tirley, I'd say you got a case on that woman," Stoney remarked.

"She is a fine specimen," Tirley replied without looking at Stoney.

"Wal, I hope ya live long enough to court her," Stoney said. "The future ain't lookin' all that bright if ya ask me."

Chapter Seventeen

We were at the top of the world. I'd been high up before, but this was somethin' else. We'd just made the ridge under the brow of Sleepy Cat Peak, and Buck was looking down the other side of the mountain.

"That cabin's right under us down the other side," Dan'l said. "I 'spect I'd best stay up here just off the skyline and keep a watch. I got a feelin' we're gonna have company."

"I'll make it as quick as I can," I told him. "You be thinkin' about where we're gonna head after I get Wheeler's money. You know the country, and we're gonna need to move fast."

"I'll ponder on it," Dan'l said. "You go do your chore, and I'll figure us a course."

I turned Sin's head and we moved down off the ridge on the east side. We followed a steep, narrow, switchback trail pocked with deer and elk tracks that dropped maybe two or three hundred feet. I found the one-room, stone-walled cabin snuggled in against the rock face where the trail leveled out on a bench. It blended in so well that it looked like it grew there instead of bein' built. Buck was sniffin' around the base of the house lookin' for mice.

I stepped out of the saddle and walked over to the cabin. It looked to be still in good shape considerin' the age that everyone seemed to think it was. It surely looked old to me, but I wasn't much of a judge. The roof was made up of wide, split wood shingles laid over split beams. There was gaps where the shingles were missin', but only a few.

I left my horses to graze on the cured bunch grass close about. I walked around to the door of the shelter and pushed it open. There were little light shafts filterin' through the gaps in the shutters that covered the windows. The floor was made of tan, flat flag stones just like Wheeler had said. I stepped in and looked around the small room. The stone walls were laid up dry, but they were so tight that not a breath of air sneaked through. The whole structure was perfectly built, and it made me admire the builder. Whoever had done the work had been a craftsman, and Pa had taught me to appreciate good work.

I stepped across the room and pushed one of the brittle shutters open. The light helped, but it was still gloomy where the light didn't reach. I walked over to the northwest corner and looked the floor over. I noticed one of the flagstones didn't fit tight with the rest of the floor. I took hold of the rock and pushed it aside. There was a square-shaped hole under the flagstone, but it was so dark I couldn't see what was down inside. I reached in, hopin' there wasn't somethin' down there with teeth. I felt Wheeler's money belt and pulled it out. It was heavy since the money was mostly in gold coin with only a few paper bank notes throwed in. I stood up and was turning back toward the door when I decided to take one more feel around in the hole. I lay down on the floor and reached as far down as I could. I felt around and was glad I'd decided to check. I come out with a cured leather bag that felt full of coins. I stood up and was gettin' ready to open the satchel when I heard Dan'l's rifle cut loose. I stuffed the leather bag in my shirt and grabbed Wheeler's belt. I ran out the open door and looked up toward the top of the mountain. Dan'l was comin' off the top fast, and I reckoned there'd be some bandits comin' soon after. I took my Henry from the scabbard and moved my horses around behind the safety of the cabin. I ran back and lay down behind a big boulder that'd rolled off the ridge. Dan'l come around the corner of the outcrop and slid out of the saddle. I figured he was purty spry for an old mountain man, and all it took to get him movin' was a passel of people shootin' at him. He moved his horses around with mine, tied 'em all tight, and come back to where I was forted up. He was breathin' so deep and hard he sounded like a tornado I once seen out on the plains of Kansas.

"They be comin', boy, and there's quite a few of 'em."

"Let 'em come," I replied. "We're in a nice spot here to hold 'em off."

"Maybe fer a spell, but soon or late they gonna figure a way around us. We got to get off this hill and down into the timber."

Just as Dan'l spoke I saw a man ride over the top. I guess he'd figured that the way Dan'l had come a rippin' down the trail that we'd tucked and run. Only problem was he figured wrong. I wasn't a man that liked killin', particular from ambush, but they come askin' for it. I let him make maybe ten steps, then touched the Henry off. He fell out of the saddle and lay by the trail. His horse come on down and settled in with our stock. It was a nice brown-and-white paint that looked like he might have some Injun blood in him. I reckoned we could always use another horse and saddle. Another man come over the top, let his horse take about four steps until he saw the first guy layin' beside the trail, and tried to turn around. He didn't make it. When he hit the dirt his horse run back over the hill. I stood up, ran around the cabin, and jumped into the saddle. Sin had heard the shots and was ready to go. He'd been a battle horse once upon a time and dearly loved a good fight.

"Stay, Buck," I told my dog. I didn't want him to follow where I was goin'.

"What're ya doin'?" Dan'l yelled.

"You get up in the saddle and get the horses ready to go.

I'll be back in a minute. I'm gonna give 'em something to think about," I yelled back at him.

I pointed Sin up the hill and give him his head. He went up the hill like he knew what I wanted. Three minutes later we topped out, and I was amongst 'em. My charge took 'em completely by surprise, and there was maybe fifteen or twenty men all bunched up just off the trail. I cut loose with my rifle and the range was close. I emptied a saddle with my first shot as I rode through 'em. I turned Sin with my knees, and come up again, this time slashin' right and left with the Henry held in my right hand. I nailed one rat-faced outlaw right above the eyebrows, and he left the saddle like he'd been shot. The majority of the horses they was ridin' was range stock and barely broke. Most of 'em started buckin', kickin', and squealin', and it was all dust and confusion. They was gettin' some shots off, but the way their horses was thrashin' around they wasn't hittin' anythin'. I topped over the ridge again and raced down to the cabin.

"That'll slow 'em down a little," I said as I rode up to Dan'l. "You figured out where we're goin'?"

"Ain't much choice left," Dan'l said and pointed his horse's head down the mountain. Buck and me followed close after.

We rode hard, slid in spots, nearly fell, and stopped to catch our wind as we made the heavy timber.

"They'll be comin'," Dan'l said. "I 'spect you slowed 'em down some, but they'll still be comin'." He looked at me, swept his hat off, and rubbed his hand over the baldness that had once been hair before he'd been scalped. "I swear, Matthew. Yer surely kin of your old man. The last time I seen somethin' that stupid was when your pappy charged the Injuns that was cuttin' off my hair."

"I had to try and cut down the odds a little and let 'em know that we'd fight if they come at us."

"Wal, you sent 'em the message, I reckon." He looked over his shoulder at the peak that loomed over us, and then down into the forest. "I 'spect we ought to split up and give 'em even more to ponder on."

"You think that's smart?" I asked. "Two sets of guns are always better if you get to a fight."

"We done this a bunch a times in the old days when we was bein' chased by Injuns. We're gonna run not fight, and this gives us a chance to split up them that's chasin' us. We'll get back together south and east of here, and when we do we're gonna hope that some of 'em have fallen out of the chase. There's gonna be some horses that come up lame, maybe some of 'em gonna get sick of the chase. They might even come across some Utes and get themselves shot up. No matter what happens, it figures that the odds are gonna be better fer us three days from now." He looked over his shoulder again and then jumped from his horse. He grabbed up a stick, smoothed out a spot in the trail with his hand, and started drawin' a map. "There's a big lake with an island in it three full days ride from here southeast. It's three days if you don't sleep more than two or three hours a night. It lays right at the base of a big set of cliffs, and ya cain't miss it if you follow the Injun trail that starts right here on the flank of the mountains. I'll meet ya on the south shore close at some big pine trees that hang out over the water. You'll see 'em." He paused a minute and looked thoughtful. "There's a shortcut that comes down off Sleepy Cat that would put them ahead of us if any of 'em know about it. If they get ahead of us, they'd have a good chance to bushwhack us. I don't figure there's a dozen white men ever knew of the trail, and half of them are dead. We're just gonna have to take the chance that none of 'em knows."

He climbed back on his horse and pulled the gelding's head around. "I'll take that Injun horse we just acquired so's I can make better time, if ya don't mind. I can switch off between 'em."

"Suits me fine," I replied. I had Sin and my blue roan I'd

traded for with the Utes. I didn't need another trailin' after me.

"Right ahead of us the trail splits again," Dan'l said, pointin'. "You take the south branch, and I'll take the east. I'll see ya at the lake in three days."

I gathered my reins and slid the Henry into the boot. We was gonna run, and I wanted my hands free. Dan'l turned in the saddle and looked at me.

"You watch yer topknot, young'n," he said with a smile.

"I'd tell you to do the same, but it's already been took," I replied. He laughed and kicked his horse in the ribs. In a blink of the eye Dan'l was out of sight, and I was by myself again.

"Well, it ain't the first time," I said, speakin' my thoughts. I looked down and saw Buck layin' in the shade, and Sin flicked his ear. "I guess I ain't completely alone," I said. I felt some better. I nudged Sin forward and the roan followed after. Buck moved out ahead of us. Five minutes later we come to the fork in the trail, and I pulled up.

"Buck," I said and patted my leg. He took a run and jumped. I caught him and pulled him up with me on the saddle. We was gonna make tall tracks in some rough country, and I didn't want to lose him. I nudged Sin with my heels, as close as I ever came to a kick with him, and he stepped up to his mile-eatin' gaited trot. The trail was fair and seemed to mostly follow the flank of the mountains. I rode for most of the rest of the day in thick timber. In some places the spruces and pines was so thick that they pushed in close on the trail and I couldn't see two feet. As the sun began to dip behind the mountains, the trees got bigger, and after a few more miles got a lot bigger. It was plain to see that some time past there'd been a fire sweep through the country. It had only singed the bark on the big trees, but all the underbrush and small trees were gone, so there wasn't nothing left on the ground but grass. Some of the trees had to be four or five hundred years old and reached a long ways up into the sky. They was so big around that I reckoned there would be just no way a man could cut 'em down with an ax. The problem was that without the brush and smaller trees a man could see for quite a ways up and down the hill. I felt like a school boy showin' up at a box social in his underpants.

I started to look for a place to camp as dark settled in. The moon was three days past full, so 'long about ten or eleven there was gonna be enough light to travel by. I'd give the horses a little time to graze and water, Buck and me would eat and maybe nap, then we'd take off again. The more distance I gained on the outlaws the better I was gonna like it.

I came across a little fast-runnin' creek that came out of the mountains and stepped from the saddle. Buck took to sniffin' around, and I took the saddle off Sin. I put the roan on picket, and let Sin graze free. He was well trained and never got off too far. I scraped together a little dry wood and started a handful of fire. Pretty quick I had the bacon on and was shavin' the last of my spuds into the grease. I bent over to stir the taters when somethin' hit me a terrible lick up side of the head. I was knocked over on my back, and then I heard the far off beller of the shot. As blackness washed over me, I had the thought that whoever made that shot had been a long ways off and they'd surely known about the shortcut that Dan'l said nobody knew. I also reckoned I was dead. I hoped that Pa would find my dog and horses and take of 'em and tell Lee I'd died game tryin' to help a friend.

Chapter Eighteen

"Good to see ya back, boy," the older man said. "Looks like you got most of what was on the list," he said, looking in the back of the large farm wagon.

"I figure one more trip to town, and we'll have everything we need to see us through the winter," the young man replied. He stepped down from the wagon and faced his father.

"Pa, I heard somethin' down at Susanville that give me pause."

"What's that, Cory?" Peter O'Malley asked.

"Uncle Tirley and some of the cousins have got 'em a fight goin' down in Colorado."

Peter looked sharply at his youngest son. "How old's the information?"

"The rider was a hard case that got run out of the territory. He said an O'Malley had told him he could ride or die. He chose to take the ride. He says he ain't goin' back. He's been ridin' for a week. He also said the O'Malleys ain't got a chance."

"He say exactly where this fight was gonna be?" Peter asked.

"Place called Animas," Cory replied.

Peter looked out across the valley he'd settled so many

years ago. He'd come to the Sierras in what was now northern California looking for fur and had found gold instead. With the gold he'd managed to secure a large Spanish land grant. The land grant had subsequently been proved up by the United States in accordance with the treaty ending the war with Mexico. Over a hundred thousand acres of timber, grass, mountains, and lakes belonged under his brand. He'd not had help from anyone except his wife and the men that had ridden and fought beside him. He hadn't seen or heard from any of the brothers O'Malley for more years than he cared to remember. He had five grown sons, and he loved them all so much it sometimes almost hurt. He didn't want to lose any of them in a fight that wasn't his. His boys were all he had left now that Elizabeth was gone. On top of all that, he was getting old. It wasn't as easy to rope a steer now as it had been just a few years ago. He had pains in places where he hadn't even known he had parts.

"How many men is Tirley and them up against?" Peter asked.

"The man said the leader, a guy named Burdett, had gathered close to fifty, and he's payin' fightin' wages," Cory replied. Peter could see the hopefulness shining in Cory's eyes. He'd been too young to go to the war, and only one of the other boys, his oldest, had gone. Cory still had the enthusiasm of youth and a lust for adventure. Peter could remember well the way he had been at Cory's age. He'd been on his own and had nearly found more adventure than he could live though. His body still bore the scars of his youth.

Peter looked off across the valley again. What would he do if fifty booted and belted men came after him and the boys? They'd fight and they'd lose. The odds were too long.

"Go get your brothers collected and round up some horses. We'd best get on the trail." Peter O'Malley had made up his mind. Tirley was still family, and he needed help.

"Where is he?" Lee said, mostly to herself.

"He'll be here soon," Frone said. "Matthew can take care of hisself."

"There seems to be so many of them," Lee said, looking down on the street from Frone's cabin window.

"Well, there's more than a few of 'em, that's sure, and seems to be more today than there was yesterday," Frone agreed.

"I feel like I should be doing something," Lee said as she turned away from the window.

"Not much a slip of a girl and an old woman can do," Frone observed.

Lee turned to look at Frone. "There is one thing we can do . . ." she started to say.

"We can go down to the street and see how many outlaws are in town," Frone finished for her.

"Exactly."

"Any of them men know ya?" Frone asked.

"There's a few, but I'd guess the one who knows me best, Burdett, is out hunting for Matt, and the rest of them might not remember me."

"Yeah, they won't remember the prettiest girl most of 'em ever seen, and I still believe in the little people," Frone responded with a smile. She got to her feet from her chair at the table and walked over to the closet. She got down an old coat and hat and handed them to Lee. "You put this hat on to cover your hair, and it's gettin' cool enough they won't think twice about the coat. Just don't look up and let 'em get a clear peek at your face."

Lee put on the clothing and looked at herself in Frone's cracked mirror. She laughed out loud at the way she looked. "If Matt could see me now he might not think I'd learned much in Boston."

"From the way Matthew carried on about you, I reckon he'd take you to wife no matter if you learned a thing or not," Frone commented.

"I so hope you're right, Frone."

"I know I'm right," Frone said as she turned toward the door. "If we're gonna do this, we might as well get started."

Frone picked up her rifle and stepped out of the cabin. "Let's go down to Sam's store. I need some things, and it's a good excuse to go downtown.

Lee closed the cabin door and reached in the pocket of the old coat. She felt the reassuring presence of her little pistol. She always hoped she wouldn't need it, but it was a comfort. They walked side by side down the dusty road to the store. When they stepped inside the mercantile, they waited until their eyes adjusted to the relative gloom of the log cabin Sam Draper had built to house his goods.

"Hi, Frone. Haven't seen you for a few days," he said from behind a long counter made of split timbers.

"Ain't been out, Sam. Too many hard cases in town," Frone replied.

"There is that," the big teamster replied. "I've counted a few over thirty here, and Burdett took twenty some with him when he went north. More than twenty and Dee Skinner." He stopped a moment and looked at Lee. "Where'd you come up with the boy?" he asked.

Frone looked over her shoulder toward the front door making sure they were alone, then she looked back to the store-keeper.

"You 'member that gal Matt O'Malley was always carryin' on about?" Frone asked.

"Lee?" he asked.

Lee took her hat off, letting her hair spill down, and stuck out her hand. "Glad to meet you, Mr. Draper," she said with a smile.

"Well, I'll be dogged," Sam exclaimed. He shook her hand and laughed. "You're just as purty as Matt said you was." Lee's blush went from her neck right up to the top of her face.

"You best get your hat on again," Frone cautioned. "You never know where these polecats are gonna be."

"They been spending most of their time over at the Elkhorn Saloon," Sam said, "but once in a while one of 'em runs out of tobacco and comes over here. They be spoilin' for trouble, and it wouldn't do for them to catch sight of a purty gal." Sam stepped in behind the counter and looked out the window. "They figure they're the law here, and no tellin' what they might do."

"I need a pound of coffee and the same of sugar while you're standin' on that side of the counter," Frone told the big storekeeper.

Sam moved to fill her order and then looked over his shoulder at her. "Tirley still likes his coffee sweet, does he?" He smiled at her.

"Might be for me, or even Lee," Frone replied.

"Might be, but you always drank your coffee black while we was on the trail, and I bet Lee don't drink much coffee," he observed.

Sam handed her the two small cloth bags and looked seriously at her. "I reckon I told you what you wanted to know about the numbers. You tell them old men not to get in a hurry to come in an' fight. There's too many of them, and they're too well armed."

"You know how Tirley and Stoney are," Frone said. "They gonna do what they want to, and there's nothin' you and me are gonna say that'll change their minds."

They suddenly heard boot steps on the porch of the store and turned. The stranger was tall and seemed thin for his height. He had a large mustache, dark hair, and was pale as a ghost. He had one short gun in a holster on his hip and another in his belt. He carried an old Spencer rifle in his hand.

"Howdy," he said in a voice that didn't sound like it got much use. "I'm lookin' for Matthew O'Malley."

"So's a lot of other folks," Sam said. "What's your business with him?"

"My name's Rogan O'Malley, and he's my cousin. Fact is, if you be friends to them huntin' him, I guess we might as well get started with it right now." His rifle had tipped ever so slightly and was centered on Sam.

"Don't be so sudden, mister," Sam said, "I'm just a humble storekeeper."

"You wasn't so humble down to Sante Fe when you took all them hide-hunters on," Rogan said.

A big smile broke over Sam's face. "I thought I'd seen you before, and they was askin' for it."

"Well, you gave it to 'em, and then some," Rogan said. "So which side you on this time?"

"I hope the right one, and it'll probably get me killed," Sam said. He looked past the man at Frone. "He's who he says he is." He looked back to Rogan. "I'd heard you'd been done under by Dee Skinner," he added.

" 'Twas a close thing," Rogan said. He looked over his shoulder through the still-open door. "Now it's my turn."

"My name's Frone, and we be friends to the O'Malleys. Tirley's up in the hills with some men. I guess they're waitin' for Matthew to get in. Then they're gonna bring the fight down on 'em," Frone said in a quiet voice.

"I got six men with me, Ma'am" Rogan said to Frone. "I'd surely be obliged if you'd show them the way to Tirley's camp."

"What about you? Ain't you goin' up to the camp?" Sam asked Rogan.

"I got me a man to kill," Rogan replied in a quiet voice. "I never held much with killin', but he took me out of the saddle from ambush, and I just can't let it stand."

"Please get him before he finds Matt," Lee asked.

Rogan looked surprised. He'd noticed her, but had paid no attention, taking her for a boy as had Sam.

"I'll do my best," he promised. "Can you tell me where Matthew was headin'?"

"Sleepy Cat Peak," Frone replied. "He ought to be headin' back by now."

"Skinner went out with quite a crowd, more than twenty," Sam said. "How you gonna separate him from the pack?"

"I won't need to," Rogan said. "He won't stay with them. He's a hunter and likes to work alone. He'll split off."

"You sound purty sure," Sam said.

"I am. He's been a loner all his life, even when we were kids." He saw the startled expression on their faces. "He's my half-brother by marriage. Pa married his mother after my mom died of the fever," Rogan explained. "We grew up under the same roof, and he hates the O'Malleys one and all."

"Mother, you've taken this as far as it can go. A lot of men are going to die if you don't call it off."

"I can't believe you'd even consider asking me to do such a thing. They killed your brothers. They deserve to die. They must die."

"This isn't the old country, Mother. You can't just call down a feud on an entire family."

"You've spent too much time in school, Laura, and that's my fault. I've given you too much, and as a result you've forgotten your roots." Marilyn took a breath and went to the window. "This fight has been going on for generations, and it won't end until either there's none of them left or none of us. They killed your father, and they killed your brothers."

Silence fell between them and Laura walked to within a few steps of her mother. "You've never told me about father," she said. "I didn't know he was killed."

"It was a long time ago, and I was with him when he died. I promised him I'd carry on the fight. I wouldn't quit until every O'Malley I could find was dead. I've been working on my promise."

Laura's hand went to her mouth as she stepped back. "You're responsible. You are as responsible for the deaths of my brothers as if you'd pulled the trigger yourself."

"The boys knew what they had to do, and they knew what the price might be. My husband and sons died for the Kurlow name, my maiden name, and I am willing to do so as well. You are a Kurlow. It is our destiny."

Laura took another step back as tears spilled from her eyes. "It may be your destiny, Mother, but it's not mine. I won't die for the name. Not now, not ever." Laura ran out of the cabin door and down the street.

"Laura!" her mother screamed after her. "Laura, get back here!"

Laura ran down the street until she was out of breath; she stumbled to a stop, gasping for air. A pair of rough hands grabbed her and pulled her behind a large tent.

"What we got here?" a coarse voice rasped in her ear.

"Let me go," she gasped. She could smell alcohol and an unwashed body so strongly she almost gagged.

The man was large and much stronger than she was. She was in trouble and she knew it. Laura tried to scream, but the man clamped his hand over her mouth so hard her breath was cut off. She struggled, kicked, and tried to strike him, but he was too strong.

"Let her go." The voice was quiet but carried a note of authority.

The hand on her face loosened, and she sucked in air with a loud gasp.

"You mind your own business, mister. I'm the law," the man that held her said.

"You'd best let her go or you're gonna be dead, law or not," the man behind them said.

Laura felt the man's hold on her loosen and suddenly she was free.

The Burdett's man who claimed to be the law tried to whirl and pull his gun at the same time. It was an awkward move, and not nearly fast enough. Laura heard a meaty thunking sound, and the smelly man fell almost at her feet. He had a very large knife sticking from his chest.

"Sorry you had to see that, Ma'am, but he gave me little choice."

She looked at the man that had saved her, and she realized she'd seen him only moments before walking into the mercantile. He was tall, thin, and had a large mustache.

"Name's Rogan O'Malley," he told her as he retrieved his knife.

"My name is Laura Beck," she said, looking into his face, "My mother was a Kurlow, which makes us enemies, it seems."

"Miss, I don't even know you, and I've never been real strong on hatin' folks just 'cause of their name," Rogan said with a smile. "Now if you shoot me or somethin' similar, then I might not like you so much, but until then we can be friends."

"You don't know how glad I am to hear that, Mr. O'Malley. I am in desperate need of a friend."

"It'd probably be wise if we got out of here. Somebody might miss this polecat and come lookin'," Rogan suggested.

"I have no place to go," Laura said in a quiet voice as they walked out from behind the tent.

"There's some folks over at the store I'm sure will help you," he said. He looked up and down the street, took her by the arm, and walked her to the mercantile.

"Frone, this gal needs a hand, and I need to be on my way if I'm gonna be any use to Matt," Rogan said.

"She's welcome to go with us," Frone replied, "and you'd best ride."

"My name's Kurlow on my mother's side," Laura said. "I think you need to know that first."

"I killed a man attacking her just now," Rogan said. "He was one of the gang workin' with Burdett."

"It's actually my mother's gang," Laura said. "She's paying the wages." She paused a moment and looked at Lee and Frone. "If you are O'Malleys or friends of the O'Malleys, then we should be natural enemies, but it's not my choice."

"We judge people according to what they do," Frone said. "We'll trust you 'til you prove you can't be trusted."

"I got to ride," Rogan said as he turned to the door.

"Hurry," Lee said. "I have a terrible feeling something has happened to Matt."

Chapter Nineteen

I didn't know it hurt so bad to be dead. My head felt like I'd been kicked by a shod mule, and there was something wet on my face. One side of me was warm, and the other side was freezin'. I reached down slow with my hand and felt somethin' fuzzy on my warm side. There was a whine, and I realized Buck was snugged up against me. It come to me right then that I wasn't dead, but the way my head felt, I figured to be almighty sick.

Buck give one of them low growls from way down in his guts, and I determined what had brought me around. Buck was tellin' me someone was comin'. Probably whoever shot me wanted to make sure he'd done a good job. There was also the fact I was carryin' a sizeable amount of money in Wheeler's money belt. I was hurt, maybe bad, and I was in no shape to try and fight off whoever was comin'.

I was dizzy and sick to my stomach, but I managed to roll onto my back and saw the sun was just droppin' behind the mountains. I had it in my mind to sit up, but when I tried the world started goin' around in circles.

"If you can hear me, lay still," a voice said quietly from behind a tree some ten feet away. "You been shot in the head, and there's a man comin' to finish the job. I'm friendly and mean to kill the man that shot you." The voice went quiet for a minute and then came again. "If you can hear me, raise your hand slow off the dog, but easy so Skinner don't see you."

I raised my hand off Buck and then slowly dropped it back, makin' no sudden moves. I had no proof the man behind the tree was my friend except his word for it, but I figured if he was the shooter he wouldn't have spoken to me. He'd just shoot me again, and probably my dog.

Skinner. The voice from behind the tree had mentioned Skinner. That had to be Dee Skinner, which made sense since he was known throughout the West as a sure-thing killer who did his dirty work from ambush and for a price.

"Keep hold of your dog," the voice came again. "I don't want him comin' over here and tryin' to eat me, and I 'spect Skinner will try and shoot him if he can. The only reason he hasn't done it yet is because he's on the other side and can't see him in the shadows.

I got a good hold on Buck's kinky hair and held on. He was growling with his mouth shut and wasn't noisy, but he was vibratin' the ground.

I must've blacked out for a few minutes and near lost my hold on Buck when he moved to stand up. I pulled him down and lay still with my eyes shut.

"If you can hear me, O'Malley, throw the money out where I can get it, and then your guns." The voice was a lot different than the first one, and seemed further away. "You do what I tell you, and I'll leave you be."

For some reason I didn't believe him. I figured any man that would shoot from ambush didn't have the backbone of a layin' hen, and surely couldn't be trusted. I just lay still, hangin' on to my dog.

I heard a horse walkin' toward me and a saddle squeak. I reckoned Skinner was gettin' down from the saddle. Buck was shakin' all over and surely wanted to take a couple of bites out of the gent walkin' toward us. I didn't dare move 'cause

I knew it would invite a shot, but I dearly wanted to see if my guns were where they were supposed to be.

"That's far enough, Dee," the voice from behind the tree said in a commandin' tone.

I heard a deep intake of breath from the other side of me as Skinner realized we weren't alone.

"I thought you were dead, O'Malley," Skinner said in an easy tone.

Least now I knew who all the actors were. I didn't know the voice, which meant the O'Malley wasn't one of my close kin, but just him bein' kin was enough.

"You missed, Skinner."

"I know I didn't miss, Rogan," Skinner replied, "and that puts you in rare company. I only know of one other man I've shot that's still alive."

"It ends here, Dee," Rogan said. "I should have killed you when you first turned bad. It would have saved a lot of men's lives."

"You couldn't have done it, Rogan. We were raised brothers, and you just never had it in you. The fact is, I always thought you couldn't take me face to face anyway."

I reached my free hand down slow and felt along my belt. My hand came across the butt of the Colt I carried in my belt. I figured Skinner was so busy talkin' to Rogan he wouldn't notice me getting my gun in my hand. I slipped it free, easy-like, and opened my eyes. Skinner was standin' on my right side not ten feet away and was watchin' Rogan who was on the other side of me. I still had hold of Buck, and his growlin' had got to the point I knew he was gonna let loose a roar any second.

He did, and it was so loud it made me jump, let alone what it did to Skinner. I guess he hadn't seen the dog layin' beside me, and when Buck thundered Skinner's eyes got big as full moons. We all shot at the same time. I didn't see where Skinner's shot went, but I knew mine had taken him in the leg somewhere around the knee. It was the worst shot I'd ever made, but I was still seein' two of everythin' and wasn't even sure I was shootin' the right one. Rogan's shot was some better than mine and took Skinner right through his vest pocket. The killer tried to bring his gun up, but I shot him again hittin' him in the other leg. As he was fallin', Rogan shot again, takin' him under the chin.

I tried to sit up but the world started rollin' again, and my guts heaved.

"Well, Matt, I always heard you was some kind of shot, but you weren't much help on this one."

"I kept him from runnin' away," I managed to croak, and Rogan laughed.

Buck was up, and he was surely gonna try and make a meal out of Rogan.

"Down, Buck," I told him. I didn't have much volume, but he got the message. His tail hit the ground and he sat still.

"Come on over, Rogan," I said. "Once he gets to know you, he'll quit tryin' to eat your leg."

I kept hold of Buck as Rogan squatted down beside me.

"Jeez, Matthew, he nearly did for you."

Buck was bein' good, so I let him go and moved a hand up to my head.

I had a bullet gouge over my right ear from the front of my head almost to the back, and I'd lost a sight of blood. I looked around and both my horses were still in sight.

"Guess that makes three of us Skinner shot and lived to tell about it. The interesting thing is all three are O'Malleys." Rogan said.

"I'd reckon the O'Malleys were just bad luck for him," I agreed.

"How'd you find me?" I asked.

"I was in Animas City a few days ago, and there was some folks there told me where to find you. I got to the top of Sleepy Cat about the time you come rippin' over the hill. I wasn't close enough to help, but close enough to hear the shootin' and yellin'. I been trailin' along since you and the other guy split, and you put some miles under the horses to-day. I could never catch up."

"I'd say you come along just about the right time," I said.

"Let's see if we can get you sittin' up," Rogan said, "I want to take a look at your head."

He put his arm behind my shoulder, and I managed to sit up. My stomach offered to climb out my mouth again, but after a few minutes I was feelin' better.

"I'll heat some water and clean you up a little. See if you can sit by yourself."

He took his arm away, and I wobbled a bit but stayed up-right. He busied himself with makin' a fire and heatin' water in a skillet he'd took out of his saddlebags.

He bathed my head, and then had me shuck my shirt. When I pulled my shirt out of my pants, the leather bag I'd found in the little stone cabin fell to the ground. Rogan picked it up and handed it to me. I'd actually forgot I had it in my shirt, and I surely didn't feel like fightin' the tie string, so I handed back to Rogan. "You open it. I found it up on the mountain," I said. He fought the tie string and finally cut it with his belt knife. He dropped to his knees beside me and spilled the coins out. They was gold and silver and rough-stamped with the heads of men with some kinda headbands the like of I'd never seen.

"Well, I'll be darned," Rogan said. "They look to be Roman or Greek," he said. "We got some in our family that been handed down for four or five generations. Where'd you find 'em?"

I told him the story, and I did it short and sweet. I wasn't feelin' up to any long stories.

"Makes a man wonder how they come to be there," he said, and I had to agree. It made a man wonder how they got to be there, and if there was any more about. He tied the little bag tight and put it in one of my saddlebags. He walked over to the creek and washed my shirt out. I still hadn't got to my feet, and I had a feelin' if I tried it was gonna be somethin' ugly.

I got my shirt back on, and Rogan threw my bedroll down beside me.

"I'm gonna bury Dee, and you're in no shape to travel anyhow. We might as well stay here tonight."

"I got to meet up with a man at a lake a couple of days south of here," I said. "He's gonna be waitin' on me."

"You couldn't stay in the saddle tonight, Matt. You wouldn't make it an hour. We'll try to move in the morning."

I didn't have it in me to argue, and I knew he was right. He spread out my bedroll, and I crawled in. I was feelin' mighty puny.

Next thing I knew there was sunlight on my face and the smell of fresh brewed coffee comin' from the pot by the fire.

"That black of yours is a handful," Rogan said. "I finally got him on a picket, but we had us quite a tussle before I got it done."

"I'm sorry, Rogan," I said. "I hardly ever let anybody else take care of my horses, and I meant to tell you Sin would be fine without bein' hobbled or put on a line. He usually won't go a quarter mile from me, and he comes to a whistle."

"I've heard of horses like that, but never owned one myself."

"I don't really own him," I replied. "He just lets me keep him company." I had a couple of cups of coffee and a cold biscuit Rogan had fished out of his grub sack. I was still seein' two of everything, and if I moved around much my stomach still tried to come up for a visit. I managed to stand and wobble off into the trees. When I came back, I was feelin' a little better.

"You up to riding?" Rogan asked.

"I got to," I replied. "I got to meet a man south of here. He'll be lookin' for me."

I held Sin by his bridle while Rogan threw the saddle on him. In a quarter hour we were workin' our way towards the ridge. It was a nightmare. Sin was an easy ridin' horse, but I was in a haze and near fell out of the saddle three or four times. We hit the top of the ridge, found the Injun trail without much trouble, and headed south. I was mighty sick, but I had a place to be, and some money to deliver.

Along about noon time I noticed there were fresh horse tracks ahead of us on the trail. I didn't reckon there was many folks in this part of the country that were friendly to the O'Malleys, and I made mention of it to Rogan. We rode loose in the saddle with our rifles in our hands.

As night closed in I knew I was near done up. I'd hoped we might be able to eat a bite of supper, and then go on by moonlight, but I could barely stay in the saddle.

Rogan could see the sickness on me and helped me down.

"I'm mighty shamed," I said as he eased me down. "A man shouldn't have help gettin' down from his horse."

"You got that right," Rogan agreed. "Good thing we're relations. I can't tell anybody about you bein' helpless without it reflectin' on me," he said with a smile.

I sat down with my back up against a wind-blown pine while Rogan did for the stock. He handed me a piece of jerky and the canteen from my saddle.

"Your dog is keepin' his face to the wind," he said. "I'd say he's caught scent of some of the boys huntin' you. We best make a cold camp and stay well off the trail."

"I got to hole up for a spell," I said. I couldn't believe what was comin' out of my mouth. "I ain't feelin' fit."

"Yeah, well you think you don't feel good, you ought to look at you," Rogan said encouragingly.

"Maybe you ought to go on ahead while I rest a mite," I suggested. "I'm supposed to meet Dan'l Potts south of here near a lake."

"So that was Ol' Potts you was with. I figured him for dead by now," Rogan said.

"He was purty lively the last time I saw him," I replied. "You witnessed the little dispute we had with those gents at

Sleepy Cat. Dan'l thought it wise we split up. We planned on meetin' at the lake."

"You're in no shape to ride," Rogan agreed. "Might be best if I get Dan'l and bring him back with me." He looked off toward the tops of the mountains and then down at me. "Draw me a map and I'll head out. There'll be a moon tonight, and I can make good time."

I smoothed out a spot on the ground next to where I was layin' and drew him a quick map. It wasn't much, but I figured Rogan for a savvy man, and it don't take much of a map for a man that knows wild country. 'Sides I just wasn't up to makin' a better one. The world seemed to be drawin' in on me. I was a lot sicker than I let Rogan know.

"I can find that," he said. "You sure you're gonna be . . ."

"I just need some sleep," I said, cutting him off. "You fetch Dan'l, and by the time you get back I'll be able to ride."

Rogan stirred up some supper in his old skillet, but I wasn't up to eatin'. I was kinda driftin' in and out, and I was cold.

Rogan woke me as he saddled his horse. "I'm headin' out, Matt. Come mornin' you'd best find a spot to hunker down and wait 'til I get back."

"I'll do fine," I managed to croak. Rogan looked worried.

He left me an extra blanket and some edibles where I could lay a hand to 'em. My canteen was on my saddle under my head.

"I'll make it as fast as I can, Matt. You hang in there."

I nodded, and he was gone. I laid my head back on my saddle and drifted out again. I was woke by Buck givin' out a low growl. The fire was gone, but the moon was up over the trees, and I could see the trail lookin' like a silver ribbon as it climbed the side of the mountain. Our camp was off the trail a ways in a small meadow, but not at all hidden. If someone unfriendly come up on me, this would surely be where my float stick got sunk. I drifted out, and when my eyes come open again the sun was just comin' up.

I tried to stand and couldn't make it. My head was light

feelin' and the world kept goin' 'round under my feet. I got to my knees and grabbed my canteen. I took a deep drag of water, sat down next to my saddle, and tried to eat a piece of jerky. I couldn't seem to get it down. Every time I tried to swaller, my throat would knot up and I'd near choke. I finally gave it to Buck, which he was grateful for. I crawled over to where my roan was picketed and moved his pin a ways so he could get at some new grass. I realized the little meadow was cut deep by a small creek that come down off the mountain. The bank was more of a cliff than a slope and dropped down maybe twenty feet. I crawled over to the edge and looked down. There was water and it looked like there might even be some beaver works. I looked around for Sin and saw he was just at the edge of the clearing with his ears up lookin' back toward the trail. It took me a minute to figure what he was doin'. I had company.

I followed his gaze and saw maybe twenty men on line comin' toward me with Bull Burdett leadin' 'em. I shoved Buck over the edge of the creek and watched him scramble and tumble down. No use of him dyin' with me. I jerked the Henry from the boot and took a shot at Burdett. I missed him, but took the man beside him out of the saddle. The world was full of sound, and I realized I was shootin' as fast as I could work the lever on my rifle. I felt a bullet hit me, then another. I fell.

I was in the creek, which was runnin' fast and deeper than it'd looked from the top. I was floatin' down and didn't have the strength to do more try and keep my nose up in the air. I heard some yellin' and there was bullets pokin' the water around me. I hit my head on a rock right where the bullet gouge was, and the world got narrow and black. I floated for what seemed like a couple of days, and them above must've lost sight of me 'cause there was no more shots. Only thing that kept me floatin' was everytime I sunk I took in a bunch of water and choked 'til I was nearly awake again. I drifted around a long bend in the creek and pulled myself up on a narrow sand beach. I heard Buck whine beside me, which was a comfort, and I went out.

When the cold brought me around, I was shakin' like a leaf in a twister, and I couldn't feel my legs which was still in the water. I crawled a few feet, took in some air, and dragged a ways further. Buck come up to me and licked my face. I tried to fight him off, but just didn't have it in me. The moon either hadn't come up yet, or it was cloudy. It was as dark as the inside of a cave. I crawled over to where the creek bank give way to the cliff face and lay up against it out of the breeze that was comin' down the mountain. I felt around my body and found a new bullet hole gouged out of my side. I found another one punched through my thigh. My leg didn't seem to be broke, but I was in serious trouble. To make things worse, it started to rain. It was light at first, and then really started to come down. I was already wet, but the rain was as cold as ice. I crawled along the face of the cliff, hopin' for a cave or even a washout. I found a hole. It wasn't big. Barely wide enough for me to get my shoulders in, but after I'd crawled in the length of my body, it widened out a little. I crawled until I just couldn't move no more. I stopped in a spot wider than the tunnel had been and had grass or somethin' bunched in it. Buck come in after me, and it was surely a tight fit with both of us. I was gettin' warmer. I figured we'd found us an old beaver bank den. I also figured that when I died in here nobody was ever gonna find me.

Chapter Twenty

"He's overdue, and it ain't like Matthew," Tirley said quietly. "I've given him two days past what I figured the trip would take at the outside."

"Matt's handy, but there's a passel of folks huntin' him," Stoney observed.

"I vote we go find him," Rosebud Charlie said.

The fire popped and a drop of coffee boiled from the spout of the coffeepot, sizzling loudly. Tirley looked around at the men standing with him. Their numbers had grown by six with the men his nephew Rogan had sent up to the camp, but they were still too few.

"Someone comin'," Lyle Hansen said from the darkness. " 'Bout a half mile down the trail."

"Can you tell if they be friend or foe?" Tirley asked.

"Can't tell, but we don't have many friends hereabouts."

Marshal Joe Bush stood up, took his shotgun in his hand, and slid into the darkness.

"We'll leave the fire up, and Tom and me will wait in the light. The rest of you can cover us from the trees," Tirley directed.

The other men disappeared, and Tirley slowly stood. He took his old Hawken in his hand and loosened his tomahawk in his belt. Tom took the thong off the hammer of his revolver and made sure it slid easily from the holster. Twenty minutes later a quiet voice called from the darkness.

"Pa, can we come in?" Mike O'Malley's voice came from the dark.

Tirley gave a sigh of relief and waved the men in. Riding with Mike were Wedge and Owen.

"Good to see you," Tirley said as the riders dismounted.

"We got tired of waiting." Owen said. "We didn't figure you boys could handle this without us."

"There might be more truth in that than you know," Lyle Hansen observed as the rest of the men came out of the darkness around the camp. "We're surely up against it. They got us outnumbered by about double."

"Well, Wedge evens that up by himself," Mike observed.

There were a few quiet chuckles and the new arrivals began to unsaddle their horses.

"How'd you find us?" Tirley asked Owen.

"A mail rider came to the ranch and told us the fight was coming soon," Owen replied. "He also gave us directions to a ladies' cabin by the name of Frone. She told us how to find you."

"We'd best get some sleep," Tirley said, after they were all gathered back around the fire. "We're gonna go find Matthew come first light." He was quiet a moment and then looked over at Stoney. "You want to ride down to town with me?" Tirley asked him. "I'd like to see Frone before we head up-country." Stoney didn't answer, but he started gathering what he'd need for the ride. Tirley smiled and turned away from the fire. Stoney grumbled some but he was rock solid, as always.

Tirley moved to saddle his pony and pulled up short as he heard the sound of pounding hooves on the trail. A moment later Frone and Lee came riding into camp in a swirl of dust. Lee slid from her horse and looked at the men around the fire.

"Sam says one of Burdett's men came into the store bragging they'd killed Matt," she said. Her bottom lip began to quiver.

"The man's name is Raskin, and he told Sam they'd come across Matthew by accident as they was comin' back to town. He said the last they seen him he was floatin' down a creek with holes all over in him," Frone added.

Tirley stepped into the firelight and looked at Stoney, then over to Marshal Joe Bush.

"Joe, maybe it'd be best if you took these ladies back to Frone's cabin. Might be good if you stayed with 'em. Burdett and his gang are gonna be feeling their oats, and things might get out of hand.

"That, and it might be best if I don't see what you do to Raskin," Joe said. Tirley didn't reply, and Joe went to get his horse from the picket.

Tirley turned back to Frone. "Any idea where this Raskin is hangin' out?"

"Sam said Raskin come in ahead of the main gang so he could make his brag to the boys that'd stayed in town. Last he saw him he was over at the saloon. He said you'd know him 'cause he was wearin' a Union Calvary hat sideways with the brim turned up."

When Joe and the women had gone Tirley looked across the fire again at his old friend, Stoney.

"We go to town and find us a man by the name of Raskin," he said with steel in his voice. "I want to get a line on where this was supposed to happen."

"I doubt if he's gonna want to tell you anything," Lyle observed.

"He may not want to tell us, but I reckon by the time we get done with him we'll know everything he has in his head," Stoney said. Lyle felt a shiver come over him looking at the two old mountain men. He wouldn't want to be in Raskin's shoes for any amount of money.

"I'm goin' with ya," Wedge said to Tirley.

"Okay, but only you. Three's aplenty for this job." He

turned to the rest of his family and friends. "The rest of ya get ready to ride. Soon as we get back we're gonna be foggin' the dust."

"They'd've never got him but for me," Raskin said in a voice too loud. "I've always been good with a gun, but I showed 'em just how good I was. Burdett was impressed. Said he'd make me his second-in-command when this is all over."

Raskin had taken three too many drinks, and no one in the saloon was listening to him anymore. He was drunk and obviously lying. He took one last slug of rye from his shot glass, looked around at the men in the saloon, and slapped his dirty calvary hat on his head. He stepped away from the bar, staggered, caught himself, and headed for the door. He stopped a moment before he went out and looked back over his shoulder. He shrugged and pushed the door open. The air was cool and pungent with the smell of freshly sawn pine. Raskin turned down the newly constructed boardwalk and walked toward the tent at the end of the street where he'd thrown his bedroll earlier in the evening. He knew he was going to have to leave town before Burdett got in. He'd made his brag, and Burdett would surely call him on it. He was sick of it anyhow. He had a bad feeling and there had to be an easier way to make a buck.

He stepped off the walk as he came to a gap between the clapboard buildings and heard a noise in the darkness to his right. He started to turn, but before he could react, he was on his face in the dirt with the air kicked out of him.

"You be real quiet, Mister Raskin, and you might live to see the sun come up," a gravelly voice said in his ear. Raskin started to move and felt a knife press against his throat.

"I'd as soon cut your throat as look at ya," a different voice said quietly. Raskin believed him.

"What say you get to your feet and walk with us a little ways," the first voice said.

Raskin rose shakily and realized he still had his gun on his hip. For a second he was tempted to grab it and try to fight his way free, and then instantly he knew better. He'd be dead before he cleared leather.

The two men walked him quickly to the edge of town behind a big livery barn. There was a small fire burnin', and a man bigger than any Raskin had ever seen was standing close by. He looked at the two men who had captured him and swallowed. If ever he'd seen two men that had been over the hill and seen the varmint, it was these two.

"Mister Raskin," one of the old men said to him, "Matthew O'Malley is my boy, and I'd surely 'preciate ya tellin' me what happened up in the hills today."

"I ain't gonna tell ya . . ."

His air was suddenly shut off along with his voice. The giant man had moved faster than Raskin would have ever dreamed and had his monster hand clamped around his throat.

"Mister, these two men are Christians and believe in lovin' their neighbors and such. Me, I'm a heathen. If you don't answer their questions, you're surely gonna get me riled up, and then I'm gonna start rippin' pieces off you and throwin' 'em in the fire. You understand?"

Raskin tried to nod his head, but the big man had too tight of a hold on his neck. He was startin' to see little stars as his air ran out. As quickly as he'd been grabbed, he was turned loose, and he sucked in a giant gulp of air. He bent over and placed his hands on his thighs, coughing and choking. He slowly straightened and looked at the three men in front of him. He was suddenly sober and scared. If he wasn't careful, his cold carcass was going to be found by the liveryman behind the barn in the morning.

"I didn't do none of the shootin'," he said in a rush. "We was headin' back to town. Your boy had shot us up some, and we had a couple of guys ridin' double. We come on him by accident at Big Piney Creek, 'bout a mile east of where it breaks out of the mountains."

Raskin told his story in five short minutes and was panting when he'd finished.

"You think my boy was dead?" Tirley asked quietly.

"He looked it to me," Raskin said.

"Let's ride," Tirley said to the other two.

"What about me?" Raskin asked.

"You do what you want," Wedge said, "but I can tell you this, I ever see you again I'm gonna tear ya in little pieces, and I'm gonna do it slow so you can appreciate it." Raskin felt the blood drain out of his face. The three strangers, one of whom was surely an O'Malley, left the light of the fire and a few minutes later he heard the sound of pounding hooves.

Raskin backed slowly away from the fire. If the three men he'd just met were any measure of the men gathered around the O'Malleys, then Burdett would need at least a hundred more than he had. Raskin was certain about one thing. He could hear California callin' his name, and he was headin' west as soon as he could get his horse saddled and his gear loaded. He wasn't gonna say a word to a single soul. He was just gonna ride.

The sun was just shedding light on the tips of the mountains when Tirley and his men rode up to the lake.

"We got to let the horses blow," Tirley said. "We'll have breakfast and get back on the trail." He stepped out of the saddle and loosened the cinch. He took note of the foam on his horse's flanks and knew they were going to have to slow down. He threw the reins up on the saddle and gave the animal a pat on the rump. The gelding immediately waded knee-deep in the lake and took a drink. They let the horses drink a little and then moved them away from the lake. Too much water too fast would ruin a hot horse. Lyle already had the coffeepot on, and Owen was shaving bacon into the big skillet. Wedge and Tom O'Malley had moved to the hillside to keep watch. There wasn't any of the easy banter usually heard around a breakfast fire.

They heard a short whistle from where Wedge had disappeared into the trees. Everyone laid a hand to their guns and a couple lay down behind some of the fallen trees. Tirley looked around and then took one of the pistols from his waist.

"This is as good a place as any for a fight. Fact, I'm ready for it." His voice was tight.

They saw two riders come down out of the trees a couple of hundred yards north. They stopped, and Tirley could see they had rifles across their saddles. They were looking for trouble.

"Owen, you and Lyle got the two fastest horses. If they break and run, you boys fetch 'em. I don't want 'em gettin' back to Burdett. I'd as soon put this fight off until we find Matt."

Suddenly, the two riders made up their minds and slowly began to make their way toward the fire.

"I know the one," Stoney said. "It's Dan'l Potts. I can tell the way he sits his saddle. He rides like he's got a hind-end full of cactus spines."

"I never knowed him to ride with polecats," Tirley remarked.

"Seems to me he owes you fer pullin' his biscuits out of the fire back a few years ago," Stoney said, lookin' at Tirley.

"Depends on how you look at it," Tirley said. "If I'd've made up my mind to charge them Injuns a minute or two quicker, Dan'l would still have his hair."

"The other one is Rogan," Kelly said. "That's his horse." Kelly gave a loud whistle, and the two riders kicked their horses into a trot. In a few minutes they pulled up and stepped down.

"You boys is a sight fer sore eyes," Dan'l said. "Rogan says Matt's been wounded and is hid up on Big Piney Creek. Rogan came fer me, and we was just headin' back to get him."

"They found him," Tirley said simply. "One of Burdett's gang says Matt's gone under. We was just gonna go find him." There was silence for a moment.

"I should never have left him," Rogan said in a quiet voice. "I wasn't goin' to, but he made a case for roundin' up Dan'l and then comin' back for him. He had a bullet crease alongside his head and couldn't sit his horse without fallin' off."

"How'd he get creased?" Tirley asked.

"Skinner," Rogan said. "I did fer him," he added simply.

"You boys might as well light and sit," Tirley said. "We got to rest the horses and get some food into us, then we'll go fetch Matthew."

Tirley watched Rogan. He was the image of his father, one of Tirley's brothers, Chagrin. Chag had been the meanest of the brothers, and rumor was he'd been an outlaw on the Texas border before there was a border. When Stephen Austin had gotten permission from Mexico to locate families in Texas, he'd recruited Chagrin to head up the newly-formed Rangers. He'd rode with them on and off for nearly thirty years.

"Yonder is Owen, and next to him is Mike," Tirley told Rogan. "They be your cousins, my boys. Up on the hill is Tom. He's one of John's boys."

"This is the most O'Malleys I've ever seen in one spot," Rogan said, looking around. "There's more cousins in East Texas I met a time or two, but they're the only ones I ever spent any time with."

"We six brothers weren't much on family reunions," Tirley acknowledged. "I was took by the Injuns when I was just a pup, and I guess I just never got straight with the family again after."

"Yeah, Pa told me," Rogan said simply.

"I was sorry about Chagrin," Tirley said. "He come up and helped me out of a spot of trouble on the Missouri one time."

"And you came to south Texas and you and Pa took on near the whole Comanche tribe, or so he told me."

"I don't know how big the Comanche tribe was, but there was fewer of 'em time we got done," Tirley replied.

Owen started dishing up breakfast and silence fell again.

Rogan looked up from his plate at his uncle and his cousins.

"Pa had some regrets in his life, and one of 'em was that we'd never kept touch with the rest of the family. I promised him I'd try to do better. I just wish it was under better conditions."

"I can't imagine a time when we'd need you more," Owen offered. "We're glad you and your men are here."

"Does seem like trouble brings the O'Malley clan together," Rogan agreed. "I just hope Raskin was wrong about Matthew."

"That makes all of us," Tirley said.

Chapter Twenty-one

I needed water. I was dyin' of thirst, and I was hot. I'd never been hotter in my whole life. I opened my eyes and it was dark. Not completely dark. There was a little light comin' from over my head. What had happened come back to me a little at a time. I tried to roll over but the beaver den was too small where I lay. I scooted forward where the den both widened and got taller. The pain was bad. Near the worst I'd ever known, and I was weaker than a newborn puppy. I groaned, laid my head down on my forearms, then struggled to finally sit up. It was dark but enough light came through a little hole above that I could make out what was around me. I was sittin' on a thick bed of grass and small twigs and there was blood on the grass. My blood.

I heard a noise back down the tunnel and reached for my colt. The one in the holster was gone, but the one in my belt, Wheeler's belt, was still there. Would it still shoot? I'd been in the water. The powder might have gotten wet. I pulled it anyhow and looked down the black tunnel.

Whatever was comin' up the tunnel wasn't a person. I was surely feelin' puny and didn't figure I could outfight the beaver if he objected to me bein' in his house. But it wasn't the beaver; it was Buck, and he had a rabbit in his mouth. I hugged him and then felt sick. I needed water. I needed food. I needed to heal, and I was gettin' mad. I'd been chased, shot, near drown, and run into a beaver den. The anger was comin' on me, but I was in no shape to fight. Not yet.

"You stay, Buck," I said to him in a quiet voice. I faced down the tunnel and started crawlin', pullin' myself with my elbows and helpin' some with my knees. The light got stronger and suddenly I popped out of the mouth of the den. On fast runnin' creeks beaver mostly dug their dens in the banks. The current was too strong for a regular beaver house to stay standin'. It was my good luck that some beaver had decided that this was the best spot to build his house. Fact was, I figured there'd probably been many generations of beaver used the den from the size of the tunnel, although I was surprised there was any beaver that'd escaped Pa and the rest of the trappers. Each beaver family had remade it, water had washed in, and over time it had gotten just big enough for me. I slid out slowly, blinkin' my eyes against the light. I held still a minute, then looked around. I could see a jay up in a pine tree, and another across the way. That was a good sign. Jays were curious, and if there was anybody about, they'd get mighty noisy scoldin' the trespasser.

I took a drink. A long drink. I sat up and almost threw up the water, but managed to hold it down. I let it settle and took another long drink. The water was so cold it hurt my teeth. I sat back and checked myself over. I was skinned, scratched, bruised, and had holes punched in me. I was alive, but I was almighty sick. I drank again and then backed toward the opening to the den. I looked at the sign I'd left. There were no footprints and I reckoned the scuff marks would be taken for the beaver. I crawled up the narrow tunnel, and Buck whined when I got back to the main den. I lay down and either passed out or slept. I woke up and the point of light over my head was gone. I slept again, and when I woke, the weak light was back. Buck was beside me and his ears were up. I reached my hand out to him to keep him quiet. I felt safe here, and I needed time. I slept again. I woke and it was darker than the inside of a black cat. Back to sleep, and when I stirred again, I was thirsty and hungry, which I took for a good sign. The light was back again, and Buck was layin' on his belly watchin' me.

I had some matches I'd dipped in beeswax not long after I'd near froze to death the past winter. I always carried them in an inside pocket of my pants. I needed a fire both to see by and to maybe cook some rabbit if Buck had left me any. I scraped some of the dry grass into a little pile and with considerable pain rolled onto my side. I pulled out one of the matches. The wax had worn off and there was nothing left on the stick. I got another out and it was the same. I was feelin' like givin' up. There just wasn't much goin' my way. I pulled out the rest of the matches and saw that two of them still had the lucifer stuff on the end. I found a small sandstone rock and struck a match across the face. It sparked, smoked a little, but didn't light. I was down to my last match. I struck it fast expecting the worst. My luck changed and it lit with a bright flare that hurt my eyes. I touched it to the grass, which quickly took. I added a few sticks and watched the smoke drift up toward the light above. I had a natural draft and the smoke, what little there was, swirled up and out. I couldn't build much of a fire 'cause I couldn't chance that the smoke would be seen or smelled by my enemies.

As the fire brightened I could see there were the remains of at least three rabbits and a squirrel layin' close about. Buck proved he could take care of himself, and maybe me too. I skinned the rabbit and seared it over the little fire. It wasn't cooked completely, but it was enough. I didn't care much about the dog spit. I just ate it. Buck watched me, and I shared the last few bites. It seemed the least I could do. I did what was left of the squirrel the same way, then I crawled down the tunnel, looked around, and took a long drink of creek water.

It was late afternoon, and as I glanced around I saw something that chilled my blood. There were fresh horse tracks across the creek from me. I drew the pistol, and looked up the bank. There was nothin' I could see, but I could tell they was fresh. I crawled back into my little den and scattered the fire. I had to keep a few coals 'cause I was out of matches, but I couldn't have the smoke.

It was warm in the den, and purty soon my head was noddin' up and down. I blew the fire to life again and then let it die down. I slept, started the fire, slept, and started the fire. I did that all night. I didn't dare let Buck out to hunt, and the remaining meat had gone bad. I was hungry, but feeling better. I'd no idea how long I'd been in the hideout, but it seemed like days. My stomach surely thought so. I had to move. I was still sore, but my wounds were scabbed over, and I was feelin' better. The hole in my thigh leaked a little blood now and again, but I was careful of it. I didn't want to break it open. The gouge out of my side was still sore and full of fire, and my head wound hurt like blazes. I wasn't well, but I was better, and I had to move. I knew if Pa wasn't lookin' for me yet, he soon would be, and he might walk right into a trap.

I made sure my one remaining short-gun was stuck down in the holster and the thong was over the hammer. I had no faith that they would touch off if I pulled the trigger. I started to slide down the tunnel and told Buck to follow me out. He 'bout ran over me. I come out into the bright daylight and lay quiet a minute waiting for my eyes to focus, then looked around. No jays, and it was quiet. Too quiet for mid-afternoon. The forest and creek always had activity from the creatures that lived there, and they all made their own small noises. The only reason they quit was if there was hunters about, either two-legged or four-legged. The way my luck was runnin' I figured on the two-legged, and they was surely huntin' me. Burdett wouldn't be happy 'til he saw the dirt of my grave splatter on my face.

I crawled slow up the steep bank with Buck close beside me. I peeped over the edge, and the first thing I saw was my blue roan horse on a short picket line. My saddle was on the ground close to a small fire, and there were two men layin' not thirty yards from me.

"I cain't believe that Burdett left us out here," the man closest to me said. He had his hat off and half of his head was bald. He also had my Henry layin' close beside him. I was surely glad to see my rifle. I sat store by it since it'd been given me by a man I greatly respected who was now gone.

"I hear ya," the second man agreed. "I had my mouth all set for some of that snake poison they call whiskey in town." He had red hair, a red face, and a broad red nose.

Baldy scratched an armpit and turned his head toward the fire and spit. "I surely like to catch that black horse the O'Malley kid was ridin'. That's the finest horse I ever seen."

"Burdett says the kid ain't dead 'til we find the body, and we ain't 'sposed to go to town 'til we find him," Red said.

" 'Tween you and me, I'd as soon be right here in this purty spot. Burdett has took to runnin' the gang like an army, and I run away from the army once just 'cause I didn't like takin' orders," Baldy said.

"The food ain't bad," Red commented, "and they left us plenty."

Well, there they were. My horse, my saddle, my coffeepot on the fire, my skillet beside the rocks that made the fire circle. My whole outfit was right there in front of me, and somewhere not too far away my Sin horse was lookin' for me.

It made me a little indignant. Fact, I was startin' to feel a fire way down in my gut. I'd surely been abused as much as one man could take.

I took the thong off my six-gun and stood up. I started walkin' toward 'em with Buck right beside me. I reckoned he was just as mad as I was 'cause he was growlin' somethin' fierce.

The thing was they just didn't expect it. They knew I was dead. They were out here on holiday. I don't think it was me standin' that drew their attention. I think it was Buck's growlin'. He had a peculiar way of growlin' that sounded somethin' like a cross between a grizz and a wolverine.

They didn't know what to do they was so shocked.

"You boys have put upon me as much as I can stand," I said, my voice loud as a Sunday preacher with a back row full of sleepers. "I remember Pa readin' to us from the Bible once about a man named Job. He had all kinds of trials put upon him, and I reckon I must nearly match him for trials and tribulations." I knew it sounded crazy, but I didn't care. Their eyes was as big as tin plates and they wasn't movin'. I needed an edge. I needed to be closer.

"I've decided I've let you push me as far as I can. Now it's time to call down the fire upon ya." Red was movin' for his pistol, but Baldy was still starin' at me like I might be Moses. I pulled my Colt and touched her off. Nothin' happened. The first shot was a dud. Buck was movin' past me on a run, and I eared the hammer back and touched it off again. The second cylinder roared, and Red flopped over onto his back. The third shot went off overlappin' the sound of the second, and I saw Red jerk again with the impact. I heard Buck's roar and saw that he had Baldy up and runnin'. Baldy had a gut on him I hadn't noticed when he'd been layin' down, so it wasn't much of a chase. Buck caught him, pulled him down, and started worryin' him a mite with his teeth. I let Buck deal with him while I picked up my Henry and checked to see if it was loaded. It was chucked clear full and felt good in my hand. I looked over at Red, but he wasn't seein' me nor nothin' else for that matter. I turned to where Baldy was snivlin' and squealin' while Buck sounded like the hound from hell.

"Buck," I said in a firm voice. The big dog backed off, but it was plain to see that he figured himself for a lion, and Baldy was a Philistine. I dug in my saddlebag and got a new cylinder for my pistol. I shucked the old cylinder out and loaded with fresh. Next I pulled out an old shirt that was clean, but gettin' mighty thin. I made a bandage for my thigh and tied it with some pidgin strings. I was feelin' better all the time.

I walked up to Baldy as he pulled himself up on one elbow. I could see by the look on his face that he was gonna say somethin' nasty, so I kicked him under the chin and he flopped back down. His eyes kinda glazed over, and I put the muzzle of the Henry right against his forehead.

"Mister Baldy," I said, in my best preachin' voice. There'd been occasions like this in the past when I'd been inspired to read to men like Baldy straight from the good book of O'Malley, but I didn't have time right now. "I need the answer to a couple of questions," I said, "and you're gonna answer them true and fast or else I'm gonna let my dog go ahead and work on you."

I surely had his attention. A Henry rifle pressed to his forehead with the hammer eared back on a cartridge had a way of makin' a man repent quick, not to mention the idea of a hell-hound havin' you for a snack.

"How many of you are still out here lookin for me?"

"Ten," he answered without hesitation. "We're spread all up and down the creek. Burdett figured if you was alive, you'd make some tracks sooner or later."

"Where'd you last see my black horse?"

"Over on the other side of the clearin' about an hour ago," He said, pointin' west.

The spot he spoke of wasn't a half mile away and uphill. I leaned back and cut loose a whistle that echoed from the trees and rocks. A minute later Sin come out of the trees on a dead run. Baldy looked amazed.

"A little trick I taught him," I said, with some pride.

"Guard him, Buck," I said to my dog. I'd never told him such a thing before, but he sat right down on his haunches and bared his teeth at Baldy. I darn sure knew the dog was smarter than the man he was guardin'.

I walked over to Sin and checked him out. He had a couple of brush scratches, but otherwise seemed healthy. I rubbed his forelock. And then his neck. He shook hard, throwin' slobbers around, and then tried to give me a love bite. I was just as nearly glad to see him.

My knees were gettin' weak, and I figured I needed to either sit or lay down. I walked over to the fire, picked up the coffeepot, and rinsed out one of the cups with the hot brew. I took a swig, smacked my lips, and looked around for some grub. I'd heard 'em mention they had food. I found it in a flour sack on what I took to be Baldy's saddle, since Dead Red was layin' on the other one. They had cured side meat, some tinned biscuits, canned peaches, and some hard candy. I sat down, opened a can of peaches, and slugged 'em down. I drank some more coffee, all the time keepin' an eye on Buck and Baldy. The man hadn't moved, and neither had the dog.

"Buck," I said, and the big dog looked over at me. "Let's eat," I said, pointin' to the side meat. He got up and trotted over to me. I had my Henry close to hand and dearly hoped that Baldy would try somethin' while I was cookin'. He didn't.

When we was full, I scooted back away from the fire and tried to figure out what I was gonna do next. There was a passel of bandits camped along the creek watchin' for me, and I figured there was plenty more some place or other that wanted me dead. The odds seemed kind of long.

I got some rawhide from my saddlebags and walked over to Baldy.

"I'm gonna tie you up so you can't cause me problems for a spell," I said to him.

"I could die out here," he whined.

"Somebody will stumble on you sooner or later, and you'd better hope it's sooner. There's still some of them big buffalo wolves that run in this country, and they'd love to make a meal of ya." I finished with him and turned back to the fire. I lifted my saddle, careful not to blow any of my wounds open and put it on the roan. I was hopin' he wasn't feelin' like showin' me his stuff. I surely couldn't stay in the saddle if he started actin' up.

I gathered up my truck and got it packed away. I crawled

up in the saddle and the roan just treated me like I was a baby with no fuss at all. I had a notion to go huntin' the boys that were watchin' for me along the creek, but I had places I needed to be. I figured to deal with them later. Sin come up to us, and I decided not to put him on a lead. He'd stay with me. We started movin' south. Slow but steady.

I rode the rest of the daylight, then stopped and built a small fire. I ate the rest of the side meat and biscuits, and took a nap. I woke to the sound of Buck growlin'. The fire had burned down, and it was full dark. I was a ways off the trail, but close enough to hear horses comin' my direction.

"Quiet, Buck," I said. I picked up the Henry and made sure I had the keeper off my pistol. Rage was building on me like a giant thunderstorm, and if they come on me, I was gonna rain all over 'em.

I could see Buck by the starlight and he was actin' funny. His head was cocked off to one side, and his stub of a tail was wigglin'. All of a sudden he cut loose with a bark. Not his battle roar, but a bark. I wasn't sure I'd ever heard him do that before.

"Matthew?"

The voice came from the trail.

"Pa?" I said back. Now I'm a man growed and strong, but when I heard Pa's voice I got to admit I got a plum warm feelin' in my gut, and my eyes kinda got misted up. If ever I needed Pa's help it was now.

They rode up to me and Pa slid from his saddle. He wasn't much for showin' what he was feelin', but he wrapped me up in a bear hug and held on for a few minutes. I didn't fight him, even though it weren't seemly, and after a minute he let me go.

"You alright, boy?" he asked me.

"I'm skinned up some, and got a couple of holes in me, but I'm mendin'," I replied.

"Owen, you want to get a fire goin', and we'll see what's carryin' on with Matt."

They were all there, my family and friends, and it was good to see 'em. Owen got the fire goin' while a man named Lyle Hansen got out a kit and startin' workin' my wounds over, fussin' near as bad as a hen with a fresh-hatched chick.

Rogan and Dan'l come over to me, their faces hard as iron.

"I shouldn't have left you . . ." Rogan started to say, and I stopped him.

"If you'd stayed, we'd have tried to fight and probably both been killed. I managed to get away from 'em, and now we can take the fight to them, only this time we choose the time and the place."

Lyle finished with me, and I changed clothes. I was feelin' some better, but tired. Bone-deep tired.

"Matt's right," Pa said. "Ya can only run from trouble for so long, and then it's gonna catch up with ya. We might as well go and face the trouble and get it over with. 'Sides, there's a young gal back at town that sorely wants to see Matthew."

"Lee?" I asked.

"She's been there for a few days," Pa said. "She's stayin' with Frone, and Marshall Joe Bush is keepin' 'em company." Pa fished in his pocket for a minute and pulled somethin' round and shiny from his pocket. He chucked it to me, and I caught it with my left hand.

"You are hereby appointed as a deputy U.S. Marshal. Joe will swear ya in when we get time. Seems that you got friends in Denver that think you'll make a good lawman."

I pinned the badge to my shirt, picked up the Henry, and walked over to Sin. Mike had switched my saddle over and the roan was on a lead. I looked around at the men and got a lump in my throat. I couldn't ask for better help. I just hoped that when all was said and done we'd all still be alive.

"Let's go," Pa said. "We'll get to town just about nightfall tomorrow night."

We didn't ride hard, but we kept at it steady. We stopped about daylight for an hour. We saw to the horses, had coffee and some biscuits, and some quiet talk. We all knew what was comin' and were a somber group. We pulled up again at noon and took a couple of hours off. We tended the stock and checked our guns over. We were just saddlin' up again when Lyle and Wedge come foggin' into camp from where they'd been on watch.

"We got riders comin' from the north, and there's quite a few of 'em," Wedge said as they pulled up.

"Find some cover," I hollered, "and we'll wait fer 'em to ride up to us."

Pa stood with me as the rest of the guys slid in behind trees and bushes. I eared the hammer back on the Henry and waited. In a few minutes we could hear the horses on the trail as the first riders came into view. They saw Pa and me in the clearing and headed our direction. There looked to be about twenty or so of them, and there was somethin' different about 'em. They didn't look like Burdett's outlaws. Their gear seemed to be in better shape, and they all had at least one extra horse tied to their saddles.

"They be friendly," Pa said. "The one in the front is my brother, Peter. I ain't seen him fer a spell."

The riders pulled up in a cloud of dust, and Uncle Peter stepped down from his horse. His shirt was stiff with dirt and he looked worn out. Fact, they all did.

"Good to see ya, Peter," Pa said in a quiet voice. "Ya got here just in time to lend a hand."

"You too, Tirley. We were afraid we wouldn't get here in time to be of any use. We heard you had a spot of trouble." He stepped down from his horse and looked at me. "This must be one of your boys."

"This is Matthew, and the rest of the boys are back in the trees lookin' down gun barrels at ya," Pa said. He waved and the rest of the fellas came walkin' out of the bushes.

"I came across Trian's boys and their hands as we came

through South Pass. They've been ranchin' in South Dakota, and joined up with us," Peter said, pointing toward the back of the group. "Names are Colin and Conrad."

For a spell we had us quite a family reunion. None of us boys had ever met Pa's brothers, let alone the cousins.

"We need to eat," Peter finally said. "We been riding hard with little sleep and eating only when we stopped to switch saddles."

"We'll build up the fire and stay here the night," Pa said. "We got a job to do, but it can wait 'til mornin'."

There was quite a herd of us. I looked around and my heart swelled. All these men had come together to help family and friends. They was ready to risk gettin' hurt or maybe even killed because they were tied one way or the other to the O'Malley family. It made a fella glad to be a part of it.

Chapter Twenty-two

"Been quite a dry spell in South Texas," Cousin Rogan said. "We decided to head north and find a piece of grass that hadn't been claimed. We had thoughts of Wyoming or maybe Montana."

"Good country up that way," Colin O'Malley said, "but the winters are hard. Man would have to put up a lot of hay for when the snow gets too deep for the cows to reach the grass."

"I've heard that the winters are pretty bad up where you're at," Rogan said.

"Depends, but most times they're long with plenty of wind and snow. That's why we took to raisin' cows and calves instead of steers. We sell the calves off in the late fall for the Kansas boys to fatten up on their excess wheat, and we only have to feed our breeding bulls and the cows through the winter."

"Makes sense, but seems a slow way to make money," Rogan observed.

"It's slower than the meat market, but takes some of the risk out of ranching," Colin said.

"We keep a hundred head or so of fat steers to sell for ready money," Conrad, Colin's younger brother, added. "We seem to always have enough to get by and put a little in the bank."

I was listenin' to the talk which flowed nice and easy around the fire. It didn't seem possible that in just a few hours we was gonna be in a fight for our lives.

"This past winter was a real struggle here in Colorado. I hate to think what it was like up in Montana," Brother Owen said.

"Probably a bad one," Rogan agreed, "but your ranch is right in a basin surrounded by mountains. You're probably always gonna catch it in the winter."

"Well, I reckon it's time to head in," Pa said from over near the timber. "I'd like to catch 'em about sunrise. If I know that pack they'll be sufferin' from drinkin' too much last night, and we need any advantage we can get."

The men moved to their mounts with their saddles. The California and Dakota O'Malleys had caught a little sleep, and we'd all rested and ate. We were as ready as we was gonna get.

A half hour later we was all in the saddle lookin' to Pa for orders.

"Dan, you take Owen, Mike, and the rest of our bunch, plus Rogan and his boys. Come in from the south. If I was you, I'd lay back in the bushes and wait 'til we flush 'em out to you. The rest of us will come in from the north. We'll give you some time to get in place, and then we'll start workin' from buildin' to buildin' to make sure we get 'em all. We don't want to hurt none of the townspeople, but we got to get all the outlaws else they'll shoot us in the back once we're past 'em."

"How're we gonna know when you start the action?" Wedge asked.

"I bet ya good gold money that you'll know when we get started," Pa said, "unless they've all pulled out, which don't seem likely. We'll let them start the shootin', but once it starts we give no quarter. They'll surely kill us if they get the chance. If some of 'em give up, we'll keep 'em safe for Matt's federal marshals." He looked at the men gathered around us in the dim light of the dyin' fire. "Once the fight is done, we'll meet at the saloon and take stock of what's to do next."

What he really meant was we'd take stock of who among us was gonna be planted under the Colorado sod. "It does no good for a man to pack up and run when faced with trouble. You get knocked down, you get up and take the fight again. You get up every time you're knocked down until you win or you're dead," I said mostly to myself.

"What's that, Matt?" Pa asked me.

"I was just considerin' all that's happened since we left the ranch on a simple little trek," I replied. "That, and somethin' you told me back before you went off to the war."

We came in on foot usin' what cover there was. We'd left the horses tied in the woods, knowin' that the work we had to do was best done with our feet on the ground and our guns in our hands. It was still dark, although there was a pink glow startin' to show over the mountains on the east. I could make out the first buildin' on the edge of town and pointed it out to Pa. He nodded and showed it to Peter. We stopped a minute and listened. I could hear an early riser choppin' some cedar wood for the mornin' cook stove, and somewhere else a door slammed.

We were out front with the rest of our bunch spread out not far behind us. We held up for five minutes or so for the light to gather a little more. As we waited, the noises of a town coming awake got louder and more persistent. Dogs started barkin', roosters crowed, and here and there were the sounds of people stirrin'. A man coughed, a woman laughed, and a baby cried. The sounds of life were ahead of us.

I got to the edge of the building and stepped into the street. There was a man standin' in the street gazin' the other direction. From the look of his clothes it was probably one of Burdett's. Buck started growlin', and I saw the man's shoulders hunch at the uncommon sound.

"Mister, I wonder if I could get you to turn around here?" I asked in a reasonable voice.

He turned in a whirl of motion, his hand going to his gun. I drew and shot so fast no one else had a chance to get into action. The first man lay dead on the street of Animas. I started movin' down the street slow, not givin' a thought to my friends behind me. I could feel the dam holdin' me back startin' to crack, and I was startin' to see red and black flashes. The rage was on me, and those that had put upon me and mine was gonna pay. I picked up the pace as I limped closer to the saloon. A man come runnin' from the alley with a rifle in his hand. He started to raise it, and someone from behind me fetched him. I realized suddenly that the shootin' had got to be steady, and there was bullets kickin' dirt around me. I run to the alley the man had came from and kept runnin to get to the back of the saloon. I could hear yellin', shootin', screams, and horses gallopin' down the street. I slid to a stop at the back door of the saloon and walked up to it careful. I knew who I wanted, and I figured he'd be in the saloon. I eased up the back steps and tried the door. It was locked. I leaned on it a little bit and heard the wood around the catch splinter. I leaned a little more and the door gave way, almost dumpin' me on my face. I fell into a room dimly lit by a kerosene lamp. There was no one around, but it looked like the excitement outside might have interrupted an all-night poker game. There were chairs dumped over and cards spread on the floor. I looked careful through the doorway, and there was a dozen men shootin' rifles from the saloon windows and doors back down the street. The noise was somethin' fierce, and the powder smoke was so thick you could almost cut it. Buck was rumblin' in his chest, waitin' for me to give the word, and I was alone against nearly an army.

All of a sudden it didn't make any difference to me if there was a hundred of them, I was surely gonna take it to them. I cut loose with my best Comanche scream, and I imagined I could see the hair come up on the heads of some of the boys in front of me that'd heard Injuns attackin' before. It surely got their attention. About half of them turned toward me, and I let them meet Mr. Henry. I yelled at Buck to take 'em, and I started workin' the lever on my rifle as I scattered empty shells on the plank floor. The battle fever was on me as I saw two men go down and a third fall over with my dog tryin' for his throat. I took a shot at a man that was linin' up on me with a rifle. I missed, but it shook him enough that he missed as well. I levered and realized that the Henry was empty. I dropped the rifle and brought up the Colt. The man had me dead to rights, but just as he lined up on me again, a shot took him through the window from outside and he fell.

I fired at a man who was aimin' at my dog. Buck was mighty busy with the outlaw he'd taken. The man I shot fell to one knee, then jumped back up. I shot him again, and this time the big bullet took him somewheres in the middle. The force of the hit blew him off his feet and back through the big window with a crash of glass and wood. I surely had all of the attention of the men in front of me, and they was all shootin' more or less in my direction. I heard the big mirror over the bar behind me crash to the floor, and the bottles lined up on the shelf were being smashed by the bullets meant for me. I pulled the Smith and Wesson from my belt and slipped the hammer so all six shots sounded like one big roll of thunder. Some of the men were down bleedin', but several of them were still standin' when my gun ran dry. I dropped it to the floor and pulled my big knife from the sheath on my belt. I started runnin' for 'em screamin' like a crazy man and slashin' the air in front of me. I could hear Buck snarlin' and chewin' on a man near the ruined window.

Suddenly, it was like they all decided at the same time to leave. They broke for the door on a dead run, and the shootin' outside picked up considerable as they cleared the batwings. I stopped and looked through the powder smoke at the destruction I'd brought down in only a few seconds. I picked up the Smith, broke it open, and ejected the spent shells. I shoved in six fresh bullets from my pocket and stuck the pistol back in my belt. I shoved a new cylinder in the Colt and picked up my Henry. There was seven or eight men layin' on the floor, and they was all bleedin' onto the packed dirt. One thing was startin' to come through to me. Burdett hadn't been amongst the men in the saloon.

"Buck," I yelled, and the big dog backed off the guy he was worryin'. I walked over to the man and realized that a dog can do considerable damage to a fella if he's given the proper motivation.

"Name?" I asked him.

He rolled over on his back and looked up at me. His hands and forearms was chewed, and he had blood on his face where Buck had bitten through his cheek.

"Villoria," he said in a voice that broke.

"Stand up," I said to him.

He tried to stand, nearly fell, and then made it to his feet.

"Where's Burdett?" I asked him.

"He said he had business with a woman up at the end of the street. Left just before the shootin' started. Somethin' about she owed him money."

"Which buildin'?" I asked.

"The hotel," he replied. He looked from me over to my dog. "I surely don't want to have that dog jump me again."

"You stand real quiet and don't show me no disrespect, and I reckon he'll leave you be."

I was stuffin' shells into my Henry and listenin' to the fight goin' on outside, which was movin' up the street away from the saloon.

"Step over toward the door," I told the man.

I knew I couldn't keep track of him and find Burdett. "You're under arrest for violation of federal law," I said pointin' at my new badge on my shirt. "You go out that door careful-like and sit in one of the chairs on the porch until I get back to take care of ya." I stopped a minute and looked at him. "Mister Villoria, if you ain't here when I get back,

I'm gonna hunt you 'til I find you if it takes me the rest of my life and yours. You understand?"

"Yes sir, Marshal, I surely do, and I'll be sittin' right here."

I truly liked the sound of him callin' me Marshal. It felt natural.

"Another thing," I said, "just a caution. As long as you sit real still, you probably gonna be fine, but if you get up and start stirrin' around, the chances of ya gettin' out of town are mighty slim. There's a number of us O'Malleys around town, and mostly we been shootin' before we ask who ya are."

"I'm gonna sit right in that chair 'til you come for me," he said. He sounded like he'd just reformed and found religion.

"Let's go, Buck," I said and walked onto the street. The shootin' had died down close about, but there was quite a war goin' on at the south end of town. I had to admit that I was more than a little jumpy, and I wasn't sure which buildin' was the hotel. There hadn't been a hotel in Animas when I'd last walked the street.

I moved north on the narrow dirt street and watched the tents and clapboard building fronts careful. There was likely still some of Burdett's people about. I got about halfway down the length of the street when I spotted a two-story raw-pine buildin' on the right hand side with a fresh painted sign that said HOTEL. It was the only two-story in town, and it was brand new.

I turned sudden-like to make for the side of the street, feelin' more than a little exposed. I was still a half block away from the hotel. The quick move saved me as a bullet whipped by my face. I heard the sound of the shot and began to run. I made the cover of a store porch just as a bullet cut a chip from a supportin' post next to me.

Buck beat me to the porch and was behind me, growlin' deep in his guts like he knew who we were after. I looked out from under the porch roof, but couldn't see anyone up the street. Whoever had the rifle was well under cover. I was stuck where I was 'till I figured out where the shooter was. I took a half step out and saw movement in one of the tents up the street. I was tempted to take a shot but I had friends in town, and I had no idea where they were. I took another full step out, and I saw the rifle come up from behind the canvas flap. I shot the Henry from the hip and put the bullet into the tent pole right in front of the rifle barrel and followed with a quick second shot. The rifle fell to the ground and a man went runnin' out the back of the tent. I snapped a shot and must have gotten close 'cause he picked up considerable speed. I probably could've killed him, but I never been one for shootin' a man in the back. I watched him disappear down the alley, and then headed for the hotel. I'd just about made the front door when I heard a woman scream from somewhere inside the building. I kicked the door open and ran inside. There was no one in the lobby, but I could hear the sounds of a struggle comin' from upstairs, and I could hear Burdett yellin' and swearin'. He had to know that things were comin' unraveled, and I was surprised he was even still in town. I started to move toward the stairs and realized that my dog hadn't come in the building with me. I stopped a minute and looked around. I figured Buck could probably take care of himself, but I felt kinda lonesome without him. I moved forward again. I was gonna finish what I started way back on the Main Street in Del Norte.

"It's started," Frone said as the sound of shots echoed from the hills.

Lee picked up a rifle from beside the door and grabbed the latch.

"Where you goin', girl?" Frone asked.

"I have to go down there," Lee replied. "Matt will need help."

"Lee, that's no place for us to be," Frone said. "There's gonna be blood in the streets."

"That's exactly why we have to be there. They need us."

"Wait a minute," Frone said. "We may have need for some

bandage stuff when we get down there." Frone went into the kitchen as Laura Beck came from the back bedroom and Marshal Bush came running in from outside. Joe grabbed his gunbelt, slung it around his hips, and clapped his hat on his head. He grabbed up his shotgun and went back out the front door at a run without a word. Frone came from the kitchen with a number of freshly laundered flour sacks and grabbed her rifle. "I 'spect these will work as well as anything," she said and put her beat-up old hat on.

"If you'll trust me, I'd like to go with you," Laura said. "It's my family that caused this. I feel like I need to help if I can."

"Come on then," Frone said. "I expect Lee's right. Those boys down there are gonna need our help, one way or 'nother."

The women hurried out of the cabin toward town, leaving the little house ghostly silent.

I took the stairs two at a time as the woman's screams became more piercing. I entered the upper hall and started down it. Another long scream rang out from behind a closed door, and I took the door off the hinges when I hit it. Burdett was standin' across the room with his hand drawn back to hit a middle-aged woman he'd crowded into a corner. He twisted around to meet me as I ran toward him. I hit him with my whole body as hard as I could and drove him against the wall with enough force to break the window five feet from us. I'd dropped my Henry when I'd hit the door, and I didn't have the time to draw one of my pistols. I knew I had to get the upper hand with Burdett quickly because I couldn't survive another beatin' like I'd taken before. I hit him in the face, knockin' his head against the wall, and then hit him twice again. He pushed me away and nearly fell. I moved in on him and took a rock-hard fist in the chest as he recovered. I moved away from him and took a quick peek at the woman in the corner. Her intense look of hatred leveled at me took me by surprise, and I lost my advantage with Burdett. He hit me in the jaw, and I went down hard. I reached down for the Smith in my belt as he drew a knife from a sheath in his boot. He saw my pistol coming level and knew I had him. He threw the knife just as I pulled the trigger. I missed him as I dodged the knife, and he jumped from the broken window to the porch roof just below. I ran to the window as he dangled over the edge of the roof, hangin' for a few seconds before he dropped to the street. I snapped a shot just as he dropped and thought I might have scored. I had to get him. I ran from the room, down the stairs, and out the front door with my Smith and Wesson leading the way. I saw him runnin' toward the alley at the far side of the hotel with blood on his shoulder. I ran after him, but stopped at the corner of the buildin' and took a look. A bullet clipped past my face, and I ducked back. I took a blind shot down the alley and took another look. Burdett was just disappearing behind the back of the hotel. I turned and ran back across the front and then down the other side of the hotel, tryin' to flank Burdett. I looked around the back corner and saw him standing by the privy maybe fifty feet away, waiting for me to show, and he had a Colt in his hand. I'd just brought my Smith up to try a shot when I caught a flash of rust-colored fur come flashin' around the opposite side of the buildin'.

It was Buck, and he was locked in on Burdett. I moved enough to catch Burdett's attention, hopin' he wouldn't see Buck, and the big outlaw raised his pistol my direction. When Buck slammed into him, I could hear the thump clear over where I was, and it knocked Bull off his feet. Buck was snarlin' and rippin' like I'd never seen him do before, and I could see Bull had dropped the pistol when Buck hit him. Burdett managed to throw Buck off and stagger to his feet. His face was covered with blood, and he had a big gash on his neck that was pumping blood. I could see he had a bullet wound in his shoulder. Burdett swept up the pistol and tried to turn it on my dog just as Buck hit him again. They fell and rolled over and over on the ground. I was gettin' close, but I knew I wasn't close enough. I could see Burdett struggling to get the gun turned around on Buck as they rolled, and I heard the shot. Burdett threw Buck off again and staggered to his feet. Buck had flown several feet. He stood up, took an unsteady step, and then fell over on his side. I was runnin' full out, and I was seein' nothin' but red. I was gonna kill this man, be it with gun, knife, or fist. I was gonna tear him limb from limb. I hit Bloody Bull Burdett so hard I rolled over and past him. I jumped to my feet to meet him as he came at me, and saw he was still down. His breathin' was heavy, and he was layin' on his face with his hands and arms under him. The Colt that had been in his hand was on the ground next to him, and I kicked it out of reach.

He was makin' no effort to get to his feet, so I grabbed his collar and rolled him over. His eyes were open, and he was strugglin' to say somethin'.

"I told ya he was the meanest dog . . ." he gasped, and then he quit breathin'.

I heard somethin behind me and turned. Buck was on his feet and suckin' wind like a fish out of water. He was all over blood, but he wasn't leakin' anywhere. I figured he'd just had the wind knocked out of him. I looked back at Burdett and saw a neat .45 hole drilled in his chest.

"I'll be darned," I said out loud. I supposed the last time Buck and Burdett had rolled over, the pistol must have got twisted, and when Burdett touched it off it was pointin' at his chest instead of Buck. "You got to be the only dog that ever killed a man with a gun," I said, lookin' back at Buck.

I remembered somethin' Pa had told me a long time ago. "What goes around comes around, be it good or evil."

It looked like Bloody Bull had gotten his payback for disabusin' Buck.

I started takin' notice of things around me again and realized the shootin' had quit.

"Come on, boy," I said to Buck and started walkin' toward

the street. I turned the corner of the hotel and saw the O'Malley clan gathered at the south end. I could see Pa, my brothers, Wedge, Rogan, and several others. They all seemed to be in good health.

I looked north and saw a sight that made me draw in my breath. Just a half block away Lee was comin' toward me on a dead run. As we met I grabbed her up in my arms and held her as close as I could without crushin' her. What lay between us didn't take words. It had always been there since the first day I'd seen her. It was strong, pure, and would last for eternity.

"There's some wounded men at the far end of the street," Frone said quietly after we'd hugged for a few minutes, "and some of them look to be ours."

I let Lee go, but held on to her hand. Frone and a girl I didn't know were carryin' flour sacks, and the girl I didn't know was packin' a rifle besides.

"This is Laura Beck," Frone said. I dropped Lee's hand and stepped away from her.

"She's right friendly, Matthew," Frone said. "She's run away from her family and feels bad about what's carried on."

I held my tongue, but made up my mind not to turn my back on Laura Beck. The Becks and the O'Malleys had no love between them.

I looked back to Lee. I wanted to take her in my arms again. I took a half step toward her and was knocked down by a tremendous blow from behind, followed by the sound of a shot. I rolled over and looked up to see Laura Beck raisin' the rifle she carried. At first I thought she was gonna shoot me again, but she fired over and past me, and I turned to look at the hotel. The older woman I'd seen earlier in the hotel room fell from the second story of the hotel, and she had my Henry still clutched in her hand. It occurred to me as things started to go kinda dim that I'd been shot by my own rifle. I looked up at Laura. She was cryin' and dropped her rifle to the street. "It's over," she said through her tears. It was the last thing I heard.

Chapter Twenty-three

The sun was shinin' bright as we stood in front of the church. Most of the townfolk had turned out and was standin' in the street with us. The big fight had happened three weeks before, and I'd been back on my feet about a week. The bullet from my Henry, fired by Marilyn Beck, had taken me in the top of the shoulder and ranged down, comin' out just below my collarbone. It had been a nasty wound and still bothered me considerable. I had my arm in a sling and had some trouble feedin' myself without sloppin' it on my shirt. Lee had been with me every day, and most every night. We talked about what we was gonna do with our future and decided that as soon as I could stand, we'd get married. I knew there'd never be another girl for me.

We'd lost five men in the fight. One of them had been the foreman of the O'Malley ranch in California who'd been with Uncle Peter for over twenty years. He was gonna be sorely missed. The rest of the men had been cowboys who had been ridin' for one or another of the O'Malley ranches. Peter himself had been shot through the thigh, and his boy Cory had lost a couple of fingers when his old rifle had blown up. Pa got himself a knife cut across his forearm when he'd been thumpin' an outlaw with his tomahawk, and Wedge had a powder burn on his hand when he'd grabbed a pistol out of a man's hand just as he was touchin' it off. We'd taken some losses and were some skinned up, but we'd mostly survived, and the family was surely closer than we'd been for at least a generation.

The outlaws had all either been killed, wounded, captured, or lit out for the hills. Marshal Bush had hauled nine prisoners back to Denver, and there were still four left in Animas who had been too badly wounded to move. We'd talked it over and decided that there had been about fifty or sixty outlaws and about forty men on our side. The man Villoria that Buck had chewed up in the saloon had stayed right in the chair until someone asked him what he was doin'. He'd told 'em that he was under arrest and was waitin' for Marshal O'Malley to come get him. Marshal Bush figured that he'd been punished enough by Buck, and Villoria swore that he was gonna go back to cowboyin' and forget about easy money. Joe figured he was a man of his word and told him to get lost, which he did in short order. Some of our guys went out to the creek where I'd been in the beaver den to see if they could round up the outlaws that'd been waitin' on me. They was all gone, so somebody had gotten the word to 'em and they'd headed for the tall timber. I'd given Wheeler's money to him, and he'd been almighty grateful. He'd tried to give me a reward, but I'd declined. He wanted to argue, but decided not to when I'd told him when he got completely healed up he could slip over the mountains to the San Luis Valley and buy some calves from us. That'd make us even.

Life was lookin' good, and the town had gathered to watch the new sky pilot hitch me and Lee to the double-harness. The new preacher had decided to have the ceremony outside, since there was no way we'd all fit in the little church. The old preacher, Reverend Gates, had finally been run out of town when he'd made some kinda unpastoral suggestions to a recently-arrived lady missionary. She'd been so offended she'd voiced her opinion to Frone, who was quick to share the information to the town gossips. It hadn't taken but a couple of days for the story to get clear through the little town, and it hadn't taken the town long to suggest to the fallen preacher that he practice his particular brand of soul savin' somewhere else, or wear some tar and feathers. The new preacher had been recruited from Utah, where he'd learned how hard it was for a Methodist minister to make a livin' among the Mormons. He was a good and gentle man and had been immediately accepted by the town.

I was standin' out to the edge of the crowd, waitin' for Lee to come out of the church where her Aunt Edna had been dressin' her up. I saw Pa and Frone walkin' toward me, and I waved at them. Pa made his way over to me, and he wrapped his arm around Frone.

"Matthew," Pa started, "we got somethin' to ask you." He fell silent for a minute and seemed to have some trouble talkin'.

"Spit it out, Pa," I said, tryin' to help him along.

"Well, Frone and me was wonderin' if you'd mind if we kinda tagged along with you and Lee, and had the preacher hitch us up when he was finished with you guys."

I was some taken back for a minute, but then I smiled at the pair. I'd figured it was comin' sooner or later. Pa and Frone had been keepin' pretty close company since we'd met up with the wagon train way back when.

"I'll check with Lee, but I reckon you ought to stand right up there with us and we'll have us a double hook-up. Fact, I know Lee wouldn't have it any other way."

"We wouldn't want to get underfoot . . ." Frone started to say.

"I 'spect you won't have much say," I replied. "Lee's purty strong-willed, and she's gonna want you right alongside of us." I paused a minute, and Pa jumped in.

"Maybe we'd ought to let Frone go over to the church and ask her," he said. " 'Sides, I need a few minutes to talk man-to-man with you." That give me pause 'cause I was afraid maybe Pa was gonna give me one of them father-son talks about the birds and the bees. My brother, Owen, had already given me some pointers, and I just didn't know if I could live through another one. Fact was, I'd rather get shot again than have Pa try and tell me about the difference between boys and girls.

Frone walked toward the church door and Pa took my arm, draggin' me off to a quiet spot under a cottonwood tree close by. "Matthew, I told you when we first started out on our trek that there was a place I had to go, and somethin' I had to do besides hunt for the gold." he said.

"I remember, Pa. I was almighty curious, but I didn't ask."

"Well . . ." He looked past me toward the mountains. "As I've told ya before when I was a youngster, I went to the mountains to trap beaver. That was back in '21, as I recall. I'd been taken captive by the Injuns before that, when I was a kid, and lived with the Pawnee for some years. When I got old enough I left the Pawnee, but instead of headin' home, I headed down to St. Louis. I guess I was still more Injun than white man, and I knew I wouldn't fit in back home. I went to the mountains." He stopped and looked back at me most serious.

"What I'm tryin' to tell ya is that somewhere out there in the north mountains you got a half-sister and two half-brothers. I was married to a Crow woman, and we had us some young'uns."

You could have knocked me over with a chicken feather. I don't know what I expected, but it surely wasn't this.

"Lots of us mountain men married up with Injun women," he said, matter-of-fact but not as an apology, "and she was a good woman. Fact is, we loved each other. I took care of her and she took care of me. I was a member of the tribe and went on many a raid with the Crow against the Blackfeet, the Utes, and even the Sioux."

He went quiet, and I reckoned he wanted me to say somethin', but I just had nothin' to say.

Finally he went on. "When I come home from the mountains and met your ma, I told her about my other family when
it looked like things were gonna get serious between her and
me," Pa said.

"What happened to them?" I asked after awhile.

"My wife, her name translated to somethin' like Dawn
Light or Early Mornin' Light, was the daughter of Red Hat,
the famous Crow war chief. I called her Dawny. She was taken
captive durin' a Blackfoot raid about six months after our
twins boys were born. I killed near half of the Blackfoot nation
tryin' to get her back. She was taken by one of my worst
enemies, a Blackfoot warrior I'd declared a blood feud with,
and when I got close to him, he killed her. It near broke my
heart."

Pa stopped talkin' a minute as his voice caught. The memory moved him more than anything I'd ever seen, except
maybe when he talked about Ma.

"I tried to deal with it and stay with my kids and the tribe,
but it weren't no good," Pa continued. "I was feelin' low-
down and mean. I left the kids with Dawny's sister and took
off. I went back time-to-time to see how things were goin',
but I drew further and further away from my kids and the
tribe. Dawny's sister was childless and the babies really took
to her. Her husband was a high-rankin' war chief and things
was goin' well for my children, and not so good for me.

"After awhile I just quit goin' back. I guess I told myself
they was better off without me, and I reckon that's true."

Pa's eyes had a shine to them. The story was costin' him
some to tell. "I decided a couple years ago that I needed to
find out what happened to them before I got to the age where
I couldn't do it. That's where we was headin' on our trek,"
Pa finished quietly.

"When were ya gonna tell me?" I asked him.

"When we left Pahgosa I was gonna tell ya, but then things
got complicated," he replied.

We were both quiet for a spell. I had a lot of questions, but decided they could wait. I looked toward the church and saw Lee and Frone standin' together with their arms linked. All our family was gathered around them. They were lookin' in our direction. I thought of my half-brothers and sister and wondered where they were. Were they alive? What were their lives like?

"We got it to do, Pa," I finally said.

Pa nodded and we started walkin' toward the church and our future. The crowd noise increased as we stepped up beside the women we loved and who was gonna be standin' next to us for the rest of our lives. I was as happy as I'd ever been, and as the preacher come walkin' over to us, I realized just how lucky I was. I took Lee's arm, and way back in some small part of my mind there was the memory of my foot fallin' through rotten wood. I remembered hearin' the sound of a tiny creek that was maybe runnin' over a bed of black sand and gold way above the springs at Pahgosa, and a bag of ancient coins found high on a mountain in a stone cabin built by hands unknown.

"We got it to do," I said to myself.